I0602791

Even Cozier Cosmic

EDITED BY

FRANCES LU-PAI IPPOLITO & MARK TEPPO

Underland Press

Even Cozier Cosmic

TABLE OF CONTENTS

THIS ONE IS FOR THOSE WHO LINGER STILL.

Genesis Revelation

~ Kate Ristau

The poet created a world
and it was good
like

      starshine
      and candy bars
      in shades of green and pink
      velvet soft
      and sticky sweet

Good.
We don't claim that very often.
That something is good.
We say it "shows promise," or "really captures the mood."
We prevaricate.
Pontificate.
We stand on the edges of nebulas and say:
"I really like what you're doing here with the rhythm."
"Have you thought about taking advantage of your syntax?"

Fuck that noise.

The poem was good.
So good, in fact,
that the poem decided to take a nibbl
How could it not
when the sun rose purple in the
  and the poet made mountains of
         destiny
      and forgotten memories?

The poem ate.
    Licking away commas
    Scratching and sniffing periods
Whole sentences   ed

   and spaces exp ded
until a white   of time and   let ers collided on   page,
storm   fury in a   create   destroy
We begin as we end but oh, the end.

   abyss calls   ,

but we create the darkness as we
push into the light—

Yes.

    time claims us all.
If the world is going to end
    Why not now
    Why not here
With cotton candy fingers melting
       bliss
          and azure waves.

⌗

For the Sea

~ Rachel Ashcraft

Maggie walks on water. The Inglemuth streets run with it. From the top of the small incline where the library sits down to her grandmother's empty house. Her shoes have enough of a sole that it doesn't reach her socks. It's been raining for four days straight and there's no sign of it letting up. The dock workers have been fortifying the coast all week, laying sandbags. Nor'easter she'd heard bandied around a little, but she had a feeling that it was going to be something much worse.

But the library comes before that, and she walks the path up to the entrance. They're a bastion for anyone who needs them. They'll stay open through the storm. The roof doesn't leak. It's a good ole building, they all say. She knows it. It's built for the end times.

Maggie's body aches with her tiredness. There's nothing for her in her grandmother's old house, expect a lingering sense of loss. She remembers what her uncle told her. *Your grandma was a tough old broad. Lost two husbands. Four sons. No teeth left, but she ate whatever she wanted. She didn't take shit and she could give it.* She uses that as motivation to get up in the morning.

"I want the library to have this."

Maggie turns from the computer screen to find two men standing at the checkout counter. The one in front holds out a small book. His liver spotted hands shake. His skin has a yellowish hue that matches his eyes. Bad liver, she hears her grandmother say.

His wrist bows with the book, but it can't weigh much. The cover crumbles and bits of it dot the counter.

There is something similar between the second man and the book, both haggard, ill-used, and flaking dandruff covers his dark sweater. His mouth is slightly open, as if he can't breathe through his nose and she cannot see any teeth, just a dark empty space. Empty gums. His eyes are the same, sunken and vacant. A man vanishing inward.

She dreads having to turn the two men away. "I'm sorry, sir, but we can only take books that are gently used." It's part of the script. Gently has a connotation of nicety: A-please-don't-take-it-out-on-me-I'm-an-underpaid-clerk sort of phrasing that was printed in bold in all the library's training manuals. He doesn't budge.

"It *is* old," she falters, wavers her hand over the book. She doesn't want to touch it. It's not faux leather. It's real and through the peeling skin she sees a sheen of metal. "They might take it down at Caveat Emptor." It's the little bookstore on the boardwalk, with its bulging shelves, and books piled on the floor.

"For the sea," the second man says. His voice booms deep and 'fathomless'. She doesn't know where the word comes from. Like waves the syllables advance and then recede. The yellow-eyed man doesn't know the second man is standing behind him, she realizes. They haven't acknowledged each other. She tries to keep her eyes focused on the first man, and his crooked finger that shakes near the book.

"I want it to have a new home." He pushes it closer to her until it teeters on the edge of the desk. "My grandfather took this from someone he shouldn't have. I don't want it anymore. At least here other people can see it."

She reaches out and touches it. It's cold. A book shouldn't feel this cold. After you handle thousands of them, you start to recognize a book not as a thing but as its own entity. Different number of pages, but always fundamentally the same. Maggie is a poet, Mikhail, the cataloger told her after she explained that books always had something of a glow about them, as if they were still in the woods, soaking up the sunlight. He'd said they were mass-produced, nothing special about them. But Maggie still believes it. And there are some that are something different. Some old ones that had been made to be special.

It's heavy and cold and feels wrong. She wants to put it down, but it clings to her fingers as if magnetized

"Yes, take it." The man with yellow eyes says. "I don't want it in my house any longer. It's an old family heirloom. His rheumy eyes fill, and she thinks of the reservoir overflowing. The sandbags giving way. Of her own grandmother and how the house can be a weight too.

The second rests a hand on his back, and the yellowed eyed man tenses, his shoulder raising almost to his ears, but he doesn't brush the hand off. He's not really there, Maggie thinks. He flickers like rain reflecting headlights.

"Would you like a donation receipt?" she manages. The script is easy to fall back on when she doesn't know what to say. "For tax purposes?"

"My debts are settled now," the man says, and waves away her offer with a shaking skeletal hand. He turns and leaves, and she hears the old door shuck into place. It swells in the summer, never settles right.

The second man lingers. She has no choice but to look at him. "For the sea." His voice is gravel. Pebbles rubbing against each other. His form wavers. *Half here, half not*, she thinks, feels her heart kick in her chest. *Please leave*, she thinks, but doesn't say. She grips the book. It's cold and wet under her hands, slimy, and she almost drops it.

He blinks slowly and when he opens his eyes there is depth, blackness parted by the green glow of water split by light. A lighthouse she thinks, calling out to all the lost ships. But under this press of water, it's too late.

The scream lodges in her throat, chokes her. She can't look away. He rots. His body bloats. Barnacles dot his flesh, skin sloughs from above his eye revealing the start of his skull. Brown liquid leaks between his gums from his expanding throat and dribbles down his chin. And then she blinks, and he's gone, and the book is heavy in her hands.

The cold of a thousand leagues of water seeps in. She puts the book in the trash and dumps the basket next to it with the day's receipts and checkout notices on top of it, so no one can see it. It will go out when the custodian comes to clean.

One can sink in different ways. And she thinks of her grandmother who knew so much death in her life. *I wrestled with the black dog. He took his pound of flesh, but he never got me in the jugular. Remem-*

ber that you're a fighter, Maggie. You're a fighter like me. She never called it depression, Maggie thinks, because it was a word without teeth. *Old people can't call it what it is. Can't look at it directly,* her aunt had said. The whole family's cursed with it. But she liked how her grandma described it. That mangy cur with its drawn back smile, and watery afraid eyes, and a lunge in every muscle.

The next day the book has been catalogued and placed in the reference archives, a small section in the back of the stacks that is always out of the sunlight. The staff can see it from the desk. The books aren't particularly monetarily valuable, but the information is relevant to genealogical research for many of Inglemuth's families. Some of the books are written by their great grandparents and tell stories of seafaring, fishing, and taming of the coast. Some of things that cannot have been.

The public library is one of the oldest buildings in the seafaring town. Built in 1820. She suspects some of the archive books have been there just as long. They leave bits of themselves behind on the shelves, they fail, and they persist just like the elderly people she's known in her life. Time takes them apart, albeit slower than other things, but all the same she sweeps up their flaking and bug gnawed pages, notes their broken spines, old fingerprints embossed in their once supple leather, coffee stains on pages, notes in the margins and doodles of ships with their wind-filled sails and many masts, maybe drawn from the libraries wide windows that look over the harbor.

Sometimes when it's particularly quiet, the library will speak. It uses the voices of the people who loved it the most. A man with a top hat is spotted reading a newspaper. Dressed in his three-piece suit, he peruses, checks his pocket watch, folds the newspaper and vanishes. Maggie always tells people that the library's ghosts are friendly. Why would you choose to haunt a library? It had to have been a place you loved. No one had ever died here, like their living patrons, they had to seek it out. It must have been a safe place that their weary feet led them back to. Sometimes she hears running on the stairs, an errant voice, a laugh like a bell tinkling, the paper doll display shifting, the paper rocking horse moving in the absence of a breeze.

The library shifts with the seasons, the wood perpetually swollen with the salt water; the doors stick in the winter, and swing open in the summer. The building seems to creak and sway, but there's a feeling that it's a place that will never come down. Something internal holds its foundation straight. The more it settles, the more it claims its spot. The library will always be here. It was here before her and it will be here after, and she wouldn't mind haunting its stacks.

The fourth director had marked a notch into the doorway for every patron that died of the Spanish Flu and recorded their names in handwritten books now in the archives. A small memorial for all the dead in Inglemuth and overseas. Some years down the line the library board had voted to fill in the cracks with resin. The notches are still visible but not sharp. They no longer catch and snag hand knitted sweaters or leave splinters in the fingers of patrons. They do catch the eye. They're a thing to comment on. All those dead, all those years ago.

There is a fire in the hearth and Maggie stands by it, but still, she cannot get warm. The cold seeps around her bones, freezes the marrow.

"This is interesting," Mikhail says. He's holding the yellowed-eyed man's book. And she's sequestered herself into the corner of his cubicle. "I had to do some digging over at the rare book's library. Apparently, this is a naval code book. That's why it's heavier than it looks. It's lined in lead." He turns the pages somewhat cavalierly. It's meant to have flag combinations to signal to other navy boats, but the cool part is it comes with its own 19th century self-destruct button. You get captured, you just toss it over the side, and *bam!* It's heavy enough it sinks to the bottom never to be seen again. You can see why something like this would be pretty rare."

"It was created to be destroyed," Maggie says.

"Yeah, pretty innovative. Who donated, it by the way? I just found it sitting on my desk this morning."

"I didn't get his name." The custodian must have fished it out of the trash.

"Well, it looks like it belonged to a man named George Farer. It's written here, pretty faded." He holds it out to her. She doesn't touch it but leans in. "I don't think the man wanted to be a sailor. There are flag combos, but there's also this." He flips to show a woman drawn in what appears to be oils. She's turned slightly away, her mouth upturned in a toothy smile. Her eyes bright and alive. "I think he is a bit more than an amateur. These are actually pretty good."

The library is more a home than the empty place she returns to each night. There are hints of her grandmother still in the house. The dish towels, the outdated mode of floral wallpaper, the scent of her perfume that has sunken into the yellow velvet couch. She prefers the ghosts at the library. People unable to move on for all the books they haven't read, those were her kind of people. When she was at the house, she read. Piles of books stacked up next to her bed. Some toppled, some sorted, and on every shelf. She doesn't touch her grandmother's favorite books. She leaves that pile untouched, hopes to see one of them cracked open on her grandma's favorite chair.

Maggie stands tentatively by the archives on her lunch break, then pulls the book marked with a handwritten *f* from the shelf. She traces the line that ends with the Farer's. A wife Della, a son, Frederick, a man George. Della and Frederick had both died in 1918 and George had died the following year. Two notches in the door frame, she thinks. One for Della. One for Frederick. George: lost at sea. How did someone come to have his book?

Maggie is the only staff in the library on the night when it happens. It's the third day of perpetual rain and wind. The library walls sing with it, a low mourning sound, and the old wood creaks like a straining ship. Rain and hail pelt the windows. The lights waver, flash and then go out with a low droning sound of dying cathodes.

The windows rattle and the floor starts to shake. Everything convulses and she drops, feeling her way towards the door. Something is tearing the library out of the ground roots and all. The building shudders under her. But it fights. She can feel its own heavy weight pushing back against the force. She stumbles, falls, cracks her knee hard on the floor, something twists wrong in her wrist. Her yelp is lost to the shrieking of the building, to the wind, to the windows that seem to buckle. The library alights as lightning streaks angry and fast outside the window. The thunder that follows breaks the world apart.

She stumbles towards the archive, a shadowy hand seeming to lead her, to grip her elbow to keep her steady, to place her hand on the old crumbling little metal book. In the boom of the thunder, she hears the words: *to the sea.*

She grabs the book. She runs. The cold rain pelts against her, hail hits her arms, her back, her head and her skin will be covered in bruises, but she doesn't feel it now. Doesn't feel the pain in her knee or her wrist. Water floods the streets. "Stop!" someone yells, but she careens down the hill, slipping, catching herself, falling so that the water fills her mouth and sinuses.

A man separates from the shadows, water drips from his duster. The same man from the library. George, she thinks. She knows it above anything else. He grabs her arm, yanks her to her feet, his skin sloughs off against hers, falls in clumps, seaweed drapes his shoulders, and his black rotten tongue bulges from his mouth.

"I know," she tries to say and then yells it above the roaring storm, until her throat is raw, and she tastes blood. And where his eyes should be, she sees his life cut short. Sees a man with nothing set sail with only the notebook, where when he finds time between his constantly running nose and eyes, because this is grief that fills the whole body, that makes his stomach turn, and his hair give way from his scalp, and his skin rebel in little red rashes that bleed, and he can't stop crying, so he draws them. His family. His son, his wife. And on those pages, there's just a little bit of them. Translated through him. How he saw them. Who they were. It's not the same, but it's more than nothing. Not the grave dirt falling from his hands, the priest drowned in his own mucus and stoney lungs so there's no one to give them a proper send off. So, he digs with his shovel that breaks on the damned rocked soil, and then digs with the handle, then his hands, until his nails peel, until he thinks his bones must be exposed, because that's how it feels, here down in the hole, with their bodies waiting up there.

He goes to sea to escape himself. And then, a great push, air so fresh and fast. He's never fallen like this, not even when everything had come out from under his feet. He wants his book. He wants his Della and his Freddy, but the book is gone from his waistcoat and the water takes his breath. And in the water, he sees only the hands that pushed him, because they thought there was something in that notebook worth having. He never had learned to swim. They wanted the codes. They wanted the thing he coveted. There was nothing in there but the faces of the dead. And the little book slipped into a jacket all those years ago sat unknown on a book shelf, a little reminder of a misdeed, until his murderer's grandson found it and George along with it. George carries the ocean tied around his leg. An endless weight, he can't escape. But he's grown strong with its weight. Stepped free from the coast, he comes to find what is his. George's hand always now on the grandson's shoulder, his body withering under the eyes of the dead as George waits, his fingers grasping for the thing taken from him.

Maggie feels something of her grandma, a shadow at her side in that long slog through the pelting rain. All her grief, always there, as black as the storm. *The black dog*, her grandma had called it. The black dog always snapping at her legs. All those years ago her grandmother had done the same. Pushed through the driving rain. *It hadn't been there then*, she said. *I couldn't feel all the loss.* Three sons buried. In the driving storm, the thing that wanted to kill her, she'd felt freed. Her grandma had shown the scars on her knees, where she had fallen on a broken bottle that day. *That day, the dog wasn't there. I realized I wanted to live. I wanted that more than anything. It was such a god damn metaphor*, she'd said with a little short laugh. A huff of a sound, never anything drawn out, but a few of those short staccatos of air that showed more mirth than a deep belly laugh.

One foot in front of the other. There was no way around it. I couldn't move faster, the wind and the water kept pushing me back, but I knew I could find him. That little boy. There in the house, too scared to move. And that put something in me. It lit something. I found him and took him to the library, and we all huddled there, and I made them tell me stories, anything, their history, their favorite memory, the things they wanted the most, and that storm tried to reach and get us, but we held it at bay. We stayed sharp and present, and we didn't let go. Her presence had saved them. Maggie often studies the portrait of her. Severe and taciturn, but something lively about the eyes. Something that said life can take and take but not me. It can't have me.

She can do this for George, Maggie thinks. Take his despair, free him of it. To wear it chained around you, to never look up from the sea floor. And she feels herself steady, her ragged breathing even out, her shaking hands around the book settle, hold it firmly. There are things outside of myself, she thinks.

Maggie grips the railing on the pier and pushes herself out onto it. She stumbles, tastes the sea air in her mouth. Feels the great vast thrashing of the ocean beneath her.

George watches, his feet planted firmly at the end of the stone pier. The book is a sharp, cold living thing in her hands. It cuts her fingers. And she thinks this is where he fell, someone took this book from him, because they thought it held something. And all he wants is it back. He'll drown the whole town to have it.

She stands at the end of the pier and lets the book go. She turns to see the figure at the start of the walkway, but it's empty.

The book floats, then sinks down, down, down and Inglemuth goes silent.

The dandruff on his coat in the library had been snow, she thinks. The man in the prime of his life, with nothing left on the land, stands on the deck of a ship just off the coast of Inglemuth. He wants to turn back and see the lights now so distant. Come home and settle by the fire. Have the dog curl by his side, his Della read in the chair next to them. Frederick watches the sea and talks about where he'll go one day. Maybe the radio is on, maybe it is off. The gas lamps glow, and his bones frozen by the Atlantic winter start to thaw.

⛊

Time To Read

~ Devan Barlow

Finally I have the time I crave
for books
only books
forever books
This library's doors welcomed me in the days
when the vines first rose from the soil
devouring all other greenery
quickly becoming
all-encompassing, umbrageous canopies
roiling, rumbling, rattling
as prey digests

Whoever established this voluminous sanctum
(long-vanished, likely vine-victuals)
left behind cupboards stocked with essentials
teas, biscuits, candles
a sturdy kettle
blankets warm enough to conceal
how cold the sunless world has grown
There are more books than I could read
in an eternity, though I do my utmost

While reading tales of battle, bravery, badinage
I noticed the vines had made their way inside
found a minuscule crack in an exterior wall
Now they twine around the once-living
wood of bookcases, impress their patterns
against wallpaper of ultramarine fleur-de-lys

The vines themselves are opaline ebony
their leaves citreous, bedizened with gleaming
silver eyes that move to watch me as I
go from shelf to cozy chair to shelf again

While engrossed in stories of sorcery, secrets, slights
one leaf fell, leaving behind a cicatrix
that healed in moments
I reached, found its trichomes
silk-soft against my skin

The wayward leaf became a bookmark when
I paused my perusal of
a carcinological tome
to rest my eyes and dream
of crabs, shells caparisoned with
chrysoprase cabochons

Woke to find the volume's covers splayed open
the leaf extending tendrils
one reaching beneath the nail of
my left index finger
but there is no pain

The vines and flowers advance
so genial, can always be convinced to shift aside
when they block a particular whodunit, anthology, grimoire
I crave
They curl over my comfortable chair
occasionally dropping leaves into the hour's
cup of tea,
contributing a pleasant tartness

Gone Fishing

~ *Peter Damien*

It was mostly still dark when Simon got up to assemble his fishing gear, but there was a bit of light coming in through the windows for him to see by. He'd done this so many times that he knew all of his equipment by touch and habit alone. The light coming through the windows had a faint greenish hue to it. Whatever the stuff was that was lingering in the atmosphere, it always seemed to flare up and get worse overnight . . . but it also seemed to mostly burn off by breakfast, so that was probably all right.

Gertrude, his cat, looked up at him from her curled up and cozy spot on his bed. She regarded him while he gathered up fishing supplies and pulled on his clothes. Then, ever the opportunist, she shifted over on the bed a little to take advantage of the warmth he had left behind, and she went back to sleep.

After he finished dressing, Simon went up the narrow staircase to his house's small attic, and then up a further ladder onto the small watchtower he'd constructed. While he scanned the horizon for signs of anything interesting, notable, dangerous, or hungry, he was also pleased to note that the green was already beginning to burn away from the air.

He went outside and loaded the boat with fishing gear, tackle, his lines and rods, and a cooler with some food in it for a bit later. Just as he was clambering into the boat and preparing to push it off into the water, Gertrude came wandering outside, her tail crooked in a question mark as she walked toward the boat, her intention clear. Simon waited patiently, which was the only way to wait for a cat. She took her time, hopped into the boat, and then settled into a crook toward the back where she could wash herself peacefully. Anticipating it, Simon had thrown a small ratty blanket back there.

He pushed off from the shore—*quietly* of course—and then rowed out into the water, the oars silently dipping in and out of the water with barely a ripple or sound. He'd gotten very good at this, over the past couple of years (or however long it had been). Once he was out there, he relaxed about the noise a little bit, and he hummed to himself. There were a lot of dangers in the world these days, but most of them didn't seem to remember how to swim anymore.

Bait, hook. Fishing line, pull back, and then cast. Legs, stretched out. He watched the small ripples on the water as they drifted wider and then faded away. Maybe the blue sky wasn't the same shade of blue as it had always been, but it was a bright clear sky this morning anyway.

He twisted his head around a little and glanced off to the south, where the blue sky was marred by a small plume of smoke. That had started going up sometime in the past couple of days, and he'd been keeping half an eye on it as he went about his day to day business. Was something on fire, or was someone cooking? It would be a heck of a cookery setup if they were, it was a lot of smoke. Maybe there was a settlement happening out that way. He didn't know how far away it was, but he *did* know that that way wasn't a good direction, so who knew how long that would all last.

The line shivered, but only a little bit. Something wasn't biting, but it was nudging around and thinking about it. Simon smiled pleasantly at the water and didn't react any more than that. Patience and a good mood, those were the keys to successful fishing. And the real nice thing about fishing was, if you showed up with some patience . . . well, the good mood would probably turn up before too long. So that was nice.

The line nudged again, and he continued to do nothing.

The sun crept up, brilliant through the foliage and then bright above the treetops, those that had leaves still. When it finally reached him, the warmth took the leftover morning chill from his bones. Gertrude shifted and rolled over in her sleep, enjoying the morning sun, and dreaming cat dreams.

A beer would've been nice. A real ice cold beer. He hadn't one of those in a long time—first for health reasons, and then for lack of supply reasons—but he always craved it when he went fishing. In the cooler was cold freshwater and leftovers from last night's supper, and that would have to be good enough for—

The line nudged, shivered, and *yanked*, and if he'd been an inexperienced fisherman, it might've come right out of his hands, the whole rod vanishing into the lake where he was not about to dive after it. But this wasn't nearly his first trip, so his grip was strong and he sat up straight, pulling back. The rod arced and bent over the water, the line pulling beneath the waves. Slowly he moved the rod back and forth, reeling some of the line in whenever it went slack.

Gertrude raised her head to watch him, he noticed.

"You're no help," Simon said affably.

Gertrude was unconcerned by this.

Eventually Simon stood and lifted the rod, bringing the line entirely out of the water and in one smooth movement, pulling it into the boat. He dropped a fish into the space between his feet where he clamped down on its back with one hand, and then pulled the hook out of its mouth.

It was a solid eight inch fish, scales opalescent and twinkling in the sunlight as it wriggled fitfully.

The moment he got the hook and his hand out of its mouth, the fish stopped wriggling and said loudly, "Don't kill me!"

Simon sighed.

"Don't kill me?" The fish asked, then declared, "Don't kill me!"

(It was just trying out different tones, see, to see which one would do the trick.)

"Well hell," Simon said, but mildly.

"Don't kill me!"

"I'm not gonna kill you," Simon said. He said it calmly, surprised that not even this inconvenience could muster any part of a bad mood anywhere in him. It really *was* a good day wasn't it.

Awkwardly, without letting go of the fish, he opened his small cooler and unpacked everything into the part of the boat that was just beside Gertrude. She watched him with disinterest and annoyance, that he was piling stuff into the space where she was busy napping. Every time the fish shuddered and moved, trying to get away, she looked at it with proper disapproval.

Even more awkwardly, Simon lowered the cooler into the water and then brought it back into the boat, sloshing some of the water out but keeping most of it in. He picked up the fish and put it into the cooler and then lowered the lid but did not shut it all the way, leaving a big gap round the edge. Just enough to keep the fish from jumping out.

"Don't kill me," the fish said, muffled, from inside the cooler. A pause, then it thoughtfully added, "Let me go?"

"I will, in a bit," Simon said, speaking up a little because probably the lid of the cooler made it hard for the fish to hear him. "But I'm not done fishing yet, and I don't wanna keep catching you, so just be patient."

The fish said nothing to this. Simon baited his hook again and threw the line back out, settling in.

Well, that was life, wasn't it. Sometimes you got a fish for dinner, and sometimes you got one of the recently-intelligent fish who could speak and who begged for their lives and who made you pretty sick if you tried to eat them anyhow.

What a world...

He took a sip from his water jug, pleased that it was still mostly cool. He settled back in and watched the morning slip by. He listened to the splash of the boat rocking in the water now and then, and also the occasional burbling splash as the fish in the cooler moved around. A faint breeze balanced against the warmth of the sun.

Some splashing from the cooler. He turned to glance and found the cat standing on the edge of the seat, just above the cooler, *slowly* extending one paw toward the water, where the fish was reacting in alarm.

"Gertie," Simon said. He leaned closer to pet her uninvited, which was of course enough to make her decide against touching the fish and sent her to the back of the boat again, where she pretended to have never been interested at all.

Simon opened a small bowl and ate some of the stew he'd brought from the night before, slurping it from the side of the container.

"Food?" Burbled the fish. "Don't kill me?"

Without a word, Simon smiled a little and threw a couple of the worms he'd used as bait into the cooler. There was a sudden slosh as the fish got them, and then it went still again.

In front of him, on the farthest shore of the lake, some shapes were moving out of the trees and along the water's edge. Deer, perhaps, which would be all right. They were sometimes as iffy—and, indeed, opinionated—as the fish were these days, but if you got one then they were good eats for a long time.

It wasn't deer though; They were two-lugged and hunch-backed and rough-moving and strange. There were maybe a half dozen of them, it was tough to tell from this distance. They were people, or they had been people. They'd been people back then, and now they weren't. He watched them shamble together, listless and veneering in their movements, bunched up together and making strange noises, wet slurps and keening cries.

They lurched along the shore and then headed back into another patch of trees, heading south, and they were gone from sight, and that was that.

Simon sighed. There hadn't been much of a problem like that for quite a while, and he hoped maybe there still wouldn't be. And if there was a problem with them? Well that was for tomorrow. Today's problem was how he was going to cook the fish he eventually caught. Grilled? Baked? Wrapped in old black-and-white newspaper, soaked in water and cooked low and slow? He focused on that instead of the shambling former-people, instead.

"Don't kill me," came very quietly from the cooler, like someone talking to themselves. Simon figured that was probably the case, so he didn't answer.

There had been a lot of fishing trips when he was younger, and they'd been nice. Then a lot of things had happened, the news had become very very busy for a while and then gone silent and life had changed quite a lot . . . but the fishing hadn't. The fishing trips now were much like the fishing trips from before, and that was good. The more things changed the more they stayed the same, eh? Simon sipped his water, closed his eyes in the warm morning sun, and smiled to himself.

The fishing line nudged.

The sun moved a little. A few clouds made an effort and then went away.

The fishing line shivered.

Simon finished his stew and half the jug of water.

Something bit the line, the hook yanked. Same thing as last time, and every time before that, except those few times when something went hilariously wrong and then he got a good story out of it. Simon fought the line, arched his back, braced his feet, kept his patient, and soon enough, well, out of the water came the fishing line and on the end of it was a beautiful fish. Twelve inches for sure, wriggling and fighting and all. He put it into the boat and pulled out the hook. The fish didn't say one word.

Simon smiled happily. Hello dinner.

The smoke, off to the south, had mostly quit. Well, who knows what that was all about.

Simon opened the lid of the cooler. The smaller fish inside stared at him and he smiled back at it.

"You have a good one, buddy," Simon said, and then he tipped the cooler over the side. The water and the fish shot into the lake. Simon imagined the fish coming back to the surface to say something to him, maybe give him wisdom or a riddle or some such . . . but it just swam off as frantically as any fish might, speaking or not. He shrugged, popped his actual catch into the cooler and shut the lid firmly this time.

He got the oars and began rowing back home. The sun beamed down on him and he hummed cheerfully to himself.

Poached. That's what he'd decided on. Poached with some of that rosemary he'd found growing wild. That would be the perfect end to a lovely day, wouldn't it.

"I prefer grilled," Gertrude said from the back of the boat without sitting up or opening her eyes.

The Breaking of the Scarlet Fever

~ *Matthew Ross*

With gratitude (and apologies) to Margery Williams

It was shortly after midnight when the Boy was taken by the Scarlet Fever. The old grandfather clock was still chiming the hours when they crept into the nursery, silent as wraiths in their red hooded robes. They picked their way carefully through the minefield of playthings the Boy had left strewn near his bedside, gliding soundlessly past the Skin Horse, sidestepping Timothy, the jointed wooded lion, and weaving a path around the model boat with the realistic rigging until they reached the object of the nefarious errand they had been tasked with. The Boy awoke not, as he usually did, to the gentle touch of Nana's hand upon his shoulder, but to the viselike grip of a rough hand clamped across his mouth. His cries were soon quieted by the sweet scent of ether. But as the Boy slipped back into Morpheus' embrace, he instinctively clutched at his habitual nighttime companion—an old stuffed rabbit, spotted brown and white, whose rich velveteen fur had grown somewhat shabby over the years, and whose once-pink nose had all the color rubbed off where the Boy had kissed it.

And that is why when the Boy was carried off by the Scarlet Fever, his Rabbit was carried off along with him.

Perhaps another toy would have been terribly frightened to find themselves plucked, in the dead of night, from the familiar confines of the nursery, and bundled off to parts unknown by a pack of crimson-hooded rapscallions. But after being stuffed into a worn burlap sack and hoisted atop the shoulders of the burliest of their abductors, the Rabbit thought it curious how unperturbed he was by the ordeal; he merely felt grateful not to have been separated from the Boy he loved so dearly.

It was a musty old sack, which still smelt faintly of cabbages, and as they were jounced along the Boy hugged him so tightly that the Rabbit could scarcely breathe. Back in the nursery, there had been many nights when the Boy had made tunnels out of his bedclothes after Nana had put them both to sleep. Then the Boy would whisper secrets to him, and they would pretend together that it was their burrow, just like real rabbits lived in. Though the Rabbit often found it difficult to breathe then too, he treasured those late-night games of make-believe—and not only because they were when he felt the Boy's love for him most acutely. Those were the moments when he felt very nearly like a real rabbit himself, and not merely a toy rabbit stitched of velveteen and stuffed with sawdust.

He did not feel especially real now, though, and the sensation of powerlessness that overwhelmed him only served to underscore his very lack of realness. The Rabbit did not know why he and his Boy had been wrenched from the comforts of their nursery and jammed into a sack like a pair of old cabbages. He did not know what destination lay ahead of them or what their captors' intentions might prove upon their arrival. He knew only that something was wrong—dreadfully wrong—and there wasn't a thing in the world he could do about it.

"If only I was Real," the Rabbit lamented, "I could find some way to aid the Boy in his peril. Rabbits aren't the most fearsome of creatures, it's true. But they're quick and they're crafty. They've teeth for biting and nails for scratching, and their powerful hind legs can pack quite a wallop!"

The Rabbit's soft little head drooped in despair. "But I've none of those things. Not even a pair of hind legs to call my own."

It was true; though the Rabbit's maker had sewn him a fine pair of forelegs, his backside was quite shapeless, and tended to assume the form of whatever surface it had been set upon.

"I would do anything to help the Boy—anything at all!" the Rabbit vowed. "I would give my life up in an instant—and gladly!—if it would help return the Boy to his family. But I fear there's nothing that I *can* do, being but a creature of velveteen and sawdust. Oh, if only I was Real…"

Many hours later, when the Boy was being coarsely extricated from his burlap enclosure, the Rabbit slipped from his lifeless fingers and fell noiselessly to the ground, landing at the feet of an unshaven member of the Scarlet Fever. As the man was contemplating whether he should pick the shabby moppet up and chuck it in the furnace, one of his comrades called out to him; they had other tasks to complete before that evening's rites could commence. So, he kicked the rabbit across the stone cobbles and, smirking, hurried to catch up to his cronies.

It was just an old stuffed bunny, after all, and hardly worth the bother. It wouldn't make a tuppence's worth of difference to the ritual's success whether the dolly mouldered in the shadows of the sanctuary or burnt to cinders in the oven. The man had a long night ahead of him, and he was loath to keep the Hierophant waiting.

The Boy awoke frightened. For despite Nana's best efforts to keep him ignorant of their existence, he knew instinctively by whom he had been taken, even before he marked the manacles which bound him to the cold stone slab or the filthy rag which gagged him. He found it difficult to remember when he had first become conscious of the Scarlet Fever, but their unseen menace had haunted the nursery for years. Perhaps it had been when he was very young, and he'd overheard his parents whispering that the groundskeeper's niece had been lost to the Fever. Or when Cook had first threatened that the Scarlet Fever would get him if he failed to eat all of his peas without complaint. Just three months past, the neighbor's son had failed to appear in the woods as he usually did each afternoon, to play at brigands amidst the thicket of raspberry canes; the Boy had known at once that he would never see his playmate again. Nana said that the neighbors had merely taken a trip to the seaside and promised that they would return by Autumn—but as she did so, she'd pursed her lips exactly as she had when she'd sworn that a spoonful of castor oil would taste just like licorice candy, so he knew that she was lying.

Nana had hushed him when he'd asked if the Scarlet Fever was coming to carry him away as well, and whether he must really finish *all* the peas on his plate, or if they might be satisfied should he manage to dispatch the bulk of them. She'd said that the Scarlet

Fever was naught but a tale that Cook had made up to frighten him, and that he wasn't to speak of them again. Then she had swept him into her arms and embraced him, until the warmth of her bosom melted all his fears away. Afterwards, the Boy did as Nana bid and never spoke their name aloud again. Even alone in his bed, with only Bunny to protect him, the Boy tried his very best to banish the Scarlet Fever from his thoughts. Sometimes he'd go so long as a week without thinking of them—and when he did, he pretended that he believed Nana, and imagined that they did not really exist.

But now that he'd been Taken, the Boy knew that he could play at make-believe no longer. He did not know what designs the Scarlet Fever had intended for him. He could only acknowledge what, in his heart of hearts, he had known all along: that the Scarlet Fever was real—frightening real.

And that no child who was taken by them ever returned alive.

Time passes slowly when one is imprisoned in the dark. But the Boy's lonely vigil ended as abruptly as it began. He heard the scratching of a matchstick, and a torch flared into being. It was followed by another, then several more, each held aloft by a red-robed figure. The Boy counted a dozen of them, their faces shrouded by hoods. Once the twelfth flame had been lit, they turned in unison and slid their torches into a series of cobweb-dusted sconces spaced evenly along the walls. The lights revealed a large chamber built of crumbling stonework which had been decorated with queer markings and images of loathsome beasts—horrid amalgamations of fangs and scales and claws, of slimy tentacles and leathery wings, all mingled together in dreadful combinations the likes of which the Boy had never seen. Both the markings and the images were illustrated in but a single color: red. Some had faded to a rusty copper hue, their pigments dry and flaking. Others seemed to have been more freshly painted, their colors bright and vibrant. A few appeared to still be dripping . . .

The Boy shivered. And not because of the damp chill which seeped out from between the stonework like a London fog.

A thirteenth figure entered the chamber and strode toward the Boy. His steps were purposeful, yet unhurried. Where the others wore woolen robes which were plain and unadorned, his was a rich satin, and had been embroidered with the same peculiar sigils which dotted the walls in shiny cardinal thread. He bore in his hands a gleaming golden chalice, studded in rubies, which he set atop the large stone slab the Boy had been shackled to. As he leaned over the chained figure, he shrugged back his hood and met the child's terrified gaze with his own.

The Boy wasn't sure what he expected to see when the man removed his hood—and yet he somehow found himself still confounded and unsettled by the visage that smiled back at him. He was a quite ordinary looking man of late middle age. He might have been of similar age with the Boy's father, or perhaps a bit older. His bald head was circled by a closely cropped fringe of greying hair, and his blue eyes twinkled behind a rounded pair of rimless steel spectacles. Had the Boy met him in more fortunate circumstances, he might have thought the man to be a kindly schoolmaster, or perhaps a country vicar.

Present circumstances considered, the Boy doubted he was either.

"Are you frightened, lad?" the man asked. His voice was unexpectedly gentle.

The Boy nodded.

"Don't be. You've nothing to fear." He ruffled the Boy's hair. "Though some of us are allotted more days upon this earth than others, we all must face our final day sooner or later, eh? And few ever get to enjoy the honor—nay, the *privilege*—of a death as meaningful as yours will be."

Writhing and twisting, the Boy struggled fruitlessly against his restraints.

"There, there," the man said, giving him a genial pat on the shoulder. "Try to enjoy these last few moments. Savor them, if you can. Chin up! I can't promise that you won't suffer, but it'll all be over soon enough."

The Boy's hearty young lungs strove their hardest to give voice to his anguish—but his cries were muted by the soiled rag that muzzled him.

In a forgotten corner of the subterranean chamber, a shabby velveteen ear lined in faded pink sateen gave a single, barely perceptible twitch.

From somewhere within the voluminous folds of his flowing satin robe, the Hierophant produced a long, wickedly curved dagger, its blade a jagged needle of obsidian glass. Thrusting it skyward, he raised it high above the prostrate form of his diminutive captive, exhibiting it before his disciples. It glittered darkly in the flickering torchlight.

In the blink of an eye, the blade plunged downward. With one swift slice, it bit deeply into the Hierophant's palm. Curling his hand into a fist, he squeezed the resulting flow of blood into the ruby-studded chalice. When he was satisfied with his contribution, he passed both dagger and chalice to the man at his left, who repeated these same actions.

As the chalice slowly made its way across the circle, the Hierophant began to speak.

"Brothers!" he cried. "When the body is sick, it raises forth a fever to burn away whatever foul contagion it has been polluted with. Such fevers are *good*! They are *natural*! For without a fever to purge it of its corruption, the body can do naught by perish."

"Why should it be any different with the body politic of our great society as a whole? Has it not also been polluted? Does it not suffer from corruption? Does it not also cry out, begging to be purged of all the vile pestilence which plagues it?"

His hooded followers stamped their feet, slowly and rhythmically, to signal their approval.

"But to whom can our society turn to deliver it from this wretched state? Whom can it trust not merely to hear its pitiful supplications, but to grant them! To cleanse it of its afflictions! To restore it to its rightful glories!"

"WE are the Scarlet Fever! WE are the remedy for all the ills our once-great society has been contaminated by. And we shall burn and we shall smolder, until we have scorched away all that has infected it, and scourged it of its frailties! Only then can it rise again, like the Phoenix from its ashes, strengthened and reborn! Unblemished! Untarnished! And untainted by all that once sought to despoil it."

The ruby-studded chalice, having concluded its circuit around the assembly, was returned to its hoodless leader, filled to the brim with their sanguinary offerings. After a brief inspection, the Hierophant nodded his approval, then placed it delicately atop the stone altar, heedful not to spill so much as a drop.

"Long have we labored," he intoned solemnly, "to bring forth the dawning of this glorious new era. Long have we toiled to complete the masterpiece which ornaments our temple." With a slight chuckle, he spread his arms to indicate the grisly murals which surrounded them. "And tonight, at long last, we shall finally harvest the fruits which we have sown."

"Nine hundred and ninety-nine times have we met thusly in this sanctuary, my brothers. Nine hundred and ninety-nine times have we opened up our veins, and nine hundred and ninety-nine times have we offered up the lifeblood of the innocent. But nine hundred and ninety-nine sacrifices are not sufficient to wake the Lord of Perpetual Anguish from his boundless slumber, are they! For so it is written in our sacred codex: Zh'eth'lel-Gruz may only be roused once a *thousand* innocents have been slain in tribute to his fell glory!"

"And you, my fine young lad," he said silkily, turning to eye the Boy once more, "have the solemn distinction of serving as that thousandth victim."

The hoodless man dipped his fingers into the chalice and swirled them about. When he was satisfied that they had been sufficiently coated in its ghastly contents, he withdrew his dripping digits and began to mark the Boy with characters and ciphers from an alphabet thought long forgotten.

He chanted monotonously as he worked, daubing his fingers in his gruesome paint-bucket and tracing crimson designs upon the Boy's person. His disciples soon joined him in his recitation, droning softly at first, but gradually increasing both the speed and volume of their infernal litany.

The torches flared as one and were suddenly extinguished, as if snuffed by some unseen hand. A heartbeat later, they blazed back to life, brighter than before. Only this time, they burned not with fire, but with sparks of some arcane energy which danced and crackled like heat lightning. They were blood-red in color, casting the chamber with a devilish hue.

Overlooked and disregarded, the threadbare toy rabbit lay, halfway tilted over, where he'd come to rest after being kicked across the cobbles. While the Boy had been straining and struggling to release himself from his bindings, the Rabbit had been ceaselessly matching his exertions, marshalling all the strength his little sawdust heart could muster to achieve its sole ambition.

"I must . . . save . . . the Boy," he told himself. "I must . . . save . . . the Boy."

He echoed this determination like a mantra, repeating it over and over and over again. But the Rabbit had never been especially adept at moving his timeworn little body—especially when there were humans about. Even after hours of his best efforts, he had only barely managed to right himself.

"I must . . . save . . . the Boy," he gasped, endeavoring with all his might to drag himself closer to the sacrificial altar. Though the Rabbit refused to give up, he teetered on the edge of despair. As the chanting of the Scarlet Fever built inexorably towards its crescendo, the bolts of crimson lightning burned ever brighter, hissing and spitting as their tendrils flashed overhead. How could he ever hope to reach the Boy in time?

As for the child in question, after hours spent desperately wishing that he might be rescued, the Boy had finally come to accept that wishes only came true in storybooks. His sole remaining desire was that he might have his old bunny there to comfort him, so that he would not have to die alone, amongst strangers.

"If only Bunny were here," he thought to himself, "it might not be so bad. I never feel as frightened or as lonesome when Bunny's by my side. Oh, if only he were with me now!"

The Hierophant raised the obsidian blade, chanting ever-louder in his strange-sounding tongue, and the Boy knew it would not be long now. He turned his head away, so he would not see the dagger as it fell . . . and when he did, he spied a small brown form sitting on the floor across the room.

"Bunny!" cried the Boy, his voice muffled by his gag.

"Boy!" cried the Rabbit, his voice breaking with anguish.

As their gazes locked, a single tear trickled from the Boy's eye. A matching tear emerged from the Rabbit's boot-button eye. It left a small wet trail as it rolled down his worn velveteen cheek.

"I'm sorry I failed you," the Rabbit whispered. "I wish I had been Real. If I was Real I would have saved you . . ."

The Rabbit's tear splashed onto the floor—and when it did, something wondrous happened. A flower sprouted where the tear had fallen; it was the most wondrous flower he had ever seen, its blooms as blue as a late-summer sky. Its petals parted, and from them stepped a fairy, clad in a shimmering garment the color of sapphires.

"I am the nursery magic fairy," she said, "and I take care of all the toys that have been truly loved by the children they've played with. I've come to make you Real."

"Truly?" exclaimed the Rabbit.

"Truly," replied the fairy. She smiled cherubically, and her entire being seemed to glow with a pale blue light.

She placed her tiny hand atop the Rabbit's head. "You see, when a child has loved a plaything . . . truly loved it . . . it becomes—"

A bolt of crimson lightning arced out, striking the fairy amidst its breast and cutting short its speech. The fairy screamed, its body jerking and twitching uncontrollably as the dark red energies summoned forth by the Scarlet Fever warred with the gentle blue halo that represented the quintessence of nursery magic. Combining together into an incandescent current of radiant violet, the twin forces coursed through the fairy . . . and into the rabbit.

There was a bright flash, and a sound like a thunderclap. The crackling arcane lightning of Zh'eth'lel-Gruz, Lord of Perpetual Anguish, vanished in an instant, and the torches in their sconces burned yet again with an earthly fire. The bewildered disciples of the Scarlet Fever lapsed into silence, abandoning their litany mid-chant, as their Hierophant slowly lowered his dagger. They eyed each other confusedly, uncertain how their ritual had been disrupted.

Behind his gag, the Boy smiled. For he could see what the Scarlet Fever could not.

The nursery magic fairy had disintegrated into a small pile of lavender-tinted dust.

And the Rabbit had been made Real.

But he had not been made Real as the nursery magic fairy had intended.

Augmented by the scarlet bolts of Zh'eth'lel-Gruz, the Rabbit was now ten times his former size. He was muscled like a panther—and bore the fangs and claws to match. Worn and tattered velveteen had been replaced by a smooth and glossy pelt, and his eyes were made of old boot-buttons no longer. They were a bright purple now, and shone with a clean and vibrant light.

In a flash, the Rabbit sprang upon the closest member of the Scarlet Fever. He fell, never to rise again.

The Rabbit leaped into a throng of his fellows—and soon the men who had willingly dripped their blood into the ruby-studded chalice gave of their lifeblood once more. For this rabbit had teeth good for biting and nails good for scratching, and his powerful hind legs had muscles like iron springs, which packed quite a wallop.

And those men had wanted to hurt the boy that he loved.

The Hierophant fell last. He tried to make a fight of it, but the Rabbit hardly felt it when he raked him with his dagger. He was too intent on seizing the scoundrel's throat and ensuring he could never bring that dagger to bear on another child again.

The Scarlet Fever may have raged for nine hundred and ninety-nine nights, but it was broken in less than a minute.

The Boy's fetters were no match for the Rabbit's powerful new jaws—a few short nips, and they soon fell away. The instant he was freed, the Boy flung off his soiled gag, threw his arms around the Rabbit, and buried his face in his fur.

"You're Real now, Bunny," he whispered. "You're Real, and you came for me."

The Bunny said nothing. He simply nuzzled the Boy's cheek. Tenderly, as a mother doe might nuzzle her kit.

They stayed like that, together, for a great long while, until they were ready to begin their journey home.

◻

The Sky Above the Corn Is Full of Eyes and Teeth

~ Erik Grove

Mom says we can't stay in the city. She takes clothes from my drawers and tosses them in the bag we bring on airplanes.

"Get your toothbrush and toothpaste from the bathroom, baby," she says.

In the kitchen, the radio sounds like screaming.

The way she's talking and moving scares me. "Where are we going?"

Mom stops packing and tucks a strand of hair behind her ear. She smiles but it seems like she's trying hard. "We're going to visit Grandma. You want to take some books?" She leaves my bag half-packed and goes to the shelf by my bed. She shows me covers.

"Not that one. *That* one," I say.

She drops the book she's holding and puts her big arms around me. She wet kisses my forehead and hugs too tight. "Okay, baby," she says. "Okay. Go on, get dressed and get your toothbrush, okay? I have to get food for Lucky."

"Lucky's coming?" I ask.

"Of course," she says. "Of course . . ."

She seems tired and I don't know why. Something's wrong but she's not saying what it is. Is Grandma sick? We don't usually visit except holidays and it's not holidays. What about school? It just started and there's supposed to be a spelling test.

I hear the jingle of Lucky's leash down the hall and Mom tells him that he's a good boy. She turns off the radio.

I put on the shirt Grandma got me for Christmas with the red cherries. Grandma always likes it when I wear the shirts or sweaters she gets me but it's too warm for sweaters. Maybe when it's dark. I put more clothes and my favorite books in the suitcase.

Outside, the sunshine is too yellow and car horns are sounding everywhere.

Mom comes back with my toothbrush and toothpaste. She zips up my bag. "Time to go," she says.

"Wait!"

I grab another book that's under my pillow and Mom takes my hand. She leads me to the garage and puts me in back with Lucky. He turns in a circle and mouth-drips on the seat.

"I want you to read your book to me while I drive," Mom says. "Okay?"

"I'm not supposed to read in the car," I remind her because I get sick sometimes.

"This one time you can," she says. "Just keep reading. No matter what, keep reading. For me."

"I'm not stupid," I tell her.

Mom clicks the buckle tight around my waist. "You know how storms come when it's hot, and you used to come into my room when you were scared?" I nod and she continues. "But you're a big girl now and you know; the thunder doesn't last forever."

I start reading when I hear the garage door rumble up. Lucky paces on the seat and on my lap and he whines. I keep reading.

"Good job, baby. Good job."

I turn the pages slow and look out the windows. People are running and lights are flashing. There's a dog we see at the park standing on the sidewalk without anyone holding his leash. He barks at us and then howls. It sounds so sad and lonely. I don't want to look anymore. Lucky lies down, shaking. I turn the pages faster.

It takes longer than it usually does to get to the highway. I'm almost finished with the book when Mom drives faster and the yellow light on my arm gets paler. Lucky presses up close and he's so hot.

My stomach feels dizzy, and I ask Mom if I can stop reading and she says I can.

"Open the window a little," she says.

The breeze smells like campfires. I fall asleep thinking about marshmallows.

Lucky licks my cheek when the car stops and I push his nose away and tell him, "Stop!"

He rests his chin on my leg and sighs dog breath.

It's dark now and where we're parked there aren't any streetlights or city sounds at all. I recognize the shape of Grandma's house, but the lights aren't on. Maybe her power is out?

Mom opens the car door and Lucky wags his tail like a helicopter. "Just a minute," she says, fumbling with my buckle.

"He needs to *pee,*" I say.

Lucky barks.

"I know," Mom says. "Just—"

He hops over me and my booster seat and slips past Mom, running loose.

"Damn it," Mom says.

I interrupt her work on the buckles. "*I can do it,*" I say.

The door to the house opens and a flashlight shines on the front of the car.

"Caitlin?" It's Grandma. She's small and thin and holding Grandpa's old baseball bat in her other hand.

Mom goes around to the front of the car. "It's me," she says.

Grandma drops the bat, and it clacks down the steps. "Thank God," she says.

"Call Lucky," Mom says and then she runs across the gravel to Grandma.

I get unbuckled and hop out of my seat. "Lucky!" I whistle. "Come here, Lucky!"

Mom and Grandma are talking in whispers on the steps so I can't hear. I get Lucky's leash and close the car door.

It's so dark and so quiet and it smells like grass. It's still warm and the night bugs go creak-creak, creak-creak. Lucky ran off into the field and I go after him, whistling and calling his name.

"Lucky! Lucky!" I kick the tall grass. "Silly dog."

Mom says that before I was born— before Grandpa got sick— Grandma had a garden bigger than our house. She grew tomatoes and cabbages and watermelons and strawberries. But now it's all grass that's yellow and goes up over my belly button all the way from the house to the fence. Mom says there's ticks in it and I'm not supposed to play there. Lucky's not supposed to either. But Lucky doesn't listen to anybody.

I call for him all the way to the big wood fence and stop when I get there. The other side is Mr. Harrison's land, and he still has a garden but mostly its corn. The inside of Mr. Harrison's house smells funny, but he has a pool I'm allowed to swim in if Mom is with me and Mr. Harrison gives permission. The lights aren't on at Mr. Harrison's either.

Tall stalks of corn on the other side move but there's not enough wind to blow them, I don't think.

"Lucky?"

Something touches my shoulder and I yell but it's only Mom. "Don't run off," she says. Her grip on me gets firmer. "Are you listening, Allison? Stay close."

I almost cry because I'm tired and I don't understand but I bite my lip instead and nod.

Grandma's flashlight lands on Lucky. He comes out of the grass closer to Grandma's house with his head low and tail swish-swishing. "Found him." she shouts, and we get the silly dog and our things from the car.

The last thing I need is the book I forgot, and I go to get it but stop on the way back and look up. The stars are different and the dark, it seems like it's moving, like it's breathing. I feel it, warm and wet on the back of my neck and I hear it, a distant soft thunder.

I run inside before Mom gets mad at me again.

The house is lit with battery lanterns and candles. Grandma hugs me and says I'm taller again and then I brush my teeth while Mom makes the bed up for me.

"What happened to the lights?" I ask Grandma.

"Not sure, kiddo," she says. "It happens out here in the sticks. It will probably all be back to normal tomorrow morning. Be sure to get your back teeth. Show me." I show her, toothpaste foam dribbling down and my mouth wide. Grandma nods. "That's good."

She tickles my back and I giggle and spit mint slobber into the sink.

The room Lucky and I sleep in used to be Grandpa's office, but he went to Heaven before I could remember meeting him. There are fishing lures in frames on the walls still and photographs of him standing in a stream with tall boots. From here I can't hear Mom and Grandma talking but I know they're up late in the kitchen at the breakfast bar because I hear their voices when I creep to the door and open it but just *barely*.

"You didn't see it," Mom says.

Grandma hurumphs and then says, "This isn't my first late night looking out the windows wondering what's coming, Caity. The people that need to figure it out, will figure it out. All we need to do is sit tight, stay calm, and look after the kay-eye-dee-dee-oh."

I've been able to decipher Grandma spelling words out loud like that since I was way littler, and I would say so if it wouldn't get me in trouble for snooping. Behind me, Lucky jumps off the bed and comes over to investigate.

"You didn't see it," Mom repeats. "The sky… The sky wasn't *right.* The color was like before a tornado but amber with a sound to it and people, people just started—"

"No use remembering it," Grandma says.

Lucky bumps me, headed for the open door, so I pull it closed quick and run back into bed and get under the covers in case they heard the slam.

I must be dreaming.

It's not quite light out and it sounds like hail or bullets bouncing off the roof. Lucky's hiding under the bed and I go barefoot to the window and pull the curtains over but all I see is night, so I go into the living room.

There's a flashlight on the table. I click it on and open the front door.

It's not hail; it's rain, I think, but the rain is too dark and too thick. I reach out and it splatters my palm. My hand comes back slick and red. I point the light toward the clouds and the small hairs on my arms stand up. It doesn't seem like clouds; it seems like when we went to the aquarium and there were things shifting in the unlit water.

Grandma yanks me inside and snatches the flashlight. She clicks it off and claps her hand over my mouth.

She sits on the floor, holding me, holding me quiet until the rain stops.

I must be dreaming.

It smells like bacon when I wake up and Lucky is sitting in front of the bedroom door. I'm in bed again. It's not raining and I'm not sure if it ever rained at all, but the curtains in the window are open. Lucky thumps his tail on the floor.

"I'm coming, Lucky." Silly dog.

Grandma is cooking on a camping stove on the back deck. The sliding door is open. I open the screen and Lucky runs out to do his business in the yard. I walk over to Grandma.

"Morning, sleepyhead," she says. "Hungry?"

The wood planks are cool and maybe damp, and it smells like rain but regular rain.

I sit on top of a big plastic cooler.

Grandma puts eggs on a plate that already has bacon on it. She gives it to me with a fork. "No juice," she says. "Sorry."

"Where's Mom?"

"She drove into town to get supplies."

"No power still?"

Grandma cracks more eggs into a pan. "They're working on it." She points a spatula at me. "You need socks, kiddo."

I wiggle my toes in her direction. "Did it rain?"

She frowns. "Broke the yolk," she says.

"I remember raining."

Grandma shakes salt into the pan. "It's that time of year," she says.

I freeze with the fork almost to my mouth; there's a dry dark brown spot on the sleeve of my shirt that wasn't there before.

Lucky barks somewhere I can't see.

"You can't let him get away, Allison," Grandma says. "Out here, he can run off and get in the road. It's not safe."

I whistle for him, and Lucky tromps back onto the deck. He's munching on something.

"Let's see what you got." Grandma stoops down to check. She pries something small and white from him and stares at it.

"What is it?" I ask.

"Bone," Grandma says. She throws it as far away as she can and Lucky barks and turns to run after.

"No, Lucky!" I shout. "Stay! Bad dog!"

Lucky comes over to me and lies down like he's grumpy. I pet him with my bare foot and sneak him half a piece of bacon.

"Scoot," Grandma says so I move over on the cooler, and she sits next to me. "Your Mom said you brought books to read?"

I nod.

"Why don't you pick one while I wash up?"

I shrug. "Okay."

"After you put socks on, little miss." She tickles me under the arm.

"Stop it!"

On the other side of the fence, something is moving around in the corn again.

"Mr. Harrison," I say and point.

Grandma takes my plate.

"I'm not done!"

"Go on inside," she says and then she uses her no-fun voice. "*Go.*"

"Come on, Lucky." I push the dog ahead of me with my knee and we go in through the slider.

Grandma closes it and turns the latch behind us. Then she goes to the front door and turns the deadbolt.

I lie on my tum and read while Grandma does the dishes. I might tell her I know how to wash dishes too, but she doesn't seem like she wants help. She keeps looking up from the sink out the window.

"When's Mom coming back?" I ask.

"Soon," she says.

That's what they say when they don't know.

"Maybe we'll play a game later," Grandma says. "You want to pick one from the shelf?"

Grandma's only got old games missing pieces. Her Monopoly has mismatched dice and no little dog. When I asked her what happened to it, Grandma told me, "Ask your mother."

"If you want," I say but I don't pick a game and Grandma reads on the couch for a while and then she falls asleep.

I put shoes on and click Lucky's leash on because he can't be trusted, and I take him out.

Lucky pulls me into the grass and sniffs around at something that has flies around it. I yank him back. "Be *a good dog*, Lucky!"

I swat the flies and move the grass so I can see. It's gross old meat with white things moving around on it. "Gross, Lucky!"

Walking though the grass there's more meat but it's scattered around. I don't let Lucky eat any of it. It can't be good for him. But where did it come from? I look up. It's lavender color almost but there aren't any clouds.

Lucky pulls so hard toward the fence that I can't make him stay put so we go close and the corn's moving on the other side again.

"Hello? Mr. Harrison?"

Lucky ducks under the bottom rail of the fence and he tugs so hard I might lose hold of his leash, so I climb through the fence too and go with him into the corn stalks.

Inside the stalks goes over my head and at first it smells sweet and good, and I remember how Mr. Harrison would tear the husk off an ear of corn. "Like dental floss," he'd say and let corn silk fall to the ground. Then he'd show me the yellow inside and take a bite just like that.

"It's tastes better raw," he'd say and smile with bits stuck between his teeth.

I tried it like that, and it was good, I guess, but I like it the way Grandma makes it with butter and salt and pepper.

Deeper into the stalks, it's different. The smell gets real bad like the trash can when its real hot. Between Lucky's barks I hear loud breathing.

". . . Mr. Harrison?"

"Shhh-shhh," a voice says from somewhere in the corn. "Quiet, girl. It's listening."

I go closer but Lucky won't follow. He sits down like a lump in the middle of the stalks. I can barely see someone a little ways away. Mr. Harrison, I think. He's squatting funny and picking at something on the ground.

"Who's listening?" I ask.

Mr. Harrison puts something in his mouth and he's slurping and crunching and slurping and crunching and spit comes down his chin and his white shirt is stained all brown like the end of my sleeve. His fingers are sticky and flies buzz around him.

"The sky," he says. "It eats and eats and eats . . ." He points a finger up, but I don't look.

"Are you okay?" I ask him.

He screams like the radio.

I tug Lucky and I run, and I would have let him go but Lucky runs too. We get to the fence and climb over the rail back to Grandma's land and through the tall grass and inside and I lock the door.

Grandma stirs on it the couch. "What is it?" she asks.

I don't say. I'll never ever say.

*

Mom comes back with bags of ice and food before lunch time.

"I got you a new book," she says, and I take it and I hug her and don't even say that I've already read it before.

The lights come back while Grandma is fixing sandwiches.

"Told you!" Grandma says.

Mom smiles. "You did." She looks so worn out. She puts a plate with peanut and jelly and chips in front of me.

"Thunder doesn't last forever," I say.

Mom reaches for me. "Come here, baby," she says, and I do. She hugs me more and makes a loud gagging noise. "You stink!"

Grandma points at me and Lucky. "Both of them need a bee-ay-tee-aitch."

"I'm not a baby," I say.

"Oh?" Mom looks over to Grandma and Grandma gives a small nod. "Maybe you need a new nickname then, huh? Are you a little bug? A little *stink* bug?"

"I'm not!"

She wet kisses my ear.

"Gross!"

"Finish your lunch and then go get clean clothes from your suit-case, bug," Mom says.

I eat the chips but only half my sandwich and Mom says that's okay she'll save it for me.

"Maybe we can play Monopoly later?" I suggest.

"After you deal with your stink situation," Mom says.

Back in Grandpa's room I sit on the bed and look at the old photos. I wish I knew him. I wish people didn't get sick.

Raindrops come down on the roof and Lucky scuttles under the bed again.

"Scaredy dog," I say but I'm a little scared too and I'm not sure why. I'm a big girl now.

I go to the window and watch the rain coming down.

"It's nothing to be afraid of," I tell Lucky and I close the curtain. Lucky creeps from under the bed and licks my cheek. I flop his ears around. "Silly dog."

"Hurry up, stink bug!" Mom calls from the bathroom. I can hear the water filling up the tub and almost smell the steam and soap.

"You're next, Lucky," I say and all he does is sigh.

⬧

They Get Down on All Fours

~ Basile Lebret

To SC Parent

The first time Susan saw the naked women she was standing by the first story window, waiting for Derek to come back home. She thought, no, she KNEW he was with some other girl and the intangible guilt that weighed upon her collar seemed heavier.

It was dark outside, yet the thirty-year-old something clearly discerned the pale stain of a body crawling on all fours, no, slithering amongst the dried branches and dark weeds. Susan didn't know it was a woman at first, and it would be a lie to pretend her worries didn't suddenly vanish, replaced by the angst one gets gripped with when cornered. Except she wasn't in some back alley. She was in her home, with the moon drooling her adamantine shine onto the always clean, always neat bed.

That night, Susan closed every door with a double lock. She hesitated over leaving the keys in the front one solely to piss Derek off.

She. Didn't. Do. It.

When she got back home on the next evening, Derek was already there, staining the couch with his greasy fingers as he ate salted peanuts.

Susan looked at him, in the electric light the Oled screen projected across his face, in the dark, and she wondered about the last time she found their couple endearing. She couldn't. They had hiked back in the days, and Derek had been so benevolent and caring. The woman wondered when everything had changed.

She had first thought of giving him a baby before remembering she never thought a kid could save a couple. She had always been adamant doing this could only fuck up the kid's life. Said these very words so many times she could almost hear herself uttering the syllable, a glass of wine stuck tightly in her left hands, a fire (or a bar-becue) roaring in her back.

Her passion for Derek had disappeared around the same time they had stopped going out. To be fair, his passion for her had vanished as soon as she gained weight. She didn't want to admit it at first, but as time had passed, she'd grappled and reasoned and finally accepted it. A full-time job with some lengthy commute will do that to you. It's important to note she didn't mind her body changing, she had always been one to adapt. Still she missed the days when she entered the bedroom and Derek looked at her starry eyed.

This was one of her most distinct souvenirs. Derek, lying in his underwear on their then-messy bed, his eyes glinting in the harsh sunlight which peered through the shades. The air, all around, full of dust particles smelled of sweat and tobacco coming from the first floor, for Derek was still smoking at the time and, yes, a tad like his dick too.

When Susan thought of this, she couldn't repress licking her own lips. If she concentrated hard enough or the images lingered for too long in the theater of her mind, she would have to go take a shower.

She missed this, yet the balance they had built which enabled them to still go to the opera and visit some exhibits, she liked that. Everyone, from the still outside looking in, said that they were such a perfect couple and she sometimes wanted to scream: "Well, my pussy hasn't been touched in three years but, hey as you say." It would have been gratuitous and nonchalant and totally unlike her. So, she never did it.

Susan was standing by the window and an oddly dark night had befallen upon the world the second time she witnessed the naked women. The complete lack of light meant she had to concentrate really hard to witness the cold, cold flesh prowling in the wilderness that extended behind the house.

This was a new suburb Derek and her had been able to buy into. Behind the rows of uniformed and boring houses laid a chaotic forest no one was acknowledging except for the kids and the teen-agers who no doubt got lost in there to mess up and smoke weed.

Susan had never even walked under the warm shadows of the trees as the sunlight basked and flickered through their leaves.

She wouldn't fathom the idea of getting in at night.

Yet here she was, staring intently outside, staring hard enough that despite the petroleum tar that was the world she peered not one but two bodies disappearing in the brushes. She noticed the second flesh thanks to the person's colossal figure. Susan was sure it was a woman this time. Being honest would be admitting Susan craved the apparitions.

Under her feet, through the stairs which led to the ground floor, she could hear the Netflix program Derek was watching, it spoke of a child predator. The room smelled of the half-burned pasta he had prepared her for dinner.

The naked bodies, the way every shade of gray reflected upon their flesh and their skin and the angle of their bones, the crevasses of their cellulite, they haunted her. She realized it as she was standing in the metro in Bibliothèque François Mitterrand, absent minded enough that she might have forgotten to get off the damned thing.

She wondered what it felt like, to crawl naked on all fours. Blurry souvenirs crept into her mind like spiders preying on mice. The thirty-year-old woman thought of the spiky feel one has when some herbs cross against their skin. She thought of the tiny sharp pain of stepping on nettles. She recalled the imbalance one has to fight when walking bare-footed on uneven ground.

Commute didn't smell of dried sweat and myriad of perfume anymore. The scent of the underbrush and dried leaves prickled through her nose. Susan felt, legitimately felt the sunshine rays that pierced and survived under the canopy and came to die onto the skin of adventurous children.

There existed a burning, not only in the thrall of her uterus but in the leather of her feet and the peak of her stomach. In the tip of her every digit.

She watched them for a third night. Naked herself this time. Her clothes strung upon the ground as soon-to-be haystacks. Later on, she would reminisce about this moment, looking at her entire body as if she stood behind herself, on the bed. In the black and white glow which spewed from the nocturnal sky she was phenomenal, beautiful. Her blisters, her bulges not smooth but rendered sharp, full of contrast thanks to the stark opposition to the blue light of the moon and the creeping stomacal darkness.

Susan could not repress a shudder as she put her right hand upon the wet ground that Derek swore he would one day turn into a legit garden. With her ass up, trying to imitate the women she had seen coming into the woods, she felt ridicule and slightly aloof. There was a clumsiness to one walking that way, and a subtle yet pregnant empowerment of having her labia on display. Part of her hypo cortex thought of it as spreading her hormones all over the place as some cat in heat and this, this kindled a hunger in her belly.

When she'd get to the end of the lawn, as the longer weeds of the forest enthralled her, and spiked her, and caressed her, she knew she'd made the right choice. Going through the twenty meters of her garden had tightened Susan's decision.

There was something exhilarating in all of this.

The blackness of the forest was another problem entirely. Wherever she'd looked, she could only see elm and oak trees whose trunk appeared white on a psychedelic background of black, gray and white. But something in her feet, in the way the slightly wet leaves stuck under her soles, in the way worms sometimes crawled in between her fingers as she grabbed the forest soil to propel her body forwards, something told her she had to push on.

She heard the cackling of the fire and the cackling of the throats before she could see them. Fighting against the angst, she continued to walk with her head low until the smoke of the fire drowned her nostrils and the warmth felt so close to her scalp, she thought she would turn Joan of Arc.

Susan stood up, as dread crept through her spine, silence befell upon the group.

She eyed every one of them, the way the fire swept upon a saggy tit, the way the darkness ate at a cellulite-ridden butt. She took in all their bodies, the one with shaved crotch, the hairy navel, the penises.

The thirty something hadn't finished her tour when the other screamed. It was not like the Gregorian chant male throat eruct among cold and damp stones. It was imprecise and shattered yet in its cacophony laid the hint of a harmony soon to be touched.

She stared at the sky and began to sing with her sisters, as all around the air smelled of smoke and ash faeries rose up to the moon, dancing to their chants.

There existed no touching at first, yet she felt invigorated. Better at work, better at life. On a whim she decided to buy herself new clothes. Garments that would complement her figure. No point in hiding, is what she thought.

Males and females began to see her on the commute. And this hadn't happened in a lot of years.

She thought of those mega churches she always laughed at, how she, for a very long time, had mocked the people who gathered and shared their grief and went into a frenzy. But a frenzy is refreshing. Moving your naked flesh as if no one else mattered under a cloudy sky, as the warmth from a hearth fight with the frost-bitten weather was something everyone should experience.

Soon, she got to touch human beings again, the grainy texture of those covered in pimples, the porous nature of the sebum ridden one, the smooth one, the dried ones, the greasy ones. There was nothing sexual in this.

The night ritual had more to do with empathy, with some ethereal link that bound them all. She knew, Susan knew not one of them would bother the other in everyday life, the common one where people gather and forget about their friend as they begin to think about insurance plans and retirement plans and business plans.

She began to hate the system which lies to us and prevents us from really caring, from really sharing, from really bounding as we fight our solitude and our depression and our angst like cornered animals in a rescue shelter. All our backs against the wall waiting for this man with a piston in his hand asserting he's friendly but we all see through his intent, and the harm he says he's doing is out of pity.

Even during her day life, she began to crave the touch of the skin, the strict feeling of the plastic fabric, and the scratched nature of cooking instruments. She distinguished better when a street smelled of shit, or of ozone, of carbon dioxide we pour into the sky 'til the sun is harsh and burns babies' skin.

Every night, she would rejoin the group, on all fours, her vaginal scent weaving a spider thread from the back door to the firepit. Not as a sign of heat, but a territorial feature.

They would scream, and chant, and scorch the earth and their bodies and they would dance to the rhythm of howling wind and the staccato of the cicadas and they'd touched one another and feel their sweat and the dry skin, and the soft lips and wrinkled eyelids.

In due time, they began to hunt.

"woman rolls sandstone"

~ L. E. Daniels

~700
million
years old—
you are proof
of epochs. against
my devolving crawl
along lawn and gravel in orthotics,
you turn one. side. at. a. time, pushed
by this middle-aged spine—nothing but
mountains had spines when you were formed.
evolution's fingers barely avoid pinning as we
heave sandy pink and tan strata of quartz, calcite,
feldspar, compacted by precambrian forces. now seated in a sunny garden,
you gaze like the face of a penultimate clock and melt slowly in the rain.

Harold and the
Colour-out-of-Space Crayon

~ *Kevin Wetmore*

One evening, after thinking it over for some time, Harold decided to go for a walk in the pale, misty moonlight.

There wasn't any moon, and Harold needed a moon to go for a walk in the moonlight.

Earlier that day there had come that white noontide cloud, that string of explosions in the air, and that pillar of smoke descending down right towards Harold's house! A great rock fell out of the sky and bedded itself in the ground beside the well next to Harold's bedroom. Harold, being a curious four-year-old went out to see what had happened. Miasma poured out of the well, but next to it appeared to be a crayon. At first, Harold thought it was purple, but it displayed shining bands unlike any known colours of the normal spectrum. These were not sane, wholesome colours, but rather strange, indescribable ones.

Harold reckoned it would be a very fun crayon to use.

So now, in the evening, thinking he would go for a walk in the moonlight, Harold used the Colour-out-of-Space crayon to draw a moon. The moon he drew with the Colour-out-of-Space crayon was like that of the Dreamlands. Although high in the sky, one could see it had great forests and oily seas. The ruins on the light side were a spectacle to behold, hinting at an ancient civilization brought low, crumbling temples to forgotten gods and unsettling, decaying shards of a once-mighty race of beings.

Harold needed something to walk on, and so he drew a path. He drew a long, straight path so he would not get lost. He set off on his walk, taking his Colour-out-of-Space crayon with him. He did not seem to be getting anywhere on the path he had drawn, perhaps because instead of the long, straight path he had drawn, the curious lines created by the Colour-out-of-Space crayon warped into strange, non-Euclidian geometries. The path he had drawn ran over the hills and through the valleys, and ran straight where the blasted heath is now; but people ceased to use it, on account of the unimaginable horrors no one ever imagined Harold would unleash during his stroll.

So Harold left the path to cut across a field. And the eldritch, ruin-covered moon went with him.

The shortcut led to the edge of a tenebrous and foetid forest. There was no vegetation of any kind on that broad expanse, but only a fine grey dust or ash which no wind seemed ever to blow about. The trees near it were sickly and stunted, and many dead trunks stood or lay rotting at the rim. As Harold walked further into the forest, all the trees blossomed forth in strange colours. So Harold decided to draw an apple tree. *The apples would be very tasty*, Harold thought, *when they turned red.* I should perhaps note, the apples would never turn red—drawn by Harold's unearthly crayon, the only colour they would ever know is one indescribable by human tongue. But Harold thought the apples were worth guarding, so he drew a Dimensional Shambler to guard the tree. It was a terribly frightening Dimensional Shambler. It frightened even Harold, and he was the one who had drawn it.

He backed away from the tree and the Shambler, and as he backed away his hand holding the Colour-out-of-Space crayon shook. Suddenly, his feet and legs wet, Harold realized what was happening, but by then he had fallen into the blue waters whose surface mirrors the sky and ripples in the moonlight. And Harold thought that the secrets of his strange days would be one with the deep's secrets; one with the hidden lore of old ocean, and all the mystery of primal earth.

He came up thinking fast and drew a boat. He quickly set sail on the black seas of infinity. Since it was not meant that he should voyage far, Harold made land without much trouble. He stepped on the shore, wondering what strange land he had washed up on. He took his Colour-out-of-Space Crayon and drew a sea-green stone idol coated in seaweed and chiseled in the likeness of Bokrug, the great water-lizard. *Now I'm in the ruins of Sarnath*, Harold thought. He did not draw any ruins, though, just only the marshy shore.

The thought of the shore made him think of picnics, and the thought of picnics made him hungry. He drew pies—nine of them, although given the inability to describe the work of the crayon other than "a colour," it was hard to tell what kind of pies they were. The pies began to turn grey and brittle, and Harold was not hungry anymore, but he hated to see even foetid, decaying, strange, alien pies go to waste. Of what fruit, no tongue can say, for it is not a word capable of being spoken by human mouth.

Harold drew a very hungry moose, a deserving porcupine, and a curious shoggoth to enjoy the pies. The moose and porcupine ate the pies and the shoggoth ate the moose and porcupine, and Harold again grew afraid of his own creations, so he draw a high wall around the shoggoth and yelled over it that if the Shoggoth was still hungry, there was a Dimensional Shambler and an apple tree with unripened alien apples a ways back down the path. He walked in the struggling beams of that waning crescent moon away from the wall as quickly as his little feet would carry him.

He thought if he went high enough, he might be able to see his bedroom window. He felt he ought to be getting to bed, and the crayon's drawings were giving him a strange headache, besides. He climbed a mountain, hoping to get to the top and see his bedroom window. As he climbed, he disappeared into the clouds until he noticed in the distance a strange, high house in the mist. None of its windows was his window.

So he made some windows. Then he drew a whole building full of windows. A strange high apartment building in the mist. Then he climbed to the top floor of the building and looked out the topmost window. When he looked from that highest of all gable windows, looked while the candles sputtered and the insane viols howled with the night-wind, he saw no city spread below, and no friendly lights gleaming from remembered streets, but only the blackness of space illimitable; unimagined space alive with motion and music, and having no semblance to anything on earth.

So Harold went back down to the street and asked a policeman, but the policeman just pointed in the direction Harold was already going and said to him, *Iä! Iä! The Black Goat of the Woods!*

Harold thanked the policeman, and then tried to draw him a black goat to keep him company, but Harold only had the Colour-out-of-Space Crayon, so the goat he drew was both indescribable and difficult to look at.

Harold then remembered that the moon was always visible through his window. Uttering ancient incantations known only to the Men of Leng who, like Harold, remember what civilized men had forgotten, Harold drew a window around that waning crescent moon.

Then Harold drew his bed and got in and drew up the covers. The Colour-out-of-Space Crayon dropped to the floor as Harold dropped off to sleep. As he slept, the colour spread from where the crayon fell to the ground throughout the bedroom, the rest of the house, and the land on which it sat. Only a dusty grey desert remained, nor has anything ever grown there since. To this day it sprawls open to the sky like a great spot eaten by acid in the woods and fields, and the few who have ever dared glimpse it in spite of the rural tales have named it "the blasted heath." But the folks in the valley to this day speak of Harold and his peculiar Colour-out-of-Space crayon in whispered tones, and will sometimes go down to the shore and leave a pie for the shoggoth that still sometimes comes up to the marshy land.

⛶

End of Line

~ Elad Haber

If I was the counting sort, like my son, I would say this is the eighty-fifth time we've been on this ride.

That's not an exact number but I like the way eighty-five sounds. High enough to be notable, but not such a big number as to be improbable. I think about asking my son how many times *he* thinks we've been on this ride, but I know that will turn into a hours-long notes-assisted fact-finding mission and I'm not in the mood.

We've been in line for awhile, but the way the outdoor portion of the line curves and loops around itself, I can see the bored employee carrying the tall sign that says END OF LINE not too far away.

It would be impossible for me to even guess how long we've been here. We are in Line-Time.

Line-Time is a strange place. It affects people in different ways. Some families seem to revel in it. They play games where they hold up their cellphones to their foreheads while siblings shout clues and the person has to guess the text on the screen. I don't know what that's called. Some people use the chance to snack and chat. There is always a place to buy popcorn and pretzels near a line so folks take the time to fuel up on saturated fats and carbohydrates. Many just stare at their phones, the occasional exasperated sigh and a peak on tippee-toes about what the hell is the hold up. Some families choose that moment, surrounded by strangers, to argue. That's always uncomfortable.

I read. My son draws or does math puzzles. Every once in a while, I glance behind his shoulder at what he's drawing and it usually has something to do with the ride. He loves this ride. Today, though, he shifts his drawing pad away from me whenever I try to steal a glance.

"Hey Dad," he says.

"Yeah?"

"How many tentacles does an octopus have?"

I think on it a moment. "Well, I think eight to sixteen would be a decent number, depending on body size." I stop. Did he say *tentacle?* I thought there was another word for that. "Hey, Brody . . ."

Just then the next people in line shuffle ahead and we move to take up their position. There's a faint left-over aroma, like someone badly needs a shower.

I shift my body far to the side to see what Brody is drawing, but he's already on a new page scribbling numbers and I forgot what I was going to ask.

It's normal to lose track of things during Line-Time.

We're close enough to the start of the ride that it's time to pack up our distractions. I shove my e-reader into my bag and Brody does the same with his sketchbook.

The interior of the building has the kind of madman aesthetic that was popular a half century ago. Every inch of wall is adorned with moving parts in bright colors. The ride itself is on these large boats with church-pew seating. The water below the boats is a disconcerting shade of black. The whole thing is weird, but like I said, my kid likes it.

We wait near the gates. Almost our turn.

"Excited, buddy?" I ask him like I always do.

"Yep!" is the reply.

As we load into the church-boats, I can hear the faint twangs of the ride's signature theme music wafting out of the dark tunnel ahead. I paint a grin on my face. *That song* as my wife likes to phrase it. Sometimes with an expletive in the middle. That (blanking) song is the reason she stopped coming to the park with us.

It doesn't really bother me. Yeah, it's repetitive and kind of annoying, but music never seems to linger in my head like it does for others. I like music, sure, but it's not that important to me and I can quickly forget whatever gets stuck in other people's heads.

Brody is smiling as the boat glides forward.

I always look for something new. As the boat crawls into the first cavernous space and the *blanking* song repeats like a mantra, there's a cornucopia of visual stimuli. Automatons with limited movements and static expressions. It's a symphony for the eyes. And I do always find something new. Some unique angle or a different perspective based on boat position. It's like a game in that way. A "Spot the Difference" style puzzle. Did that clown always have a frown? How many hula dancers are usually there?

As we snake around the space, I notice the hairs on the back of my neck rising a bit. Something funky in the air.

And that's when I see it. Dominating the back of the room, alive with swirling mists, an octopus the size of a building. Its eight to sixteen tentacles pulse and gyrate. Unlike the fifty-year old automatons that occupy the space, this thing *shines* like something newly constructed. It turns its massive head and twin purple eyes flip open. I think I hear it growl.

I wrench my eyes from the octopus to Brody, who is awestruck. The octopus yawns open a massive mouth. It swallows the boat in front of us. I try to find some words. Something to shout, to scream, to pray for someone to help us.

But the damn song keeps going as if nothing has changed and the boat inches closer and closer. I'm not proud of it, but I close my eyes.

There's a loud munching and crunching sound.

I open my eyes. A dude near me is going to town on some popcorn. His kids are trading pop-it's and candy. We're in the middle of the line, I can see the guy holding the sign but the sign itself is blocked by some thin trees. Brody is sketching and I've got my e-reader open but I don't remember what I am reading. In fact, I'm not sure how we got back in line at all.

"Hey buddy," I say. Brody looks up. "Everything okay?"

"Yep!" he says and goes back to his drawing.

Line-Time is weird. Sometimes you lose track of time and sometimes it slows down until you can feel arduous seconds ticking by. I feel like I'm somewhere in the middle. I focus on my kid to kill some time.

"What are you drawing?"

Brody hesitates for a moment, which is odd. Usually, he can't wait to show me his work. Then he gets over it and shrugs and spins the sketchbook around.

It's a picture of a man, but not a regular man, more like one of those blank-looking dolls that resemble a person without any of a person's signature features. A crash test dummy kind of man. Next to the man is a series of numbers and mathematical equations.

"Oh," I say. "Neat!"

Brody sighs. "Yeah, it doesn't turn out well for him though."

Concern pinches at the corners of my brain. "What do you mean?"

He shrugs again. "You'll see." Then back to drawing.

Reverberations in Line-Time are the barometric pressure in the air that indicate a coming storm. It's a scratch at the back of your mind, trying and failing to remember something.

I sneak a couple of more glances at Brody's sketchbook. I see what appears to be a bartender. A dancing couple. More random numbers on the borders of the pages like some secret language. He flips the page and gets back to drawing like someone possessed. His hands move in a blur, his fingertips black from chalk.

At the gates again. "Excited, buddy?" I ask him.

A pause. His expression is vacant, but just for a moment. Then the smile comes. "Yep!" he says.

On the ride, the music in an endless loop, we pass through the first chamber and no massive octopus tries to eat us. I sigh in relief.

But then in the next room, I notice changes. A winning hand in the Spot in the Difference game. Usually, this chamber is devoted to the Asian cultures, but instead it looks like a homage to fantasy stories. One side of the room has volcanos and quaint hillside communities, strangely small. On the other side is a patchwork inn from every elf and wizard story written in the last half century. I recognize some of the characters now. The patron at the bar, his facial features not quite filled in. A bartender surrounded by drinking glasses. A couple dancing.

As the boat crawls forward through the snaking path around the chamber, a scene plays out in the inn. There's a freestanding door. It opens and a new character dressed in black enters. Purple trim on his hat and trousers, but everything else is the color of midnight. He raises his arm. Something is in his hand. It doesn't compute because it doesn't match the genre, but it looks quite clearly like a handgun.

There's another iteration of the man in black. He's closer to the bar now. The gun in his hand cocks back and forth as if it's firing.

The other figures react. The man at the bar flings his chest forward and back as if he's being repeatedly shot. The bartender tries to duck under the bar but instead falls back in a flurry of broken glass, which then reassembles and he goes through the futile attempt again. The dancing couple in the back fall on top of each other. Again and again.

And then, hidden partly in shadow near a wall, the killer in black is in a posture of struggle. Arms and other misshapen limbs appear to be erupting from holes in his body. The boat turns a corner before I can see what else comes out of him.

I hear a tight and quick giggle. I look down. It's Brody, he's smiling but not in the joyful countenance of ignorant youth. There's a darkness in that giggle. He catches me staring. His smile scares me.

The world around us swirls and speeds up then slows down and we're in line again.

The guy holding the END OF LINE sign is just a few feet away. I try to catch his eye, to share my wordless sympathy for his dull work, but he doesn't look at me.

Besides, I have other things to concern myself with.

I touch Brody on the shoulder. "Hey buddy," I say. "Do you notice anything strange going? Like, how are we on this ride again?"

Brody's voice still has that youthful lilt of innocence. "We're not on the ride, silly. We're in line."

I feel like I need to press the point. "Yeah, but we were in this line not that long ago, right? We already did the ride. Maybe you want to go do something else?"

His expression is blank.

"There's that new rollercoaster. The line is long, but the ride is amazing."

Blank, but also the first hints of frustration.

"No," he says. "I want to ride this one."

"Are you sure? Lots of other options."

I can hear him growl a little. "Yes, I am sure."

"Okay, okay."

He goes back to sketching. I try to glimpse what's he drawing but his fingers are moving so fast, it's all a blur. On one page, I see boats piled on top of each other like a highway wreck. I see fallen trees and animals with red holes in their chest. Some kind of conflagration, bodies strewn on the floor. All the pages have what looks like a random collection of numbers scattered about, like toys strewn on a messy bedroom floor.

I look around to see if I recognize anyone else on the line. Are we all repeating this nightmare or is it just Brody and I? They're all wearing their signatures themed shirts, hats, ears, backpacks, so it's hard to differentiate but I'm pretty good with faces. I don't recognize anyone. Just us, then.

Back at the gates. The previous group of riders approaches on their boats. They're all smiles and laughter. No scattered blood on their clothes or the shocked faces of those who just witnessed a tragedy.

We'll be fine. This must all be in my head. Too much sun, not enough hydration. I should have gotten more sleep last night.

"Excited, buddy?"

No answer this time. Brody is expressionless as he climbs onto the pews. A pair of adults without a kid in tow sit down next to us. We're at the front of the boat. Brody leans forward to grasp at the boat's edge. He squeezes the metal in anticipation.

We glide into the first chamber and it's all normal. I recognize the characters and their placements. Nothing out of the ordinary. Same with chambers two and three. I sit back and relax a little. We'll be done soon.

And then there's a screech from below us and the boat stops. The boat behind us bangs into our boat with a twist of whiplash, just a bit. We all look back as loudspeakers come on and a pre-recorded message explains a ride stoppage. It's surprisingly cheerful.

Brody is grinning and the adults next to us are smiling too as if a ride breakdown is a noteworthy thing. Some people take out their phones and start recording.

And then another whiplash as another boat collides with the sudden traffic jam, this one also pretty short. But there's more boats coming. The next one slams—hard!—into a boat and all of us lurch forward and then back. The first stuck boat, ours, appears to be caught in something. It spins in ways it's not supposed to. It's only a matter of time before—

A splash. Some kid has fallen in the water. His dad jumps in after. The water should be a foot or two, ankle-deep, but they haven't come back up.

"Where are they?" someone shouts.

More screams from other boats as additional collisions throw people overboard. I look around us. We're actually not far from a maintenance ledge. There's stairs and I even see an emergency exit door.

I grab Brody, whose eyes are wide, in excitement or fear, I don't know. "We gotta get out of here!" I shout. I lead him to the edge of the boat. "I'll go first." I take a step and then jump. I land on hard ground. I reach my arms out and beckon Brody forward. He lands on the edge.

I help our row-mates to safety as well and then turn to lead Brody to the emergency exit.

But he's not there.

I turned away for him for just a few seconds.

Where did he go?

"BRODY!"

From either side, there are access paths into the background of the ride. He must have escaped into one, but which one? I pick one side at random and rush through.

This is the side of the ride no one is supposed to see. The scenery has raw wood on the backsides and numbers and simple equations written in sharpie. There are wires snaking on the ground. I step over them while trying to survey the chamber for any hint of Brody.

Sometimes there's a break in the backgrounds and I can see the automatons, but something is wrong with them. They look beaten and broken. I don't know if it's just the angle but it looks like someone went on a rampage and targeted these poor, brainless, repetitive automatons. Some of them have holes in their chest and fake blood on the floor. A few are clutching their middle sections while pieces of their insides hang from their bloody fingers. A couple are prone on the ground in abstracts of pain.

"BRODY!" I shout again.

Ahead I can hear the crackling of a fire. I climb over some wooden blocks behind a fake building. Strips of red, yellow, and orange paper flutter in the wind. Then one of the strips catches fire (*real fire*) and suddenly it's everywhere and I feel the warmth like a wave. I don't stop. I can't. I push through the fluttering paper.

And Brody is there, surrounded by blackened and burned bodies of automatons. I can tell these are the ones that are supposed to indicate a "perfect" world, beyond color and nationality. Except they are unrecognizable now.

Above us, holes appear in the sky. They are nothingness black with smoke like threads around them, shining like that octopus with the glistening tentacles. The ever-present music shifts and twists as if it's being swallowed. The floating black holes ensnare my gaze. I can't look away. Something wet and sticky and purple emerges from the holes. A tentacle. Do I hear some kind of laughter?

Someone shakes my shoulder and my eyes break from the holes in the sky. It's Brody. His cheeks are tear-stained. His expression is a mix of guilt and fear and it breaks my heart. I hunch down around him to hold him and close my eyes and hope that...

The heat, the cackling, and the looping music is gone.

Nearby, the cruel joke that is the END OF LINE sign is being held up by some guy with a fake smile.

Brody's face is still in shock. He's looking around like something might come and attack him. I wipe some soot from his cheek.

"Hey buddy," I say, willing a calmness to my tone. "How many times do you think we've been on this ride?"

His eyes light up. He sniffles and wipes his nose with his sleeve. He's already reaching for his sketchbook. "Well, we'd have to do some research to find out."

I attempt a smile. "That's fine," I say. "We've got time."

Sewing the Beginning of the End

~ Phoenix Bourgeois

Robert "Bobby" Junior's shoelaces dragged across the overgrown stepping stones that lead to the cottage at 433 Elderberry Lane. The aroma of sun-soaked honeysuckle only reminded him that while his friends would be playing baseball, he would be stuck indoors all day with Mrs. Beatrice Davis. Bobby kicked a rock. Mrs. Davis was ancient and she smelled like dates and fish sticks.

Her front porch creaked at his approach. A faded, once-sunny yellow exterior cluttered with mossy firewood, piles of crystals and colorful rocks, cobwebs, and wild clinging ivy. Bobby lifted the heavy, brass door knocker. It was shaped like a wriggling mouse that dangled from the mouth of a proud cat. He cursed his parents. Why did he have to volunteer here? And on the *first day* of summer? It was all so utterly, totally, catastrophically unfair.

He knocked once. Twice. Three times.

Bobby cried out as an unkindness of ravens scattered from the ivy in a frenzy of feathers and haunting, rasping croaks. "Gaaah!" he yelped, squeezing his eyes shut. He wanted baseball, not birds! He warily opened his eyes and jumped at the presence of Mrs. Davis standing in the doorway.

His heart beat harder than the time he had hit a triple.

Mrs. Davis lifted a toothy smile, squinting through old coke-bottle glasses thick enough to light a hill of ants on fire. The creases of her eyelids sagged as if with the weight of her life. She wore a quilted cloak and a pair of worn hand-sewn bunny slippers. Long strands of frazzled pepper hair fell past her shoulders. Heat wafted out, despite the record high temperatures.

"Hello, Deary," said Mrs. Davis. "Do please come inside."

She ushered Bobby into the dim cottage. He followed her through a hall lined with peeling floral wallpaper. His heart steadied with each step. It smelled of stale tea leaves and cinnamon, mixed with a distinct, metallic scent like rain on rusted iron. They entered a small living room with a roaring fireplace. *Jeez!* Didn't she know it was June? Bobby pulled at his collar. He wished he could crack a window, but they were all covered with frilly layers of thick curtains.

Mrs. Davis lowered herself into an overstuffed armchair and gestured for him to do the same. He plopped into the chair, stirring a plume of dust from which a moth fluttered up and away. Bobby flinched, turning his gaze to the steaming tray of tea and biscuits between them.

"Help yourself, Deary," said Mrs. Davis. Her smile crinkled like night folded around the edge of a crescent moon. She picked up a half-finished quilt and a needle and thread. "It is so, so kind of you to sit and talk with an old woman like me," she said. "Do you have any hobbies?"

"Well, I like baseball," Bobby said, as he scooped a sugar cube into his chipped porcelain teacup. He thought of Katie and Benjamin at the diamond with all of his other friends and scowled. He swirled the tea with his fancy silver teaspoon and watched the crystals dissolve into the steaming void of black liquid. Life was *so* unfair. He took a scalding sip of bitter tea before hastily rattling it back onto its saucer.

Mrs. Davis leaned forward with a knowing look and dashed three more sugar cubes and a generous splash of cream in Bobby's cup. He took another hesitant sip and was delighted by the wonderful transformation. *Malty caramel, sweet, earthy nutmeg, intoxicating vanilla, and Mother's fresh baked lemon-berry scones.* It somehow smelled like fresh grass and pine tar. His next drink was a gulp.

"Would you be a dear? Hold this for me?" Mrs. Davis asked. She placed a thimble on Bobby's free index finger before he had time to respond and started to sew. "Do tell me more about baseball, I just love to hear about hobbies."

Bobby felt a pulse in his fingers. It was probably from the heat.

He shrugged and took another gulp of tea. *Wow is this stuff good!*

"Baseball is the best," he said, excited. "I'm better than anyone on the team and all my friends say I'll go pro when I'm older." Mrs. Davis was surprisingly easy to talk to. He told her about his team members, about the feeling of sliding into home base, his crush on Katie Sue, and the sound of his parents cheering in the stands. He felt a nostalgia that didn't feel quite like his own. As if he had stepped far into the future and was looking back on his boyhood from a life long lived. A wistful yearning to return to a time that was now. Bobby shook his head back into the present. He was playing a grown up. An actor too consumed in his role. The sensation of time passing melted down his spine.

"I'm going to practice all summer to perfect my . . . " Bobby trailed off mid-sentence, unsure of what he had been trying to say. The recesses of his mind sounded in distant alarm under the crackle of the fireplace and the humming of Mrs. Davis. The warm feeling in his chest whispered that he needn't worry.

Bobby looked around the room. He realized with regret that his teacup was empty. The cat on his lap purred, digging its claws in and out of the quilt stretched out over his legs. Bobby blinked. Where had the cat come from? How had the quilt gotten so big? Time had passed, but he couldn't be sure of how much. He stared, transfixed, into the cat's tranquil, black orb eyes and found himself stroking her soft fur.

He jolted at the dull, throbbing pinprick sensation at his fingertips. It felt as if he had fallen from the top of one dream into the bottom of another. He wiggled his fingers—his arm must have fallen asleep. "You sew really fast," Bobby said in astonishment. The vast expanse of quilt covered the entirety of the room. Folds of it pooled around him.

In response, Mrs. Davis only sewed faster.

Bobby wondered when he could leave to go play baseball. Poor Mrs. Davis was clearly senile, and the quilt was getting heavy.

"Are you making this quilt for your grandchildren?" Bobby asked.

Mrs. Davis hummed in absent agreement, her wrinkled hands moving with impossible speed. The stitchwork appeared to shimmer. Specks of light reflected off her glasses like sparks of cosmic stardust flashing past the magnified planets that were her eyes. His ears buzzed with static. He wrenched his gaze from her and the intricate patterns of the quilt to lean over the edge of his chair. He peered beyond her silhouette and felt the world slide rapidly away.

The quilt spanned endlessly from and through the splintering periwinkle door frame—simultaneously swallowed and expelled from the deep, vast, unknowable shadows of the quaint country kitchen that lay beyond.

Dust circled the room. Rose like steam from whistling floorboards. Fell from the ceiling like a thousand dazzling stars.

The needle flashed. But Mrs. Davis wasn't holding any thread.

Bobby felt suddenly small in the infinite folds of the ever-expanding fabric. Everywhere and nowhere. Here and now.

"More tea?" asked Mrs. Davis.

Robert reached forward with wrinkled hands and thought he would love more tea.

Your Black Apron™ Meal Kit Has Arrived

~ Luke Elliott

Welcome to Black Apron™, the world's first meal subscription service that combines healthy eating with esoteric power drawn from the luminiferous aether! This week's offering is: "Mushroom & Goat Shepherd's Pie."

INGREDIENTS

16 oz Potatoes
1/2 cup White Cheddar
8 oz Mushrooms (A modified species—cook for glowing surprise!)
1/2 oz Coagulated Goat Blood
1 Onion

1/2 oz Herb Mixture
1 tsp Minced Garlic
Tomato Paste
Veggie Stock Concentrates
6 oz Carrots
10 oz Ground Goat*

**Our goat is what really makes gives this dish that Black Apron™ magic. The protein is locally sourced from an isolated Puritan village where black-furred Billy goats tempt the daughters of local farmers into joining pagan groups that hold their orgiastic black masses deep in the heart of a twisted wood. Humanely butchered!*

BRING FORTH

Large Pot
Large Pie Pan
Salt and Pepper
Butter
Black Apron™ *Occult-Stylings* Cooking Apron

Assorted Lit Candles
Potato Masher
Olive Oil

1 - COOK POTATOES

- Dice **potatoes** into 1/2-inch pieces: place in a large pot with **salted water**. Bring to a boil and cook until tender. Meditate (1-2 min) on the lightless soil which cradled these tubers from infancy until harvest, keeping them isolated in darkness and blind to the colorful flower basking in the sunlight above.

- Reserve **1/2 cup potato liquid**, then drain and return potatoes to pot. Keep covered off heat until ready to mash.

2 - PREP

- Trim and quarter **mushrooms**. Strip and dice **carrots**. Peel and dice **onion**.

- Heat **drizzle of oil** in a large pan over medium-high heat. Add **goat**. Cook, breaking up meat into pieces, until medium-rare. 2-3 minutes.

- If you hear a deep voice, speaking from just out of view, ask if you would like to **"live deliciously?"** answer, **"Yes"** for maximum flavor! Transfer goat to paper-towel-lined plate.

3 - COOK VEGGIES

- Heat a **drizzle of oil** in the same pan over medium-high heat. Add **mushrooms**. Cook stirring occasionally until visibly glowing even in bright light. Allow any **extrasensory glimpses of an eldritch realm beyond imagining** to imbue your body with arcane energy. 5 minutes.

- Add another **drizzle of oil** to pan, then stir in **carrots**, **onion**, and **salt**. Cook, stirring until softened and mushrooms fill your nostrils with a phantasmagoric blend of aromas. 5-7 minutes.

4 - MAKE FILLING

- Stir **butter** into pan, then add **herb mixture** and **coagulated goat blood**. Cook, stirring, 1 minute. Stir in **tomato paste** until incorporated.

- Add 3/4 cup water and **stock concentrates**, scraping up browned bits. Set aside 1 tsp of the resulting blood sauce.

- Stir in **goat.** Breathe in the essence of his dark soul, welcoming it to penetrate your flesh without reservation or restraint.

- Bring to a boil: reduce to a simmer and cook until thickened. 2-3 minutes.

- Don't allow any sudden, intense **sexual arousal** to distract from cooking—you don't want to burn anything!

5 - MASH POTATOES

- Mash drained **potatoes, half the cheddar,** and **2 TBSP butter** until smooth and creamy, adding splashes of potato liquid as needed. Season with **salt, pepper,** and any **tears shed in defiance** of the stifling restrictions, societal or spiritual, that frustrate your daily life.

6 - SPREAD POTATOES

- Heat broiler to high.

- Once **filling** has thickened, transfer to pie pan. Spoon **mashed potatoes** on top: spread in an even layer, leaving a narrow border.

- Sprinkle mashed potatoes with **remaining cheddar** and the tsp of **blood mixture** you set aside in step 4.

- If you find yourself in the presence of a bipedal goat-human, proclaim either, "Ave Satani!" or "Vade Retro Satana!" Your preference.

FINISH & SERVE

- Broil **Mushroom & Goat Shepherd's Pie.** 3-4 minutes.

- Let rest at least 5 minutes, then divide between plates. Remember that any hallucinations are likely to be mild and brief, brought on by the mushrooms, and not the culmination of an occult ritual. **It's a metaphor!**

- For optimal results: serve upon an altar under direct starlight. Consume nude while carousing with your dearest friends and lovers.*

Black Apron™ is not liable for any complications or afflictions resulting from fornicating during or after the consumption of "Mushroom & Goat Shepherd's Pie," whether of the flesh or of the spirit. Nor does a Black Apron™ recipe imply co-signature for any agreements made with any infernal beings.

UP NEXT

We've delved into the briny depths and returned with a bounty to share: "Seared Coelacanth with Lemon-Ambergris Sauce." Your ingredient package will include a carven idol of the Great Old One most popular in your region!

The Nameless Boy and the Automatic Vegetable God

~ Jon Lasser

The boy stood, feet planted in the sand, screeching whenever the tepid ocean licked his toes.

"Stay out of the water," Toby Peng shouted at his two-year-old son. He half-expected a sea serpent to emerge from the unfathomed ocean and drag the boy—still nameless even within Toby's own heart—to its sour-smelling depths, but the boy hadn't yet learned to be afraid.

He bit back the urge to run out into the sand and save the boy from the sorts of imaginary threats a father saw everywhere. No wonder the nurseries locked children away for so long. They just wouldn't listen, no matter how many times you repeated yourself. Toby found himself always on the lookout for new terrors to befall his son, ones he could protect the boy from on his own. That task was as hopeless as their situation so he hunched his shoulders and ran through scenarios where he would somehow be able to save the boy from whatever lived in the water or anywhere else on this uncharted world.

Commander Wooten, their jailor, watched Toby out of the corner of her eye even as she pretended to survey the red and cyan jungle that lay beyond the beach. She wouldn't stare head-on at it; whatever she imagined there seemed to fill her with the sort of fear the boy's heedless play incited in Toby, the limitless oceanic terror that kept his son nameless. Toby wasn't afraid of staring at the jungle, an angry particolored braid from which no noise emerged. He tried to follow a single strand to see where it would lead, but it all looked the same and he lost track.

Toby's stomach rumbled. Yesterday, they'd crashed in the darkness, tumbled onto the beach, and stayed close to the burning craft, its acrid smoke seeping into his dreams. After six months of antiseptic recycled air, none of the planet's unfamiliar scents hit him as hard as the smoke, which might have meant death aboard the ship. Did Wooten know he'd sabotaged it? Did every prison commander have piloting skills like her? Toby hadn't expected any of them to survive, but now he was desperate to keep his son alive.

The boy screeched again as the water jumped and shivered, silver like crumpled shielding in the sunlight.

Wooten crouched, reaching for the pistol she'd lost in the crash. Toby leapt up and stumbled through the sand toward his boy, but before he'd covered half the beach, the water stilled itself.

He waited. Nothing happened. Geology or monster, the threat had fallen silent.

Toby took the boy's hand and led him away from the lapping waves, toward the burnt-out wreck of what had been the command module. The breeze carried a whiff of ash, of the ship that had been their shelter through the interstellar wastes.

"I don't know what I'd do without him." Toby sat back down next to Wooten, hands still shaking.

"Is that why you stole it?" Wooten asked, meaning his son. "You could have had another. After you give one up, you're allowed another." Everyone had to feed the Empire's inexorable spread across the vastness of interstellar space. Some children became people; most were only a renewable resource.

"Suzanne died in childbirth." He'd stolen the child from the nursery out of instinct, too deep in grief to understand what he'd done, how he'd set himself against the Empire. How was it possible, even as humans spread among the stars, that a woman could still bleed to death during that most fundamental act—one that so often served the empire? "Any other child wouldn't be the same." It was the only part of the truth she might understand. Maybe one day she'd recognize why he'd crashed their ship rather than allow them to take the boy back.

"I'm hungry." Wooten leered at the boy and licked her lips. Every muscle in Toby's torso twitched as he held back. She could take him in a fair fight, no contest, and then who would protect the boy? A copper and mint-scented wind gusted toward the beach from the jungle.

"I'm cold," Wooten said. "And hungry. You gather wood. I'll get a fire started." She handed Toby a pair of purple safety gloves extracted from the wreckage, but didn't take her eyes off the boy. Perhaps Toby could outrun her, outswim her, but not with the boy. Even if he could, where would they go?

As if in answer, a scream came from the jungle. Not a human scream, nor any animal Toby'd ever heard or imagined. Something without a throat, only a ululating, resonant cavity and teeth like reeds. Almost musical.

The boy scrambled up a pile of what remained from the ship's heat-ablating skin, which had sloughed off the ship like a snakeskin when they crash-landed. He rolled down to the sand then, laughing, scrambled up to the top again. He wasn't afraid of falling, of Wooten, or of whatever waited in the jungle. Whether or not you ennobled the boy's obliviousness with the word "innocence" it seemed like a worthwhile trade for the fear that twisted Toby's gut whenever he shrieked.

"Come on, boy," Toby shouted and stood up. His son came up the beach and smiled beatifically, obeying his father's command for once. Maybe for the first time. The boy knew only a few words, but he didn't need any to charm Toby, whose heart welled with satisfaction. He'd made the right decision, taking the boy, even if he wasn't sure how it would all work out. It was his job as father to make it happen. The boy trusted him, completely and unjustifiably. "We're going into the jungle."

"We?" Wooten put a hand on Toby's shoulder before he even registered her standing. "The contraband isn't going anywhere. You are."

"I'm not going anywhere without my son." He sat back down. "Get your own firewood."

"The hell you're not. When J-E gets here, do you want me to tell them how you resisted my authority?"

"When J-E gets here? Are they even coming? We need to—"

"They're coming." She spoke with such certainty. Once upon a time, Toby had trusted The Empire like that. And why shouldn't Wooten? They'd raised her from a baby, and she trusted it the way Toby's son trusted him.

Toby stared into the cloud-roiled sky. Had their distress call made it through the atmospheric interference? Was Justice Enforcement on its way? Or had the Empire at long last failed Wooten? What would it take for her to realize if it had?

"If they're coming they'll find us wherever we are." For her that was a promise; for him a threat. "We should find a continent, a larger island at least, with more resources." If this was a family, however unwilling, he and Wooten had to provide.

"You saw it, Peng. In the water." Toby hadn't seen more than a splash and a flash of light, but whatever Wooten had seen spooked her. "We're not going anywhere. We'll stay on the beach and wait for J-E." She looked away from Toby, towards the jungle, and shuddered.

He watched her silently. She was just as afraid of the jungle as she was of the ocean. The jungle wasn't vast, but if she wouldn't go in, maybe it was big enough. She wouldn't kill him until she had her firewood and something to eat. If nothing else, Toby had to protect the boy from that. His hands shook.

He'd only wanted his son. Now he'd destroyed a Prisoner Transport Vessel, and was defying a sworn officer of the Empire. Where did it end? Why not flee into the jungle?

"Come on," Toby called, but the boy was gone again.

His son had climbed up on the wrecked spacecraft while Toby was distracted, and swung from the wrecked superstructure as though it was monkey bars. "Get down," Toby called. His heart wasn't in it, even though if the boy got hurt all this was for nothing. They'd lost their medkit in the crash, along with so much else.

The boy ignored him. Once upon a time, parents had raised children themselves, without the nurseries. No wonder so many children had died young. How must it have felt, to lose children who wouldn't listen? Toby's heart ached just imagining his son falling, his neck twisted too far. It wasn't safe, being alive. Toby couldn't protect the boy from everything, but he had to. He bit his cheek and fought down panic.

Toby shuddered and looked across the water again. Without the boy he might swim for it, sea monsters be damned, and see if he could make it to another island, one with more resources—maybe even an unregistered encampment. With the boy, he had to figure out how to survive here with Wooten. He stood.

Wooten tugged him back down to the sand. "Where do you think you're going?"

"I'm going to get him down from there. Before he hurts himself."

"What's the difference?" Wooten smiled slyly. "If he falls, it saves me the trouble."

Toby shivered. She'd hinted before, pantomimed, but he felt like she was going farther now.

"You'll have to go through me to get him," he said quietly.

"I know." She gave that same smile again.

She wasn't wrong about how little Toby's life mattered, or the boy's. Still, he shuffled down the beach to his son.

The boy looked at Toby, whose heart filled with everything he couldn't put into words. Up welled the way he fought his desire to smother his son with affection and protection, and how difficult it was to let the boy grow naturally; the way Suzanne stared out from those open yellow eyes, so pale against cream-colored skin, how he smelled like cardamom, like she had, and how those eyes and that scent meant nothing and everything, all of Toby's intentions snuffed out when she died both gone forever and brought back in the boy.

But these were feelings, not words or thoughts that Toby could nail down, and he turned them away as he had every other time. He would ignore that rumbling in his soul, even as it had brought them together to this place against all reason or conscious intention.

Instead, he smiled back at his son.

"What's this?" he said. He grabbed one of the white-metal ribs.

"Space ship!" The boy grinned broadly.

"That's right. It's not a fitness block—"

"Space ship!"

"But you're climbing it." Toby shook the rib, which came loose in his hand. "It's not safe, see. You could get hurt. You don't want to get hurt, do you?"

"No," the boy said, shaking the struts. He knew what words would make his father happy, Toby thought, but didn't understand what they meant or what he should do. "Hunny! Hunny!" The boy patted his tummy. Who had taught him that gesture?

"We'll eat soon. Right now, let's go for a walk, okay?" Toby worked the loose strut back and forth. The segment looked to be about a meter long. Light and strong.

With a snap, it came off the structure completely. Now Toby had something Wooten didn't: a weapon.

Another eerie scream emerged from the jungle, like the whistle of a tea kettle running dry and sputtering out atop the cook-flame.

"Peng," Wooten shouted, "Come here. Bring that bat of yours." She still watched him, hadn't let her guard down. Damn. He trudged up the beach, kicking sand like a petulant child.

"What?" Peng asked.

"That scream. It's dinner. Go into the jungle. Find it. Kill it, and bring it here. And give me that bat." She grabbed it from his hands.

"What am I going to kill it with?" He reached for the spar, but she pulled it farther away.

"Your bare hands. A stick. I don't care."

"Why don't you go?" But he'd already decided he would go, if she'd let him take the boy. Trapped between her fear of the jungle and her fear of the ocean, Wooten wasn't going anywhere.

If he could find food, if it got them through the next several days, maybe they'd find help. As small as the jungle was, perhaps it could keep them safe from Wooten. If not, maybe he could talk her into taking their chances on the water. If they had food, and built a raft, perhaps they could make it somewhere there would be food other than the boy.

"What are you waiting for, Peng? Get in there!" Wooten sneered, but he didn't care. "Bring me dinner, and some firewood too."

"Come on, boy!" Toby's son wobbled over. Wooten scowled but didn't say anything this time as the two of them plodded toward the jungle, to find whatever animal had made that terrible noise.

The whistle had guttered out by the time they reached the edge of the jungle, as though the fire had burned away all of the water in the kettle, left to scorch in the cook-flame.

Come on." Toby tugged his son's hand. They needed to get out of Wooten's sight before she reconsidered. They plunged into the trackless jungle.

Only a few steps out of the pale aquamarine light and into the rose-tinted dim, the noise began again. Toby held his son's hand

and followed the quivering note deeper into the jungle. His son came along without hesitation, trusting his father more than he feared the strange, overgrown place so different from any he'd ever been or seen.

Out of Wooten's sight, Toby surveyed the jungle from up close. There wasn't much that looked like food or wood. Gloves on. He knelt, swallowing his urge to gag, and ran his hands through the organic matter on the jungle floor. Crumbly beige plates dissolved as Toby picked them up, emitting that minty scent Toby had noticed on the beach. Up close, it smelled a little like bananas and yeast soaked in turpentine. The plates didn't seem like bark or leaves; a fungus analog, perhaps.

He stood, looked up. What made this a jungle? The soaring shapes and their fecund promise. The height came from a reef-like accretion of those fungoid plates, red and cyan. He broke off a fresh one. It didn't crumble, but also didn't seem to have much substance to it. Low energy density. It might kindle a fire, but wouldn't sustain one.

He tugged on the delicate traceries he thought of as creeper vines, but they too wouldn't burn long even if he could ignite them.

Where were the animals? The scream resumed, sounding at this distance like a fan with a bad bearing. Maybe Wooten was right; the screamer could be dinner. They had to find it, or else risk the fungus plates.

"Boy, stop that!"

Toby's son had dropped to his knees and poked at the awful crumbs on the jungle floor with his bare hands.

"No!" shouted Toby as his son stuck a handful into his mouth. Toby blanched. What if the fungus was toxic? What if there were bugs in it? Then again, there wasn't any reason to imagine that the screaming beast would be any less poisonous to humans.

The smell didn't seem so bad when Toby knelt again. A little putrid, like a ship with failing scrubbers, but more like a good salt pickle. He picked up a handful of sawdust-like crumbles with his left glove and poked at it with his right.

"Come back here," he shouted, one eye on the boy, who had begun to crawl farther into the darkness. His son looked back at his father and smiled, but went no further. The boy needed a name. One would come soon, Toby thought. It was on the tip of his tongue.

Something moved in Toby's hand. Not just fluttered in the breeze, moved against it. Locomoted. Where did it go?

There it was, slowly looping through the hummus, moving not side to side but over and over like their spaceship tumbling through the atmosphere, hurtling toward the beach.

And there was another, all different, inflating and deflating relentlessly to move in a single direction. It reached the purple glove, then turned around and headed toward the other end of his palm. Toby took his tweezers, collected fifteen wee beasties in a specimen bag.

How many had the boy eaten already? Toby shook a handful of the bugs from the specimen bag and popped them into his mouth. They crunched, but didn't taste like much of anything. Was that good or bad?

Toby stood and stumbled over to his son. He took the boy's hand and they walked deeper into the jungle. More than once, they encountered an impenetrable wall, where the two colors of growth had grown so full that Toby couldn't push through. These thickest stands weren't so large that he couldn't find a way around them as they pursued whatever beast screamed so implacably.

The beast didn't move. The sound came from a single location that Toby and his son approached. Could it move, or was it fixed in place like an insect trapped in a spider's web? At last, they thrust through an array of cyan fans and found their screamer.

A wet, glistening fungal mouth, tiny flying beasties clouded the air before it, flitting near then into the cavity from which they did not emerge. When the insectoids stayed away, the sound guttered out; when they flew in, the voice revived. With the noise came the coppery wind, the mushroom's alien breath.

No animal, the jungle screamer, no intelligence Toby could discern. Only a mindless cycle of consumption and expulsion, the buzzing insects feeding the blind deity of the alien jungle. No different, in the end, from the Empire's constellation of worlds that would consume the boy, or Toby himself.

He couldn't kill the jungle, nor the Empire. Like the buzzing creatures that fed this automatic god, he could fly into that vegetable maw and be consumed, or he could drift farther from that mouth until he reached a safe distance. It neither knew nor cared whether it digested him specifically, but would likely furiously resist any assault. It wasn't worth discovering whether he could provoke it. Better to slip away.

Would attacking Wooten provoke a response from the Empire, or was it as heedless of her fate as the mouth to a single mushroom crushed beneath his feet? She certainly presumed that a thousand worlds would leap to avenge her, but how could that be?

Toby's stomach rumbled. Time to test another possible food. He broke off a small lobe from one of the growths and chewed deliberately. No alkaloid bitterness, which was good, but not much flavor, either. It would fill his belly, and it might not make him sick, but would it give him strength?

He chewed, and a thousand eyeless jungle faces screamed.

Toby nearly choked on the mushroom. He spit it onto the jungle floor. The scream guttered out. He tore another lobe of fungus off a tower and chewed it. The jungle screamed again.

The boy, who'd been rooting around in the dirt, leapt up and clung, sobbing, to his leg, trusting his father to protect him. Toby promised again to try.

"Ssh," he said, but the boy kept crying. "It's all right." He put his arms around the boy. "Nothing's going to hurt you."

Did they do it this way in the nurseries, lying to children? He'd never lied to his son before, but the boy was terrified. He should be terrified: they had no chance of survival, no chance at all. But the boy didn't know that. All the boy knew was that his father held him, his father made everything all right. He'd keep making everything all right as long as he could.

Toby felt the tingling first in his fingers, then his legs. His stomach cramped and he fell to the ground. He couldn't stand up, couldn't cry out. He felt everything, but couldn't move.

His son knelt carefully, then lay down next to him. The boy didn't know his father had been poisoned by some unknown neurotoxin. That he was about to die as the paralysis worked its way through his chest muscles. His not-yet-stopped heart broke again.

If his son hadn't been there, Toby would have welcomed death. Surely he'd gasp for air as the last moments came, but he felt no pain now, no cramping, no nausea. This had to be a better way to go than what awaited them with Commander Wooten.

Wooten. She'd really eat the boy. Not because she was evil. She just didn't see him as human yet. At that age, he was raw materials. When she looked into the boy's eyes, she didn't see the light in his eyes that Toby saw there.

If she would eat the boy, Toby had to kill her. If he survived. He *had* to survive. Without his father, Wooten would eat the boy for sure—or the boy would die in this jungle while Wooten, paralyzed with fear, died on the beach.

Toby tried to breathe in. His chest didn't rise. He tried to breathe out, but his chest didn't fall. In again. No movement, but was that tingling sensation his imagination? Out, and another tingle. He closed his eyes. Maybe if he slept he wouldn't feel it when his breath stopped.

When he woke, his son lay against him. How long had it been? He couldn't see the sky, but everything bore a distinct aquamarine cast, even this deep in the jungle.

Toby put his arm around the boy and rolled over before he understood that the paralysis had worn off. He wasn't dead. Without food, they'd be dead soon enough. Wooten would see to that. Unless—unless they killed her first.

Toby had never killed anyone before. Never wanted to. She would force him to choose between his conscience and his son, and he would choose the boy. Still, he would treat her with respect. She wasn't raw materials any more than the boy was.

He shook the boy, who cried out as he woke but smiled as he saw his father. Toby's heart welled again. He'd been saved again, saved to protect this wonderful boy.

"Time to wake up," Toby said. "Time to go back to camp."

"Hunny, hunny," the boy answered.

"I know. Give me a hug."

The boy hugged him, and their hearts thumped with joy. They'd make it somehow.

They trudged back through the jungle, brushing away the strange growths that grabbed at their faces. When the last uncanny tendrils fell behind and the crumbly soil turned to sand, Toby shielded his eyes from the blinding beach. Toby crumbled a fresh piece of fungus in his pocket, and the jungle screamed obligingly.

Wooten looked at him, crouched in a shooter's pose, as though she'd forgotten she had no sidearm. The spar lay nearby, but out of her reach. He walked calmly until he stood between her and the weapon.

"Don't eat the mushrooms," he said. "They're poisonous."

"What's the screaming?" Wooten hadn't moved.

"It's nothing," he said. "Just the mushrooms. They don't like being eaten." He didn't look at the club, but felt where it was, just outside his peripheral vision.

"That doesn't sound like mushrooms."

"Go look yourself," he said. "It's harmless, so long as you don't eat its friends."

Wooten didn't move, but continued to stare into the jungle. Toby crumbled the mushrooms, raising screams from the automatic vegetable god, and she jumped, just a little.

Blood pounded in his ears. His fingers tingled with adrenaline and hard breathing. He grabbed the club and raised it above his head, then hesitated.

"Peng," said Wooten, "Don't do it." She stood up and stepped back from him.

Toby motioned her to stop, then turned toward his son and knelt. "Go to the beach. Go play." The boy ran away, laughing, as though he couldn't hear the terrible vegetable screams.

Wooten smiled. "When J-E comes, you'll drown in an ocean of hurt. I'm going to tell them—"

"Shut up." Toby brandished the club.

"You're not going to hit me with that. I'm smarter than you. I'm faster than you. I'm stronger than you, and I've got an entire Empire—"

Out in the ocean, the sea serpent roiled the waters. Wooten turned to look.

He swung the club like a football bat. It connected with the side of her face. She yelped like an animal, then fell silent. She crumpled, and made a muffled sound as she landed hard on the sand. He hit her again, to be sure. The club splintered into countless metal fragments.

It didn't feel momentous. Not what he'd imagined at all. Maybe the empire was right, and everybody wasn't much more than raw materials. (No. Commander Wooten had possessed hopes, nurtured ambitions. She'd been as much as person as Toby or the boy. Even so, it had been a question of survival.)

Toby looked toward his boy, who still played on the beach with nearly inhuman focus. He hoped the boy hadn't seen what he had done. Toby wasn't that kind of man, but times were desperate.

The mushrooms fell silent while he dragged her body down the beach, past the remains of their ship, toward the water. He would throw her body into the sour ocean, and with any luck the tide and currents would take it out to sea, or sink it. Or the sea serpent she'd so feared would consume her remains.

The boy ran over. Toby moaned. He'd hoped to avoid this.

"Dada! Dada! Lady nap!" The boy pointed at Wooten's inert body.

"We're saying goodbye to her. Can you say bye-bye?"

"Bye-bye." Mercifully, the boy didn't yet understand. He would, one day, if he survived.

Thank the lucky star, the boy hadn't learned to ask questions yet. Where was she going? Why was she going? Why didn't she wake up? He couldn't lie about what the boy didn't ask, what the boy didn't desire to know.

"Hunny hunny, Dada." He patted his belly again.

"Me too, son." Toby grunted as he dragged the body down the shore. The boy tugged at his leg again.

"Hunny hunny, Dada," the boy repeated, a whine creeping into his voice. The boy had been so good, so patient, for so long. Toby's hunger and thirst were nothing compared to his son's, but the boy hardly complained. Not even as much as Wooten had.

"Let me finish—saying bye-bye to the lady. Then we can eat." That was a lie, wasn't it?

Maybe he shouldn't drag her to the waterline. He could keep her on the beach. She might have been injured upon crashing. Killed, even. Blunt-force trauma caused by banging around inside the spacecraft as it came down onto the beach. Not murder, just an accident. Could J-E know the difference? They were so hungry. Surely they could they be forgiven if—

Toby dropped to his knees and vomited on the beach. There wasn't anything left in his stomach, really, just a thin acid trickle that burned long after his stomach had stopped heaving.

He shouldn't have done what he had already to protect his son. He'd done bad things. But his son was worth it. Toby dragged her body back toward the ship.

Another scream emerged from the forest, louder than before, more forceful. Ululating, consonantless, unwavering and breathless. Goosebumps rose on Toby's arms, on the back of his neck.

The boy followed, capering across the sand, his footsteps erasing the lonely track of Wooten's body. One day, the boy would think back in terror and disgust on what his father had done. If he was lucky enough to survive to the age of reason. If Toby was a good enough father.

The great ocean lay silent. Would anyone come looking for them? If J-E insisted. If they could spare the resources. Until then, he and the boy were on their own.

Something in the sea leapt out. Not a serpent, a whole school of fish arcing above the surf. Surely he could fashion a fishhook out of—something. Some bit of the ship, perhaps. Were they paralytic, like the fungus? They'd know soon enough.

The boy tugged on his father's pants. Toby picked the boy up and hugged him fiercely. Whatever the cost of that hug, of future hugs, he was glad to pay it.

"Chance." He said it out loud, testing the feel of it. "Chance Peng."

Chance said nothing, but looked into his father's eyes. The boy's eyes seemed brighter, more alert. The fungal screaming ceased, and the fish jumped, glittering in the dim aquamarine light.

Toby put Chance down. They walked across the beach, hand in hand, toward the ship that perhaps held their salvation among its wreckage.

◻

From This Day Forward

~ Tyler Battaglia

It'd been about half a week since Darius had come back. More precisely, it had been four days since he had returned, meaning that it had been thirty-three years, five months, and twenty-six days since Darius had died.

Not that Carson was keeping count.

Still, every morning for the past four mornings, Carson had been waking up to find Darius asleep on the couch, somehow not having disappeared in the night like a dream. Instead, Carson would exit his tiny, lonely bedroom in his tiny, lonely apartment, and find that his home was slightly more crowded than it had been shy of a month before. There had been the cat, for a while, but otherwise it had just been Carson in the apartment. And now . . .

And now, Darius.

Carson tried to be quiet, walking across the room, but Darius stirred anyway. Carson froze, then turned to face his . . . his what?

Darius. Just Darius.

"Good morning," Carson said, and he hated the sound of his own voice. It was cigarette-raspy, an old man's voice, rough and aged from decades of chain-smoking. He had never kicked the habit, and now it was frankly too late.

When Darius spoke, on the other hand, it was a young man's voice, never touched by the inevitability of time. Nor had his smile been touched by it, either. "Morning, Carce."

Carson stood stock still in the middle of the living room for what felt like eternity but was only a fraction of an instant when compared to the long, long time that he had waited to be able to say all the things that he never got to say to Darius. But the only thing he could muster up the courage for was, "Would you like some coffee?"

"I'd love that, man."

Carson nearly winced, wondering about the elephant in the room, wondering if it was as painfully obvious to Darius as it was to him. He didn't ask, and instead turned and walked into the kitchenette and started a pot of instant coffee. Not exactly refined taste, but he was living off a shitty job that couldn't wait for him to retire, and he'd never had much company before. Give or take a friend or family member who decided to remember he existed.

No, there hadn't been many people since Darius.

Carson stared blankly at the coffee pot for a moment, then turned around and dug through the fridge for cream. He made their coffees almost mechanically, not looking up when he felt Darius's eyes on him. He remembered how Darius took his coffee, as if it hadn't been decades since he learned: a lot of cream, a little sugar, barely any actual coffee. Big contrast to Carson, who now took it pitch black, as bitter as he needed.

When Carson turned around, Darius was in the doorway of the kitchen. Carson was careful to pass him without touching him, walking past him with slow, deliberate steps, trying not to spill any hot coffee on himself as his hands shook, unsteady and weak. He set the mugs down on the table, sat down more abruptly than necessary, but waited until Darius took his seat—with more grace and ease than Carson had left in his old, tired body—before he picked up his coffee to drink.

He had to set it down a moment later as a series of hacking coughs built up in his lungs, dark coffee sloshing out of the mug and onto his hand, scalding it. It hurt almost as much as the violent coughs that shook him, spattering stained gobs of spit onto the table. He smelled the metallic stink of rot that followed.

Darius looked at him the whole time, not touching his coffee. "You sick, Carce?"

Carson thought about the elephant in the room while he tried to weigh how blunt he deserved to be, but this truth was one Darius didn't need to be sheltered from. He picked up a napkin to wipe the hot coffee off his hand. "Lung cancer," he said. "Found out a week ago that it's . . . I always thought it'd be the other thing."

"The other thing?"

Carson stared Darius dead in the eye for a moment. *Ha*, thought Carson. "Never mind. You still don't remember anything?"

"I remember you."

"You know that's not what I meant."

Darius shrugged, pushing his coffee mug around the table, narrowly avoiding the rusty brown spittle. Carson saw him lock eyes with his coffee, a lighter spot where the cream hadn't fully mixed in staring back at him. "Yeah, well, I don't remember shit about . . . where I've been or whatever. I remember us, and I remember you're all I have."

Fuck. Carson looked away, then said, "You were all I had, too, Darius."

There was a heavy pause. Darius picked up his coffee and took a long sip before frowning at it.

"What's wrong?" Carson asked.

"Tastes funny."

"Maybe the cream's gone bad," Carson said. He dared to pick his coffee back up, hoping his hands weren't trembling anymore. "I haven't cooked with it in a while. Mine's fine, but it's real coffee, and yours isn't."

"Hilarious." Darius smiled at him.

Carson smiled back.

Raising the Dead
by Carson Bennett
. February 20th .

It's been one month since the phenomenon started in the city: the dead are apparently coming back to life. Earliest reported events were minor: beloved pets emerging from the ether, apparently unharmed by either illness or accident. The incidents have now escalated, and some reports are coming in of loved ones returning . . .

Carson knew that, growing up, he'd been a privileged little shit. He'd admit it, now, as an adult. As a kid—and he was a stupid kid for most of his life; even having been a legal adult for the past nearly forty years, he'd still been a stupid kid for much of even that—he'd not wanted to acknowledge it. As a gay boy growing up in the 1960s and 70s, he'd thought life had sucked. That there was never any escaping from parents who knew too much and smiled more. From sisters who wanted to treat him like one of the girls. From the torturous words and actions of peers who would spit on him.

And it *had* been bad. He'd faced his fair share of terrible people. But the truth was, given the circumstances, Carson had been fucking *lucky*. Even if it had taken more than Darius's death to teach him that. It had taken surviving a genocide of queer men, somehow relatively unscathed—barring, at least, the emotional scars of losing friends and loved ones... and Darius. It had taken finding a stable enough career, so long as no one asked, and no one told. It had taken quitting the military right before the Gulf War and landing on his feet at the local paper where he then worked through war and recession, growing into old age with a secure enough pension. He just had to wait out his days in relative solitude. That was all he'd ever had to do. Hold on, head down, let life pass him by.

And then Darius had knocked on his door, shivering and frightened like a runaway kid, thirty-three years dead. So even though he'd initially been scared shitless, he had let Darius in and gotten him a towel and tried not to stare too hard.

He'd reported on the events, of course. He'd known that it had been a possibility. He'd expected the *cat*, not Darius. At least, he hadn't allowed himself to think of the possibility. Thirty-three years was half a lifetime. His lifetime, anyway. Not Darius's. Darrius had never had that long.

But here they were. Carson and Darius.

Together again.

<hr>

Letter to the Editor
Anonymous
. March 3rd .

This is clearly a sign of the end.

Dramatic? You might think so. Yet, the dead are rising, and we are embracing it, when we should at least be asking ourselves *why?* And I'm not confident that should mean

> reading the Bible for answers. Our prayers haven't been answered. No, we should be looking to something far worse than any god you think you know.
>
> We should take this very seriously . . .

The hardest part, Carson had found himself thinking in those first few days, wasn't staring at Darius and wondering what the fuck was going on, it was keeping from Darius what the fuck was going on.

Darius had been a prime twenty-seven when he'd died. He'd been mostly out of the 'stupid kid' mindset, even if Carson hadn't been, but he'd been a young guy. Optimistic, full of life. Until the end. When he got sick.

Only Carson had shown up for the funeral, and he'd lied to the priest and said he was a dear friend, that was all. Just a friend. He hadn't been sure that any preacher would have been willing to bless the ground otherwise.

But it meant that Darius was *still* optimistic, full of life or something like it, now that he was back.

Carson didn't want to watch his spirit die all over again. What was he supposed to tell him? It was bad enough he'd told him about the cancer thing. He wouldn't have been able to hide that for long, anyway. Not with blood in the sink.

Carson should have remembered that Darius was always smarter than that.

That, and the cat made life harder.

"Hey, Carce," Darius was saying, calling Carson out of daylight reverie. "There's a cat in your yard. You recognize her?"

Carson paused and looked over at Darius curiously. Darius just gestured at him to come closer, so Carson took his tired old bones to the window, standing a careful but respectable distance from Darius, and saw the little black-and-white cat circling the old oak tree in the corner of the yard. It looked up when it saw the blinds moving, and it saw Carson and Darius there. Carson couldn't hear the meow, but he could see the vigour with which it must have let out its cry before it ran up to the door.

A moment later, there was a scratching on the back door. Carson jumped. Carefully, he opened the door. The cat bolted in.

"She yours?" Darius asked.

Carson delayed agreeing. He stared the cat down. "Sugar?"

The cat looked at him and started purring. She weaved around his ankles, rubbing up against him as if she had been wondering where he was. As if she'd lost sight of him, that was all.

He saw the dusting of white across her otherwise black fur that told him for sure that this was Sugar.

"Yes," he said. "She's mine."

Darius looked at the cat, then Carson. "Thought she'd died."

Carson hesitated. Surely, by then, Darius had read the news. Carson didn't have a TV, or much technology for Darius to think too much about, at that, but he *did* have newspapers, including the one he wrote for. He couldn't hide it forever, could he?

"I thought so, too."

Opinion: How much longer?
by Carson Bennett
. April 1st .

. . . I'm not agreeing with the anonymous letter-writers that have been writing in droves to say we should panic, but there are points to be taken from the fear-mongering. Should we be taking this for granted? Can we expect more time with our loved ones to come without a cost? Should we make every moment count, or should we take it all with a grain of salt? It's unreasonable to count the days, when surely, we already were.

But there is no end in sight, is there?

Carson was on the couch reading when Darius returned from a short run.

Carson had been scared to let Darius go too far at first, and it was anyone's guess as to whether that was to protect Darius or his own heart. Not that Carson expected Darius to drop dead a second time if he learned what was going on, exactly.

So far so good.

Carson looked up from his book when Darius walked through the living room, pacing as he drank from his water bottle. The cat eventually joined the trot, following Darius's feet at a safe distance.

Carson was either envious or attracted, seeing Darius sweaty and healthy and alive, but he watched until Darius caught him watching.

There was a moment of silence when their eyes met, and Darius stopped his pacing.

"You know," Darius said slowly, "you better not think I don't notice."

Carson swallowed hard around the tickling in his throat. A coughing fit would be ill-timed. He struggled to breathe, nonetheless. "Notice what?"

"That you're older than I remember. That you act like there's eggshells on the floor. Or that I've been here a few weeks now and not a soul has called except your boss at the paper."

There was another pause.

Carson asked, "Your memories are clearing up, huh?"

"A bit. Sort of. That's not the point, Carce."

"Well, I mean, if you're remembering my age…"

"It's pretty obvious you got old on me, man. You're *sick*."

Carson avoided saying that sick had nothing to do with age. That a man as young and healthy and lively as Darius himself could become sick in what felt like no more than a heartbeat and die in another.

"You have to realize—"

"—that this is all real fucking weird? Yeah, I realize. But I'm not talking about that right now, since I'm sure neither of us has any fucking answers. I'm talking about the fact that you're alone. More than that, you're *lonely*."

"You expected something else?"

"I expected you to try to live a little, man. Without me."

Carson winced. "I don't think you know what you're talking about."

"No, guess not." Darius huffed a breath, then crouched to scratch the ears of the cat, who was watching them both, concerned. Darius very clearly looked at Sugar, not at Carson. "I don't know, man. I just know it seems pretty shitty to be alone when the world's this fucked."

Carson was going to say *I'm not alone anymore* when the cat recoiled and hissed, swatting at Darius's hand.

Darius retracted his hand quickly. Carson saw a flash of red blood. "The hell, cat?"

"Sugar," Carson scolded as he stood and scooped her up. The cat let out a meow of protest but didn't squirm. She stared at Darius from out of Carson's hands. "What's gotten into you?"

The cat, obviously, did not answer. But she and Darius locked eyes for a concerningly long moment.

Carson was almost afraid to break the silence.

Letter to the Editor
Anonymous
. April 10th .

Last week, my mother showed up at my door.

I'm sure that you all expect me to say that I welcomed her. That I let her into my home to meet the grandchildren she never had the privilege of meeting the first time, before she died. That my cold heart melted, and I saw this was a blessing.

But I remember watching her struggle to breathe on her deathbed, barely responsive as early onset dementia took everything from her, even her last words. I remember the life fading from her eyes. I remember her being stolen from me. And I remember accepting that.

I don't know if her coming back would have brought back her ability to recognize me, to form coherent words to say she loved me, if she would have even understood that these children are her grandchildren.

I slammed the door on her and closed the curtains and ignored her weeping outside.

I don't know where she went, but I'm glad that she was gone before my kids got home from school. I don't have much time left to live, I heard that from the doctors already. Even got a second and third and fourth opinion. I don't need my children exposed to more death than they're already going to have to be.

I started thinking, though.

> Has anyone tried exhuming the graves of those who have returned?

Carson was so overcome with his violent hacking that he almost didn't hear Darius calling his name.

"Carce, get out here!"

"Just a minute," Carson called back. He wiped his mouth with the back of his hand, then examined the colour of the phlegm before he thoroughly scrubbed his hands under the tap. He stepped out of the bathroom and headed to the living room where the patio door was. He'd left Darius out there. Darius had been trying to keep himself busy with gardening lately, and Carson didn't know what else to do except encourage this novel hobby of his. "What is it?"

"What is *this*?" Darius asked. Not accusatory, but genuinely concerned, pointing to a hole he'd dug in the ground near the tree. He was surrounded by flowers—purple ones, mostly, which Carson remembered was his favourite colour. They'd picked them out at the nursery together. Violets. Hyacinth. And trailing purple blossoms and tall spears of magenta, which Carson was sure were invasive from an article he'd written a few years before but couldn't bring himself to say no to. He didn't have the heart to say no to Darius. Some of them were wilting already, besides.

Even surrounded by purple beauties, Carson was filled with dread as he approached Darius and the hole. He was halfway there when he paused, afraid of what he'd see there. How long had it been? Six months? A year? Enough that—

"Carce?"

"Yes, I'm coming."

Carson took his time with the last few steps, head spinning. How could he explain this?

He got to Darius's side and looked in the hole.

The smell was enough to nearly send him coughing, gasping for breath. He barely suppressed the hacking, his lungs burning with the effort.

The cat hadn't rotted enough for the patterns in her fur to be mistakable. They looked like they were moving, though. Like bugs were crawling under the surface of her skin, causing the speckles in her fur to pulse with something else's life. Carson felt sure that at any moment, something would burrow through her flesh and crawl out.

"I—"

Darius looked like he was about to ask him again, what is this, but his eyes trailed past Carson to the screen door, which Carson had left open.

Carson turned slowly, joints crying out suddenly, as if every part of his body wanted to deny what he and Darius were about to see behind them.

Sugar trotted down the porch steps and into the yard. She meowed as she approached them, then nuzzled up to Carson's legs, purring.

If the smell of her own rotting corpse bothered her at all, Carson couldn't tell.

Opinion: Respecting the Dead
by Carson Bennett
. April 20th .

Is there no respect left for the dead?

I know local laws have been passed to make it easier—and cheaper—to request an exhumation of a dead body, as if seeing the corpse in the ground will change anything at all about the fact that your loved ones seem to be alive and something akin to well, but what are we hoping to accomplish? The bodies are still in the ground, rotting. We've verified that. The bodies are also above the ground, breathing.

We can see that with our own eyes.

What is digging up the body going to do to bring you comfort? No, we're just disrespecting the dead—twofold. The dead that we buried, and the dead in our homes.

Do I understand this anymore than anyone? No.

But I don't want to wait for the other shoe to drop anymore.

Carson had called in sick again, but he was worried that his excuses were getting thinner. He hadn't told anyone at work about the lung cancer. Maybe it was obvious that something was wrong, but he hadn't even told his family, so why would he tell his boss? It was his own damn business, and he was tired of answering questions.

Come to think of it, only three people knew about the lung cancer: Carson, Carson's doctor . . . and Darius.

Which was maybe why Darius was perched on the coffee table, watching Carson where he lay on the couch, barely moving, barely breathing. Darius was barely moving, but he *was* breathing.

"Carce?" Darius asked after what felt like a lifetime.

"Yeah?" Carson's lungs burned with the effort of saying even that.

"I think we need to talk."

Carson laughed, his voice wet with phlegm. That hurt worse than the word. "Are you breaking up with me?" The joke felt thin. There hadn't been anything to end for over thirty years. No, this was a different end.

"You know that's not it."

Carson took a few laboured breaths, each one sticky and clinging to his throat, aggravating the raw wounds left from so much coughing. "Then what?"

"I don't know, man. A lot of things, probably. Why I'm here. Why Sugar is here. Why you're not telling anyone that you're dying."

"I'm not dying."

Darius laughed this time. It sounded as wet as Carson's, and for a second Carson panicked, irrationally afraid that the lung cancer had spread to Darius. Even if it had somehow evolved to be contagious, Carson had been too scared to even touch Darius, no matter how much he wanted to. He couldn't have given him shit all. "Then what the fuck is *this*?" Darius asked.

"I don't know."

"Yes, you do," Darius said. "But *fuck*, it's so unfair, Carson. I don't know why the fuck I'm here, but I'm just—I'm back just to watch you die." Cruel words bubbled to Carson's mind, but he was too weak to say them, even if he had wanted to hurt Darius. But he didn't have to. Darius provided them himself: "I guess now I know how you felt."

"Dare . . ."

"No, Carce, don't fucking *say* anything. This is fucked up. I don't know if there's anything else to say. Maybe the gods are punishing me. Us."

"For what?"

"For loving you? I don't know. Maybe they were right all along, that we were being punished. Maybe that's why I died. Maybe that's why I came back. To torture us some more. The gods hadn't had enough."

Carson began to cough. He waited until the worst of them, and the worst of the pain, faded before he tried to reply. His voice sounded bloody. "Do you think the gods are so cruel?"

"Seems pretty fucking cruel to me."

"I always kind of hoped that the gods still loved us."

Darius bent over where he sat on the coffee table. He covered his face with his hands. Carson watched him just breathe for a few long moments. He felt jealous. Eventually, Darius said, "I don't know how you can still think that. That there's any god at all. That we're not just out here, all alone. After everything, while you're *dying.*"

"Are we alone, though? I got to have you back, if only for a little while."

"Just in time for *me* to watch *you* die. If that's love, then *fuck that.*"

Neither moved, and neither answered. Not the young man, thirty-three years dead, nor the man in the last grips of life. Neither could quite meet each other's eyes, anymore.

It wasn't like either of them had anything left to give, anyway.

Carson Bennett, 1963-2020

Carson Bennett, a long-time employee of the paper, died this past Friday from accelerated lung cancer, which he had kept from his colleagues. Carson had lived a long and storied life, and previously held a career in the military. He was loved by all of us at the paper, where he had written many articles and opinion pieces. His intellect was surpassed only by his empathy.

While no family could be reached for comment, and Carson is not survived by a wife or children, we are assured by the dear friend who was by his side when he passed that Carson will be missed.

My Sweetest Oblivion

~ *Maxwell I. Gold*

The end was sweet,
wrapped in fur and stardust,
a comfort that tickled my fragile consciousness
as if it were nothing less than some store-bought toy;
unwrapped slowly and thrown about in the deepest,
most desperate voids
blanketed by entropy, salt, heat, and frozen comforts—
back and forth
I found myself its plaything.
The pawprints plastered on my brain tissue,
neurons jockeyed like stars
in the purple-webs,
Oblivion became my sweetest joy,
despite their finality
closing in on me
every moment,
every scratch until I was lost,
forever tangled in some thistledown darkness.

⬥

The Last Surf on a
Black Sea of Infinity

~ Chris J. Karr

The night-gaunt propelled itself through a black and dying universe. The last star had finally winked out and the timeless entity enjoyed a fresh coolness on its black wings, now that it was no longer blistered by electromagnetic radiation.

Other than its fellow dark flyers, the night-gaunt was alone in this new cosmic darkness. There were no sleepers left to fuel the Dreamlands or its creatures, and as the mortals perished, even the Outer Gods and Great Old Ones faded into oblivion without believers to sustain their existence. With its shiny inky-black skin, faceless profile, horns, and wide leathery wings, the night-gaunt was often mistaken as one of the eldritch monsters of the expiring universe, but it had less in common with those predators than they shared with their prey. The flyer simply *was* for many cosmic lifetimes before those who arose in this universe, and it would continue to *be* for many more cosmic cycles after this universe and its monsters ceased to exist.

Even so, the night-gaunt contemplated how much longer *it* wished to remain in this empty reality. It was becoming bored. This was not the first time it had faced this decision, and it would not be the last. While its memories of previous universes had blended and blurred, it recalled the genesis of this one. The explosion of matter and energy had been spectacular, and the cosmos that congealed gave rise to mortals, gods, and the hidden realms that their prayers and dreams spawned.

As it reminisced, a subtle vibration prompted the night-gaunt to change its flight path. It relished banking off the gravitational waves of three nearby black holes dancing around each other. The gravitational waves emanating from the triad provided the thrilling boost that the flyer sought as it searched for its next home. Once it coasted into a quieter region of spacetime, the night-gaunt detected a distant cluster of several smaller singularities which might be what it was seeking, or at least an entertaining region to navigate after far too long spent traversing the staid cosmic void.

As the flyer coasted to its destination, it considered what made this universe's Dreamlands special.

Unlike the universes preceding it, this one had produced many species and races with innate talents for storytelling. Yithians, Mi-Go, humans, and "star spawn" all employed stories to communicate and relate to each other. Here, while the allegorical denizens slept, their storytelling seeded and cultivated subconscious sagas as their minds used dreams as a means for untangling and making sense of the waking world.

The night-gaunt was as sleepless as it was timeless. While it lacked the capacity to visit as a Dreamer, its unique composition of dark matter allowed it to shift between the waking and sleeping worlds. Where the waking realm was saturated with scalding electromagnetic radiation, the Dreamlands provided a refuge. There a black flyer could bask in the mental energies pouring in from sleepers to embody and ensoul the land, cities, creatures, and personalities in the Dreamlands. Night-gaunts do not hunger or depend on feeding the same way that mortals and gods do, but they do find purpose and motivation to continue in the dreams of the sleepers. Consequently, they spent most of their time in the subconscious dimension, only venturing out into the waking world when absolutely necessary.

Sleepers' dreams would often combine and merge, producing rich and textured Dreamlands where the flyer replenished itself in the energy and emotions flowing from the Dreamers. It lacked a face, the night-gaunt, so it did not see, hear, or smell. But it could "taste," and it sampled the beings and settings it encountered. There was always a new feast to be had in the Dreamlands.

As the stars went dark one by one, the races that had once sustained the Dreamlands vanished. The feast of energy and imagination that the faceless flyer had become accustomed to was a little bit smaller and little less rich as the eons progressed. This process began gradually—a species lost once every epoch or so—but accelerated until the Dreamlands consisted of nothing except eroding lands and crumbling cities, devoid of any life or intelligence. The night-gaunt recalled when the Dreamers sustaining Nodens vanished. The flyer's ancient friend did not vanish all at once, but sublimated into the void, his sad eyes last to fade from existence. The inert remainder of the Dreamlands soon followed suit, and as the last dream-substance evaporated, so did the night-gaunt's ability to access that now-null realm.

The cosmic surfer felt no loss or remorse at the dying of this universe. Any sentimentality it may have carried had long since been weathered away after the first few universes it witnessed sprung into being and inevitably expired in their natural cycles. While the meaning and vitality of *this* cosmos had already been consumed by the maws of ravenous collapsed stars, the night-gaunt found joy and satisfaction in the knowledge that there it would be part of a new reality soon. That said, the dark surfer hoped that it might remember this cosmos for longer than it remembered the others. This universe had been one of its favorites.

The night-gaunt pushed forward and did not slide along the gravitational waves aimlessly—it combed the black cosmos for its next home. It knew that as this universe was being picked apart by cosmic scavengers, beneath each unidirectional membrane, the seed of a new universe was gestating from remnants of this dead one, all of that energy and material coalescing into a single point that would glow blindingly violet to those with eyes to witness it. The night-gaunt's unique composition would not save it from becoming trapped in the gravity well of a black hole, but it would exclude it from being incorporated into the singularity at the center that would soon blossom into a new reality.

In searching for a new home, the traveler skimmed along the boundaries of each singularity it encountered to determine which suited it best. Once the night-gaunt choose one, it would dive within and wait patiently for the new cosmos to spring forth.

If the night-gaunt had a mouth like the Dreamers, it would describe the character of each universe as a distinct "flavor." Smaller black holes would generally produce bland realities with few Dreamers and boring pedestrian gods. Those had a pleasant, if unremarkable seasoning. Larger singularities—like those that occupied the centers of long-dead galaxies—produced overwhelming cosmoses of chaos. From experience, the night-gaunt knew of the cacophony of violence and misery that emanated from mortals and deities in these colossal realms, drowning out beauty and intention. Those flavors were overwhelmingly rotten and bitter. The night-gaunt had already found many candidates representing both kinds of realities. It chose to continue seeking something between those two extremes—a new cosmos that would have enough conflict to add drama and stakes to the Dreams within, but not overwhelmingly so that it would result in Dreamers that were prisoners of fear and anxiety, with little room for true creativity to bloom.

The night-gaunt encountered a choppy gravitational region as it approached its destination: a singularity that was the product of several smaller ones colliding. From the vibrations that emanated away from the event, the dark surfer finally felt some opportunity and potential. Collisions of this sort produced universes with a solid balance of calm and chaos, from which inventive sleepers could emerge to craft breathtaking new Dreamlands, and conjure forth majestic pantheons of new gods and monsters.

The night-gaunt weaved and ducked, surfing the chaotic waves until the collisions ceased, and a single black hole now sat gently spinning in the center of what had been several before.

The black flyer glided along the event horizon, and approved of what it savored. Before it irreversibly dived beneath the membrane to discover how this new universe would unfold, it silently thanked the dying cosmos that had been its most recent home, and allowed itself one final moment to appreciate the monsters and dreamers and gods that made it exceptional.

In a Bottle

~ *Buffy Mitchell*

Someone gave it to a friend of a friend who shoddily wrapped it up as a White Elephant gift for Christmas last year. The novelty item peeking from within the red and green striped bag would be at home next to a lava lamp sitting above a massage chair that always had someone in it who never intended to purchase anything, shouting about how they wished they had the money. Sharper Image went out of business so long ago, generations of people don't recognize the name, so their wares are all but antiques. The way the light flickered from within the open bag with no real pattern told me the batteries must be nearly dead. Still, it had to be mine.

And so, it was.

Part canning jar, part beaker, the smooth blue glass is on my desk beside my sticker-covered emotional support water bottle and the hand-painted candle I can never light. A metal tag dangles from a thick braided rope deeply embedded into the cork stopper. "Lightning in a Bottle" is etched into the front, making it nicer than most other things bought from aisles with Chia Pets. The back of the tag reads "Take care."

It started a week after the party, on New Year's Eve. Sounded like an odd knock, but some people like to do that. Like saying *present* instead of *here* when getting called on in high school—just trying to be different, stand out or whatever.

I shouted to see if my pizza had miraculously arrived early, but no one answered.

Without looking in the peephole, I opened the door. A woman with green hair and a lip ring fell into my arms, heavy and quick. She smelled like cake and cigarette smoke.

I did the normal thing of shaking her, shouting at her, asking her if I should call someone. Then, I checked her pulse. With no wounds or blood, I thought she must have had a seizure or heart attack.

My first instinct was to call the police. I had just started to dial when a whisper like a devil on my shoulder told me to put the phone back in my pocket.

Thanks, I whispered to nothing in particular, as I dragged her to my trunk.

My devil was keeping me in check. There is no statute of limitations on murder.

Some poor woman came next. Just a stranger who would be declared missing and missed by someone, somewhere. I didn't connect the two at first, because she was a mess. An arm was on my front porch by the fake flower pot I keep my hide-a-key under. A nice leather bag with lipstick too dark for me laid abandoned on the steps. The soles of her shoes had melted into the bristles of my custom welcome mat. It was disappointing. I'd just swept.

Logically, I should have called the police the week before—with the pizza girl. It's clear I had nothing to do with either of these women's deaths. But the whisper was more insistent this time, and having the police search my house would be more than disastrous. Arizona still has the death penalty. Again, I appreciated the whisper, which felt less like my internal devil and more *other*.

Cleanup took so long the stars glittered by the time I was wrapping her up.

The drive to the quarry was quick that night. No traffic or flashing lights, just the open road and a heart thudding so loud it drowned out my janky air conditioning.

I'd nearly forgotten about both incidents until a friend came for Game Night a month later. He was burned so badly, I could only identify his watch. Seeing his body, I wished the trips were part of Susan's weekly ritual and not mine, wished she was dealing with the death of one of her closest friends. She had everything. She could stand to lose one or two people, I'm sure.

Sure, I did the *one* thing to deserve this. I thought no one knew about it. In hindsight, I think that's why it chose me.

Like cats, we think we have a say in our lives. I thought *I* was choosing *it* during that White Elephant party. After all, who was bouncing in their chair to steal it? Who was chewing on the inside of their cheek to fuck over Susan Bartlett?

Susan, who ended up with a mouse-eared shaped waffle iron—*a waffle iron*, for goodness sake. Still haven't heard the end of it. That night was exhausting with her bemoaning how she rarely got what she wanted. All the while, her gaudy sweater was flashing at me. Wealthy, hot wife, big house, endless supply of dumb parties to fill her social calendar. I had no doubt Susan got everything she wanted.

She dodged a bullet getting that probably still untouched waffle iron I'd use every week. Imagine her driving in her shiny red pumps to the quarry. It's more than laughable. Or maybe Susan already had a guy for that kind of thing. Broke people like me haul their own bodies, though.

But it didn't consider my economic status. Somehow, it sensed what I had hidden in my basement.

Nothing about my excitement was authentic, manufactured electric energy drew me to it. It knew I would keep it's secret because I'd never expose my own.

I know you're thinking, *It's just fake lightning in a bottle, Brit.* But you're wrong.

A predator lives in that bottle. An old entity, dark and needy. Or maybe it's just a tendril of a god, with bits of it spread across the world. The confines of the glass are like a swaddling blanket, keeping it warm, until it doesn't want that anymore. When it wants fresh air, the cork is no match. I doubt much of anything would be.

Merely a suspicion at first, I had watched it crackle and felt the charge in the air grow, only to ease when another dead body awaited me. I couldn't prove it yet, hadn't seen it for myself, but I'd *felt* the change.

So a month later, I knew what was coming. My hair was standing on end again. I couldn't sleep. I had to stay alert. So I popped pill after pill after pill. I stayed awake for four days, using the last of my sick days to be home when it happened, to stop it.

It caved before I did. In our game of chicken, I won—if you can call that winning. In its jar, the lightning slowly changed from a pale yellow to a neon blue. One bolt pronged off into an electric root system, some not much more than tiny fractured sparks. No longer able to be contained, the frantic energy shoved the cork up and out of the bottle.

I was a deer. Like a deer, the car had no interest in me.

The entity moved through the air like an inchworm. A pressure caused by fear or the tendrils suffocated me as I followed it, did nothing to stop it, despite my earlier bravado. It slid between the seams of the doorway, crackling with anticipation. Bright blue filled my living room as a guttural scream ripped from whoever was just beyond the threshold. The sound cut off almost as quickly as it started, but it reverberated in my bones for hours after.

It came back a springier, pale yellow once more. The many electric appendages were fading away as it slid into the bottle. One remained long enough to jab at the cork and pull it back towards the mouth of the bottle.

With that, it returned to its original single bolt, and the air went back to normal. Wordlessly, I stood and moved to remove the fifth victim from my porch.

Purple and brown jagged marks marred her skin. Unmistakable cause. There is no longer a point in hiding itself from me.

In order to keep my own secret, I must spend the rest of my life covering up this dark entity's needs. I must accept *The Lightning*.

My shoulders rolled forward, and I knew it sensed my new resignation, knew that the fifth victim would end up being a blip in the body count.

Electricity bounced around the glass jar. There was a childlike happiness to the action, as if it was giddy about our future together.

Good night, I whispered into the dark. *I'll see you in the morning.*

⋈

Forget All Thy Troubles

~ *Andrew S. Fuller*

It was still dark outside when she took Galen to the airport. She drove in pajamas and kissed him goodbye inside the warm car. She was looking forward to a weekend by herself. On the way home, a long freight train blocked the road until any chance of getting back to bed or to the gym had passed. By the time she made it home, the alarm clock had been ringing for thirty minutes, the dog awake and anxious. She took Bartleby out to do his business, trying to keep her eyes open. She only had to make it through Friday. As she dressed in business casual, the shimmering points in the sky faded under the bright relentless influence of the nearest star.

On her eighteen-mile morning commute, a trailer truck overturned on the highway and several hundred home furnishings shattered across all three southbound lanes. She texted her team to let them know. There had been a time not long ago where everyone worked from home. Many of her friends still did so, but her employer had not taken a vote on the matter. Now she waited in unmoving traffic, both hands wrapped around a travel mug full of her homemade amaretto mocha. The bumper sticker on the vehicle in front of her said SOMETIMES DEFENESTRATION IS THE ONLY ANSWER, and she said amen to that.

She found the last available space at the far end of the parking lot. There was a tray of freshly baked brownies in the breakroom, and it was still early but she took one because it was Friday. With a middle layer of caramel, bless the baker, the snack did not survive the walk to her desk.

When she opened her laptop there were no meetings in her calendar, but within fifteen minutes there appeared four urgent mandatory invites on her screen. One of them for 12:00 P.M., because some persons are complete monsters who do not know the concept of lunch. At least the 2:00 P.M. was a virtual, and she could keep the camera off, get some work done. The vent above her desk released frigid air and the occasional dust bunny onto her keyboard, one into her freshly poured coffee before she replaced the lid.

In the first meeting she listened to the sales team speak for over an hour on their latest maximizing whatever conference, and felt like the only one in the room who saw the folly of a panicked and frankly impossible plan for a sudden pivot in direction. Immediately afterward she stayed in the same conference room to run a training for a subgroup of team leaders on how to format and submit reports. They had one question, but asked it a dozen different ways. She reminded herself to breathe and blink, take sips of coffee, and that it was Friday. Cup of coffee number three joined the sugar in her otherwise empty stomach. It tasted of lukewarm despair with a shot of mania.

The next hours were lost to chats and merges and process testing and assembling a presentation deck, along with several co-workers stopping by to follow-up on an email, and she found herself scowling at the spreadsheets open before her and at the entire restless world in general. She was surprised to find her fingers composing a time-off request email to her supervisor and hitting send. Well, it could be true that one of her extended family was ill at that point in time. She refused to breathe until a response came. Fortunately it arrived within two minutes. Half-day of PTO approved. With an additional note reminding her to finish the presentation by Sunday evening.

At precisely noon she enabled out-of-office notifications, donned her sunglasses before leaving the cubicle, and made it to her automobile without encountering any opposition.

And why the hell not, she thought as she pulled out of the parking lot at the dangerous speed of seven miles per hour.

On the way home she thought highway traffic would be better at midday, but it slowed to a stop before the curves. For over ten minutes she sat in lanes of unmoving cars. A quarter mile ahead, the flashing lights of emergency and police vehicles surrounded a large dark spill or maybe a sinkhole. Exit 295 was a few hundred feet away, and, urging herself not to worry too much about it, drove along the shoulder, then sped up the ramp to escape the congestion.

A small brown sign with white lettering pointed the way to an

HISTORIC DOWNTOWN DISTRICT, and she thought that made sense, for several of the suburbs had been townships at one time, though no town name was included. It sounded quaint and inviting, and the navigation app on her phone insisted this was an alternate route.

Tall fir trees flanked the road as it climbed a winding incline. This was surprising to her because she felt like the view from the highway had always been a steady sequence of commercial buildings backed by rows of housing on every hill. For miles, the occasional wooden gate appeared among the large tree trunks, less often a leaning skeletal barn in an uncut field. She did not mind, finding it all colorful and wild.

Forest aromas seeped into the car, bringing with them a sense of renewal. She felt far from home and on a new adventure. The high pointed tips of trees curved above her like a closing mouth, and she raced to escape, laughing, *oh no you don't!* The road narrowed and crumbled at the edges. A large elk watched her pass, and she looked too, both their heads turning at once.

The gasoline gauge indicated less than a quarter tank. This did not seem correct but it was more than enough to make it home, even if she had to take backroads all the way around the city to I-205. Two crows swooped back and forth over the car hood, cawing up a ruckus, and just as she began to worry, flew off.

The forest relented briefly to a sparse main street and she slowed her vehicle out of courtesy, though she could not help looking. There were no cars present except the tireless rusted shells occupying a lifeless gas station. The pumps had no hoses, and next to the boarded-up door sat a vending machine for a soda that she was sure was no longer being made. There was more sky here, and delicate clouds rippled over like great inhalations.

Next to the gas station sat an old general storefront with unpainted siding and wooden sidewalk, worn and faded gray by seasons. The modern electric sign on the façade declared ANTIQUES, WINE TASTING, TEA, FRESH PIE, and GIFTS. Her roaring stomach reminded her of the two meals she had already missed, so she parked in front of the place. She abhorred saltwater taffy and licorice and fudge, and was thankful not to see any of these listed.

✳

Night awaited her when she came out of the store, which was somewhat surprising. She called behind her a thanks and apology, in hopes she hadn't kept the owner too long. The brown grocery bag was full and what all she had bought escaped her at the moment. Her plan was to snack as she drove. She looked forward to each treat.

The dashboard clock said 10:08 P.M. She checked her phone and it said the same. Now this was very difficult for her to believe. She gasped at the thought of Bartleby having an accident, missing dinner, being alone. A weary fog settled into her mind and she shook her head slowly. Her limbs felt like fallen trees.

She groaned aloud and started the car. Then she tapped open the navigation app. The car icon spun and spun in the center of the small screen, with no other visible roads or features. There was no reason to panic, and it made sense to go back the way she had come. She pulled out carefully into the small road. Halfway through the u-turn, she saw the remarkable Victorian era house in the adjacent extended lot, elegantly illuminated by several soft lights in the yard.

She was not surprised to see her arms make the turn a full circle, and she found herself in front of the tall house. Stained glass and ornate trim of exquisite detail decorated every surface of the place. The dense hedges were neatly pruned, while an arbor passage led past a sculptured fountain to a back garden. Arranged near the prolific rhododendron was a set of iron lawn furniture that she imagined quite pleasant in the late afternoon. Lastly she noticed the post lantern and hanging sign that read NEPENTHE INN, an AUTHENTIC BED AND BREAKFAST. She hesitated out of consideration again, before she turned off the engine and went to inquire.

The doorbell was a twisting spindle with internal spring in the middle of the wide door flanked by beautiful leaded glass. Almost immediately a woman with curled gray hair answered wearing an apron and an expression of delight. The aromas of allspice, molasses, and cardamon drifted onto the porch. *No worries at all,* the woman said with warm laughter in a voice reminiscent of her favorite aunt, and repeated several times as though they'd already had several exchanges, already climbing the curved staircase, motioning to keep up, then along two hallways with glimpses of unoccupied rooms featuring wide beds under glowing sconces, and then up another set of smaller stairs to the third floor where she turned the skeleton key and gestured an invitation into the beautiful unfurling suite with dimensions seemingly larger than the those of the house.

So in awe of the original wardrobe, kitchenette, canopy bed, and several features, the guest did not see the hostess depart. The iron room key sat, warm to the touch, on the nightstand next to the rotary dial phone and stained glass lamp. It seemed a journey to cross the room, though it was a heavenly walk with shoeless feet on the deep rug depicting a great forest full of dancing animals. She opened the only other door and discovered the bathroom was at least half as large as the suite, complete with double-headed shower and separate platform bathtub, two sinks, a separate bidet, a makeup dresser with lighted mirror and cushioned bench, and its own balcony. The bathrobes were silk, and as soon as she wedged a chair under the main door knob, she changed herself into one.

She had a fleeting thought of how much this single evening might cost. Her phone alerted her to an incoming message. Without looking, she powered it down, and spun around and around with eyes closed, letting the device cast off in some unknown direction, allowing herself a long grateful sigh.

The packed grocery bag sat on the hall tree bench next to the door, and though she did not recall bringing it inside, she did not mind, and proceeded to dump its contents onto the bed's ample duvet. She did not recall purchasing every item but the selection delighted her. Here was everything she desired.

She found drinking glasses in the kitchen cabinet, clean and spotless, and a corkscrew in the drawer along with other utensils including a kitchen knife of impressive quality. As she poured a glass, she recalled the shopkeeper mentioning the bottle was from a small vineyard in the next valley. The label was simple and formal, and the pinot noir was superb. She enjoyed the wine out on the larger balcony. The forest cut away part of the night sky strewn with millions of stars, embellished with the prismatic spine of the vast lonely galaxy. She felt absolutely meager and lost among it all, and increasingly relaxed with her position.

The wine made her smile at nothing and everything in particular. She went and started the bath water before pouring another glass. Then she used the good knife to cut a generous piece of strawberry rhubarb pie. She ate each delicious bite with her fingers. Next she unwrapped the smoked cheddar and rustic sourdough bread, tearing each portion with her teeth, for there was no one else around, thank you very much. Half of the loaf was gone before she whirled and ran to the bathroom. Thankfully the bathtub was large enough that the water had only reached a third of its depth. *Well, whatever shall I do while I wait . . . ?*

She poured a third glass, which she enjoyed with dark chocolate-covered peanut butter cookies. These snacks were wrapped in parchment paper and locally made. *Perhaps,* she thought, *by someone I have recently met in this beautiful secret place.* She giggled at length about this observation.

In another kitchen drawer alongside napkins and toothpicks, she found a few long candles, raw and simple with a honey scent; and a small wooden matchbox stamped with the house name. The pewter holders were not difficult to locate, bookending a shelf with old editions of well-read books, many familiar titles from her childhood. Fond memories of dragons and spaceships soared through her mind.

Arms and hands full of candles and wine vessels and the knife for protection, she made her way back to the alluring bath, growing more comfortable every moment with her circumstance. On the way, she noticed the last unopened package on the bed, spherical and wrapped in colorful tissue paper with a ribbon tied into a generous bow. *Oh please take one at no charge,* she vaguely recalled the shopkeeper saying, indicating the basketful by the old analog cash register. They smelled heavenly, of ancient woodland groves and undiscovered fields, with oceans over the next hill. She freed one pinky finger from her armload and caught the package through the ribbon's loop.

Setting her drink aside, she arranged the candles around the steaming tub before lighting them. She opened the octagonal windows, and breathed the pure unsullied air as she moved with the moon's glow over the cool perfect tiles.

Once she turned off the electric lights, she placed the expensive chef's knife within reach, and removed the lustrous robe. Sitting on the edge of the great tub she untied the package ribbon and carefully removed the tissue. Gently she crumbled the shape within, inhaling the luxurious aromas, feeling the soft and sharp texture, gazing at the shimmering minerals across her palms and fingers. Soap suds grew from the bathwater and created a soothing terrain. Her skin whispered to her that it was time.

The heat rose in welcome as her body entered the bath. She sipped the wine until it was depleted and sank back, her vertebrae nestled into the cool curve of porcelain, her limbs floating in the prickling pool, until water filled her ears and the voices of her mind quieted. She watched the mountains of suds tremble with the rhythm of her heart.

Surely she was allowed to forget for a few minutes. Forget the emails and office bureaucracy. Forget the dying species and boiling planet. For just a few minutes, forget the abounding cruelty and injustice, the dismantling of civil rights, all the letter writing and phone calls to senators; screaming into the closet and crying at the accumulating corruption and slaughter. Forget what's-his-name and that dog. For only one single minute. Slowly she felt the world recede, and smiled for no one but herself.

In each small bath bubble there opened an eye, bright and ready, constellations gazing upon her. She looked back at them with a last moment of worry. But that fear passed, as she exhaled.

And they rose together on her gentle swirl of breath, leaving nothing behind, no form or shadow in the still water. They floated calmly away from the container and across the surfaces; a weightless multitude loose and tranquil, drifting upward and outward, unwinding into the hushed extent of the night sky; beginning their unhurried migration to fill the sweeping dark between every distant star.

The Family Death

~ *Megan Lee Beals*

We were a young family; my husband, our cat, and me. Our death was young and inexperienced. She was only there to usher away crinkle legged spiders from the closet, dusty moths from the threshold of doors, and the ants we crushed beneath our thumbs before they could lead their fellows to our cupboards. I saw her often out of the corner of my eye, flitting their spirits away and tidying the house of their ghosts. I told my mother, knowing she would be so proud. That I'd moved out and established myself well enough to have a death of my own. I told her it was a kind death, with a face like the grandmother I only knew in pictures; high cheekbones and cat-eye glasses and that meticulous pile of blonde curls on her head that must have taken hours to pin in place.

"She looks like your grandmother Edith?" she asked, and my face grew hot. Perhaps it wasn't so kind then, to bring up the mother she lost when she was still in college. But she pulled on a smile after a long deliberation and patted my shoulder. "Do you want to hear something stupid?" she asked. It was the start to an old routine. The question she'd always ask if I wanted a dumb little joke to lighten the mood. I nodded, because I always did. It was my role in the routine. "She was a generally happy person, but when she was mad, your grandmother had a scowl that could scare death to death."

I hugged her, and as we pulled away, she urged me not to look at it straight on. To let our new death busy about her work unbothered and never invite her near. But I needed our death. The cat was sick. He had been for months, and she was nowhere to be found.

So I sought her at the vet. I signed the paper and it seemed so small. A single page, a paragraph I could hardly read, a name and a date. It seemed that invoking death should require more words.

A grimoire and robes and chanting that would bring her to me, but words meant nothing to death. It was the drugs that forced her to me.

The cat and I were alone in the exam room when she walked in through the wall. Her skull was bare and smiling, her skeletal body was cloaked in a black shroud. I put myself between her and my cat because she did not deserve to see him after she left him suffering for weeks. He was lying on a towel in the center of a metal table. His breath was labored, rattling, and he did not stir at the sight of her.

"You're late," I said.

Admonished, our death covered her face with fleshless hands. Static buzzed in my ears and behind my nose. When the world refocused, she looked like a poor memory of the pictures of my grandmother. Hair too long, eyes too large and rimmed with too much black.

'I can't be late,' she said. I'd never heard her speak before. The voice was gentle and soft, and it came from behind my head even though I watched her lips move with the words.

She was correct. The cat was still living, but only just. I had to help him stand earlier that day. I held him upright as he drank from a shallow dish. To think of it started my tears again, and I stuffed a handful of tissues to my face. The table around his towel was already littered in paper and snot and tears.

"He's in pain," I growled through my body's racking. He had yowled through the morning until I took him in my arms and read aloud the nearest book to us, flipped to a random page. I had hoped my voice was a comfort, but he was too ill to signal if it was. "You're supposed to take away pain."

She nodded solemnly and folded her hands neatly over the black lace that hid the skeletal body beneath her shroud. 'Would you like a flashback? I'm very good at flashing lives before eyes . . . Remember all the times you were sick and he'd press his head to yours?'

I could see his whiskers brush the tops of my glasses and feel the cold pressure of his nose on my forehead.

"Stop."

She blushed. 'Right. You don't want to hear about sickness. Sorry. That's okay, there are so many happy memories! What about the time he chased off that stray who tried to kill your friend's turtle?'

I bit the inside of my cheek until I tasted blood as I fought the memory's resurgence. I couldn't bear to see him that young.

She carried so many tiny deaths out of our house, flies and spiders and mice, so that I could discard their bodies without guilt. She was not inattentive, but this was my cat. He deserved more than spiders. And she fled when I needed her most. "You're supposed to be here for him."

She bent to the cat on the table and cooed. 'Hey, Ike.'

His head almost lifted. He blinked slowly, and kept his eyes closed. I touched the fur at his back, afraid that the weight of my hand would be too much for him.

'Remember that mouse you caught under the bookshelves...?'

I pushed her away. "He doesn't need a fucking flashback! Don't you speak cat? Tell him it's going to be okay. Tell him it couldn't last forever! Tell him I'm sorry and I'll never get over him and that I'll never forgive myself for signing the paper..."

'Oh,' said death. 'Oh darling, I don't speak cat. I'm your death.'

I spluttered. "Then why are you here? To tell me it's his time? Like that'll make it hurt less?" It was past his time. He'd survived so many illnesses before. We'd survived, with foul tasting antibiotics and years of saline drips. I couldn't borrow any more time.

'No,' said death. 'I know every moment you shared with him. There is no sentiment that will replace that. You are going to hurt. I'm here so you don't have to hurt alone.'

"So you're here to tell me that everything dies. And everyone hurts. And his life amounts to nothing in the grand scheme of the universe." It was so easy to hate her.

'There is no scheme,' she whispered, and a perfect tear ran down her porcelain face. 'Every death is enormous. Every death remakes the world. It puts a period in the lives of those left behind.'

The hate bubbled over. "You. Fucking. Suck."

Her face fled, and a shocked skull covered its teeth behind skeletal hands. 'I don't know what you want from me!'

"How long have you been doing this? You're supposed to be our death. You've seen every moment my family has shared, and all I get are a couple of memories designed to make me cry?"

She fiddled with the edges of her shroud. If she had lips still, she'd be chewing them. 'I'm really sorry. It's my first big death, and Ike is such a good cat . . .'

"He's the best cat," I corrected as I stroked his skinny side.

'The best,' she agreed. 'I just wish I knew what you needed.'

"I needed you two days ago. Peacefully, in his sleep. Not shivering on a table and crying because he can't walk more than three steps without falling."

'He wasn't ready then.' Her eyes met his and she put her face back on to give him a gentle smile. 'He's such a good boy that he doesn't want to leave you. He hates to see you cry.'

"God dammit." That opened the flood of tears again. I pulled more tissues from the box.

'Do you want to hear something stupid?'

The phrase rocked through me and stopped my tears. I pinched my eyes closed and nodded. Yes. I always want a joke.

'It's actually fortunate that you had to come here.'

My fingers clenched and I glared at her. Hard enough to scare her to death, but she continued.

She smiled at me and casually slid the box of Kleenex into my purse. 'Your house is all out of tissues.'

It was so stupid and petty and small, and I was so close to the gallows that I burst out laughing.

Ike stirred beneath my hand and pressed his nose into my palm, happy again to see a break in my tears. The veterinarian came back into the room with her sedatives prepared. She looked past the family death standing by my side. She would not see her. The veterinarian had her own family and her own death that would come in time.

"Are you ready?"

I shook my head and answered. "I'm going to miss him so much."

Death wrapped her arms around me as I held Ike's head, and together we said goodbye.

The Unrelenting Grind

~ John Klima

~ John Klima

FOUR DAYS BEFORE THE RITUAL

Later this week, we fight an Elder God to free the Black Goat of the Woods so she can put out the sun. But today is laundry. I'm not about to let the end of the world throw off my schedule.

The Center holds up to forty residents, but we only have thirteen at the moment. The Center's industrial-sized washers and dryers make the task less onerous but it's still unrelenting. And I make residents do their own folding. That is too much picky shit for me to be bothered with.

All the same, I'm not able to start laundry until after the evening shower shift is finished, so it's well after midnight when I wrap things up.

The residents are required to label their clothing so we can sort it after it's clean. Jessica helps me deliver the laundry to each resident's room. After a quick cigarette, we sleep for a few hours while the overnight shift prepares the fresh tinctures needed for evening rituals.

THREE DAYS BEFORE THE RITUAL

As the sun, our future foe, rises the next morning, Jessica heads into town to check our mail and pick up supplies for the week.

I make breakfast.

All the residents are in a good mood this morning, even Jason. He's the star of the ritual and if he makes any mistakes, everyone's efforts are fucked. For the last few weeks, he has not been dealing well with the pressure. But today it's like everything is fine and there's nothing to worry about.

He's acting a little delusional but at least he's eating. Unlike two seasons ago, we haven't brought out the table to strap him down and force gruel into him. If he's weak from hunger, he won't be able to perform the ritual. He's eaten so little since his arrival four months ago that I wondered if he was on some sort of hunger strike. Later I learned from Mabel that he was nervous, and his stomach was upset.

Today, however, Jason's eaten so much at breakfast that I worry we'll have the opposite problem: he won't be able to perform the ritual because he's stuck on the toilet shitting himself. I mention my concerns to Matthew, who can also perform the ritual, but he waves me off and assures me that Jason will be fine.

With everyone off to their studies or quiet contemplation after breakfast, I settle into washing the dishes. There are always so many dishes. It's all I can do to get the dishes washed and put away before I'm making the next meal, which makes more dishes. We tried paper plates and plastic silverware one season, but too many acolytes complained about the environmental impact.

The staff used to be bigger, but now it's just Jessica and me. Jessica treats the work like a job rather than a calling. Whenever she complains about everything she has to do, I just shake my head and remind her that we all play a part in the Center's role in support of the Black Goat.

I like it when things are routine. I don't mind repetitive work. Jessica hates it and prefers to run errands in town. She's just as busy as I am, but dishes and laundry are such Sisyphean tasks that it's hurtful when she throws my preference for routine in my face when I make any mention of feeling tired and sore from constantly washing dishes.

Today Jessica complains that it's been weeks since she's been able to get a decent manicure.

Rather than shoot back a spiteful comment, I pull Jessica aside and tell her what I think is going on with Jason. She holds eye contact with me for an uncomfortable amount of time and then just nods her head. She'll keep an eye on Jason and make sure he's prepared. But she'll also make sure that Matthew is ready to go.

The Center doesn't have a set midday mealtime, so the struggle is to create a meal that can sit and allow people to come and go. Things like shredded pork, taco meat, lasagna—even a hearty soup—work well for midday. Everyone can get food on their own schedule or skip it altogether if it doesn't fit into what tasks they are trying to accomplish for the day. I offer a prayer of thanks to the benefactor that he made sure that this group of acolytes doesn't have any allergies or food aversions.

I really want tacos, but if I've learned anything over the years, not adhering to Taco Tuesday is disastrous. I can wait until then. I've recently made use of an app that randomizes meal choices. Today it lands on lasagna and garlic bread. It's easy to prep and it can sit forever, giving me a chance to check the fire pit. If repairs are needed, there's still time to bring in a craftsman before the ritual.

The pit will be lit around 3:00 A.M. on the next new moon. The benefactor installed a gas line four years ago after a ritual started without a lit firepit. Jessica and I plan on starting the fire naturally, but it's important to know the gas line is working even if we don't use it. There's no need to light the Center on fire because we didn't check for leaks.

The acolytes' cloaks are dry-cleaned and ready for the ritual. We'll put them in the acolytes' rooms the night before.

The firepit looks great. All the stones are in place. The carvings are scrubbed and readable. Jessica did a great job cleaning up the mess after last season's attempt at the ritual. I thought she'd never get all the gore and viscera scoured out of the deep cuts in the stone.

Peter and Shari have done excellent work preparing the wood pile. All the firewood is nearly identical in shape and size. The wood's been well dried out so it should light with minimal effort.

Evan removed all the stone benches over the summer. Who would have thought that benches would create so much chaos and destruction? But when an acolyte tripped over a bench and into the fire, it didn't take much for the conflagration to spread. It's hard to know if it was due to being lost in the moment, an intentional sacrifice gone wrong, or if it had been an attempt to poison the ritual.

A member of staff wondered aloud whether someone had infiltrated the Center to usurp the ritual. They were summarily dismissed.

The benches were repurposed as stones lining the paths in the Foliate Head Garden. Daniel helped Evan get that all sorted before he left, heading north a few hours to Monhegan Island or some such place.

When I arrive back in the Center, I note that Peter has cleaned up the midday meal. I'm surprised but it's not unexpected. Often the acolytes relish menial work so close to the ritual as a way to settle nerves or clear their heads.

This means that I have even more time in the afternoon than normal. Jessica is off on some errand or other, and I don't have time to search for her to discuss what's happening.

I spend the afternoon with the latest Colleen Hoover.

As I'm prepping curry for dinner, I overhear some acolytes mention that Allison ordered sandwiches from Amato's.

That's the second time today that someone has stepped in and done my job for me. It's not completely unheard of—there was that group several years ago who were feverish in their doting on the staff—but this sort of behavior is always suspicious so close to the ritual. If the acolytes were truly focused on the ritual, we'd be knocking on doors to get people downstairs to dinner.

While I'm cleaning up the unnecessary prep, Jessica wanders into the kitchen and says she has made reservations at The Front Yard for dinner. Her treat. We shouldn't leave the compound this close to the ritual, but I won't turn down Chef Memo's bouillabaisse when given the chance. Maybe I can get the recipe from him for future meals.

While we're being seated, Jessica glances at my low-cut top and rolls her eyes. She knows what I'm playing at. We both know that Chef is not giving up his recipe for anything.

Dinner is delicious and Jessica is a delight, but we are unable to come to any sort of an accord about what might be happening.

I have a growing suspicion the acolytes are getting cold feet and trying to focus their minds on other tasks.

Jessica, on the other hand, is convinced that the core issue is Jason. She feels he hasn't learned the ritual. At all. All the acolytes she's spoken to have the same concern, she tells me, and so they don't see any reason to continue research and practice. Jessica claims that they're trying to show appreciation for all our hard work.

Jessica's still young; she hasn't been at the Center as long as I have. You get to the other side of forty and you can tell when people are nervous and when they are nonchalant. The acolytes are nervous. If I'm being charitable, when I was her age and had smooth skin like her, I was just as oblivious about people.

And of course I didn't get the bouillabaisse recipe. Why should anything go the way I want it?

TWO DAYS BEFORE THE RITUAL

I can't find Jessica anywhere. Today is trash day and I had to wrestle all the bins to the street on my own. I wasn't sure if it was also recycling, so I brought those bins out just to be safe. I was sweating and dirty and barely awake.

Jessica's not bad at her job. In fact, she's the best housing officer the Center's had during my tenure here. That's why I'm really more concerned than angry.

So instead of Jessica doing the final check-in with Jason, it's up to me to take up the slack again.

As I approach Jason's room, I hear two voices in urgent conversation.

I open the door instead of knocking and find Jessica hastily getting dressed while Jason has his back to both of us while he reviews notes.

I hold her with my fiercest gaze and state that this is not the time for extracurricular activities. There is a Center to care for and preparations still need to be made for the ritual.

I turn on my heel and head to the kitchen.

Jessica catches up with me and starts apologizing. I stop her and ask if he was any good. She stammers for a bit and then I clarify, not in 'was it worth it' but in a 'would you like this to be a regular thing' type way.

She laughs and says no. It was adequate. Better for him than for her, because afterwards he seemed to be more focused on the ritual than she'd seen him in weeks which was why she did it in the first place.

So it wasn't a fling. It was done in service of the Center.

That meant we could proceed as planned. Pancakes, bacon, and fresh-squeezed orange juice. Bring the bins back inside. Errands in town. Prep tacos for lunch. Clean around the firepit. Sharpen the knives. All the unrelenting, unappreciated things we do so the ritual is a success.

Jason spends the day focused on the ritual. On preparation. On growing his strength. Getting all the phrases down perfectly. He looks ready. The others follow suit and get ready, too.

We received a large donation from a booster in the mail. I'm grateful, of course, but honestly it's too late. It could've meant hiring back a cleaning service, but after the ritual it won't matter.

I'm more excited that everything is falling into place.

Dinner was pizza from Seacoast Pizza and Pasta, but that was part of the schedule. A present from the benefactor.

In past years he's made the trip to see how everything is coming together but this year he decided to stay at his summer home. Most of the current acolytes at the Center have never met him. That didn't feel right to me, but I don't question his methods.

This is a good job, even if it's meant to bring about the end of the world.

ONE DAY BEFORE THE RITUAL

The day before the ritual is the easiest day of the year. Every hour of the day is set down in the grimoire; no deviations allowed.

Breakfast of plain toast and English Breakfast tea. 7:00 to 8:00 A.M.

Quiet meditation. 8:00 to 10:00 A.M.

Light exercise in the yard (jogging, yoga, or tai chi for example). 10:00 to 11:00 A.M.

Directed chanting. 11:00 A.M.to 12:00 P.M.

Lunch of plain chicken breast with broccoli.12:00 to 1:00 P.M.

Martial combat practice from 1:00 to 2:00 P.M.

Break into groups and rotate through twenty-minute routines: self-flagellation, ice water baths, and inversion therapy. 2:00 to 3:00 P.M.

The grimoire notes free time for the acolytes, but this time is better served in meditation and self-reflection. 3:00 to 5:00 P.M.

Dinner of clear broth and crackers. 5:00 to 6:00 P.M.

Black Mass. 6:00 to 9:00 P.M.

Bed at 9:00 P.M., to be woken at 4:00 A.M. for the ritual.

The whole day is set to keep their minds active and their bodies ready. No one knows exactly what will happen should the ritual be successful. The closest the Center got was in March of 1936 when the ritual caused the Kennebec River to flood. Ice floes leftover from the harsh winter brought down several bridges along the Kennebec, including the one the acolytes were standing on to perform the ritual.

Of course, the local papers wrote it up as a horrible, albeit unusual, natural disaster. The grimoire distinctly states that rising flood water is the first sign of a successful ritual. It's likely that the next stages of the ritual failed because the acolytes were swept away in the ensuing flood. Notes from a staff journal at the time confirm this:

> *A translucent figure came into focus as the ritual wound down to its end. Its full height should have been obscured by the clouds, but we were able to see the figure as if it was an overlay on reality. Its many limbs brushed the sky and the ground simultaneously, making the clouds give forth a torrent of rain while the ground shook beneath our feet. The Kennebec River rose quickly, pushing heavy ice floes towards the acolytes' bridge. Shadowy creatures capered on the ice floes, directing them at the stanchions of the bridge. Before anyone could react, the bridge and the acolytes were gone.*

The flood destroyed much of the benefactor's property. It took until the 1950s for his wealth to rebound. The Center as it stands today was built in 1951, near water, the ocean instead of a river, but on solid ground to avoid the flood interrupting again.

The ritual has been held more than fifteen times at the current location, and it's never come close to the glory that was almost reached in 1936. This means that the sad reality after those failed rituals is that the Center is full of tired and hungry acolytes. Acolytes who no longer believe, who no longer have faith.

The benefactor is a patient man. He has nearly unlimited resources. He has been able to extend his life well beyond the norm. But the turnover rate after each ritual is discouraging. At some point, surely even his patience will run out.

Jessica and I refuse to speculate about that. We just work here.

THE RITUAL

I've found it best over the years to just stay up until it's time to start the ritual. Jessica insists on getting sleep. When Jessica heads off to bed, I tell her if she isn't awake to light the fire, she has the responsibility of waking Jason and the other acolytes.

The sky was clear when I lit the fire, but dark clouds roll in quickly. I can see lights on in the Center. Looks like Jessica is doing her job.

I should have brewed coffee, but instead all I have is the awful, canned cappuccino that Jessica insists on stocking in the refrigerator. I guess it's better than nothing.

Before I finish the drink, chanting from the house grows louder.

Jason enters the area first, but he's eschewed his robe and walks out to the fire pit naked.

The tattoos of the ritual mark his body in stripes and swirls.

The other twelve acolytes follow, wrapped in comfy robes, smoky breath puffing out as they chant.

Jason stations himself on the east side of the clearing facing the new moon with his back to the fire. Jason will start ritual as the sun rises to bring about its demise.

Jessica excitedly accepts a canned cappuccino. The woman has no taste. She hasn't stopped yawning since she got here. I need her more awake in case someone needs to run to the house and get something.

The acolytes drop their robes to the ground. Jessica rushes to pick them up. I have faith that we won't need to clean them ever again.

The acolytes approach Jason, knives gleaming in the firelight.

The first acolyte chooses a tattoo and traces it with her knife, carving flesh. Soon she's joined by others. It doesn't take long, and the tattoos disappear under all the red.

Jason performs admirably. A normal person would collapse by now, but Jason remains upright, his arms raised to the sky. His voice rings clear through the cold morning air.

If I wasn't overtired, I would say that I see an enormous figure in the distance.

If I wasn't overtired, I would believe that I feel the ground shifting.

But even with the unsteady earth, all I can think about is cleaning those knives and laundering the robes and preparing the rooms in the Center for the next group of acolytes and making the first of many meals. And the dishes. Washing the dishes never ends.

⋈

Before the Beginning

~ *Brian U. Garrison*

God twiddling their thumbs.
God inventing hands just before that.
God, heavenless, wondering what to do for lunch.

God wishing for a dictionary to look up the definition of lunch.
God realizing a few other things that are undefined.
God knitting for the first time.

God inventing their neck just after that as a place to hang a scarf.
God feeling fashionable.
God doubting.

Cue the beginning.

God, companionless, just before that, foreseeing how this could
    all spiral wildly out of control.
God releasing it all anyway.
God wondering what to do for lunch.

¤

The Oral and Maxillofacial Surgery Center Sends Best Wishes for Your Birthday

~ *Daniel David Froid*

For many years, an orthodontal clinic in a small town in Indiana has sent me a postcard on my birthday. It's the same one every time, showing an anthropomorphic slice of white cake topped with frosting in a lurid pink shade, its lips curled in a wild grin, its feet kicking outward as it dances against a rich blue background. The smiling slice is ready, eager, to be devoured. HAPPY BIRTHDAY! Even after several new addresses and a move across the country, the clinic has somehow managed to keep tabs on me. This trite missive gives me an odd jolt of joy; it's one of those things to which I look forward, a tradition, just like my choice of cake (lemon poppyseed). But it's also the sole remnant of that nothing town that we hated so much—a reminder that it has not quite let us go.

My wisdom teeth were extracted at the clinic when I was twenty-seven, a little older than most. The removal had, in fact, been necessary for quite some time—at least a year, and probably longer. Like an idiot, or like a graduate student with a laughable stipend and an insurance plan that could only be described as nefarious, uncertain of how much it might cost me and afraid to ask, I put it off. The ache became ever more intense and impossible to suppress as K. and I wrapped up our master's degrees and selected doctoral programs. We undertook a long and challenging move across several states, both of us having found programs at the same university, which, it turned out, offered marginally better benefits. During the move, I popped ibuprofen to numb the pain, with mixed results. We arrived in town after nightfall and found a shitty hotel at the outskirts; the landlord couldn't meet us until the following morning. In a humid room beneath a balcony where skinheads spat and laughed, perhaps at us, I chewed my way through tasteless pizza, aggravating the pain. We opened cans of ginger ale, our last resort after discovering that the state's peculiar liquor laws forbade the purchase of alcohol after 8:00 P. M. on Sundays, and raised them in a toast to this place that was already welcoming us so heartily.

We rented a house in disrepair. Just as soon as we arrived, the dog peed on the carpet. She seemed to do it with pride, defiantly meeting our eyes as she thrust her crotch at the floor with expert precision. Home at last, her gaze said. The landlord laughed and immediately mentioned our security deposit. Too broke to go scouting, we had rented sight unseen. Now we learned that our landlord had recently purchased the aging property from an elderly client. He quickly led us through the cramped, low-ceilinged rooms. The wooden floors were scuffed and stained an ugly brown. The vents on the floors were abnormally large; arranging the furniture would prove a challenge. "Water's not turned on right now," the landlord said and shrugged. "We'll try to take care of it by tonight." He said something about some work that needed to be done in the basement as well. Then he left us to unpack. Across the street, a family was moving into a house that looked even more rundown than ours.

The first night, as I collapsed on the bed and tried to fall asleep— sweaty and unwashed, still without access to running water—I heard a low sound that I struggled to identify. I lifted my head from the pillow and glanced around as though to find its source. It sounded like static. As I continued to listen, however, it coalesced into something else, or I tuned into its frequency. It was chaotic, as of several voices raised in screaming. The tone suggested violence, exquisite pain; though specific words were indecipherable, I imagined howls of agony and sorrow hurled desperately into the void. I noticed a peculiar effect as though the sound grew gradually quieter, spiraling into a brief pause, before roaring back to a high volume. I asked K. if he could hear anything, but he was already asleep. Eventually, I managed to join him, but the sleep was fitful.

We finished unpacking the next day and rejoiced when the landlord called to tell us that we had running water. It was less thrilling to turn on each faucet by turn and wait for the brown muck to turn clear. As I stood in front of the kitchen sink, the voices began again. Or had it taken me this long to register that they had been there all along? The noise followed me as I walked from the kitchen to the miniscule living room and the bedroom, where they seemed to be loudest. I found K. in the bathroom and said: "Do you hear anything?" He paused in front of the cupboard he was wiping down, turned his head to listen, and shook his head.

"There's this sound following me around," I said. "It's like static." I described it that way despite that I had already begun to think of it as howling; it seemed safer, more closely tethered to reality.

K. shook his head again. He said, "Are you okay?" I didn't know what to say. I made a feeble excuse about being very tired; he gave me an odd look for a moment and then turned away. K. has always tended to be more sensible and to have little patience for my flights of fancy. He turned back to the cupboard.

It occurred to me that the sound could be a symptom of something. The pain in my mouth that I continued to ignore—could it somehow induce aural hallucinations? I thought not, and felt like an idiot just wondering, yet it seemed almost possible. Random, discreet googling—"wisdom teeth sounds," "wisdom teeth pain hallucinations," "teeth hurt hearing noises"—made me feel even dumber, and exposure to strangers' uncertainty, fear, and poor medical literacy, bared online, did nothing to deepen my understanding of what was happening or to ease my anxiety. Why, anyway, did I think to connect the two? I suppose my toothache was the only aberrant detail about myself to which I could point. I knew that I needed to have four teeth removed, and I wished to chalk up the noise to my stress about that, the move, and the start of my Ph.D program.

Our first few days there, K. and I walked around the neighborhood to familiarize ourselves with it. I found that, the farther I got from the house, the quieter the voices were. But you might say that other, realer voices grew even louder. After the landlord asked us, early on, "So, you two brothers?" we correctly intuited that his words presaged something more. I don't think we ever gave him an answer, permitting his mind to take him where it would. We lived in an ugly neighborhood, with squat houses covered in flaking, greasy-looking paint. When the leaves fell, I hoped it would look a little nicer or, at least, picturesque, but it turned out to be like hanging seasonal decorations on a dumpster. Stubby, dingy buildings blighted the entire town. Every store looked like a throwback to the '90s at its most squalid and desperate. Pick-up trucks with confederate flags waving in the back congregated in front of the dollar store several blocks away. Every face we encountered looked sallow, weary, and a little disturbed and had mostly belligerent things to say. The denizens appeared to be constantly on the move. In our first months there, we must have seen five families move in or out on just our street. From the start, we hated it there and felt guarded and alone.

We tended to stay indoors. But inside we felt restless too, for the house was too small for us two finicky, idiosyncratic men to get the space we needed. We fought a lot, fought over whose turn it was to do the dishes or to give the dog a bath or to go to the basement. Its dirty concrete floor and walls were enough to depress anyone. And one unfinished wall allowed us to peek into the house's foundations, clotted by dirt and seasoned with mold. We grimly joked that that was where we would store the bodies. We only went down there by necessity, rushing to the washer and dryer to do what was necessary and then right back upstairs. For me, the static down here raged even louder than in the bedroom.

K. had a special fear regarding the basement's secondary exit. The house, so very old, had a battered, haphazardly sealed cellar door sticking out of the ground in the backyard. In one corner of the basement loomed a shadowy stairwell that led up to it. The landlord averred that the door was sealed, but light shone through it plainly, and when it rained the evidence filled a bucket in the stairwell. K. worried about what manner of thing might intrude on us through the cellar door—robbers and worse. He had fears, too, but they were lodged within the real. I shared them, but I was too distracted by my teeth and the noises to give them my full regard.

I began to have frequent dreams that I was wandering in the house I now lived in, except that the rooms stank very badly—the pungent odor of rotting food—and were far too large. The doors (or, rather, door, for I never broached the threshold of the living room) appeared always just out of reach. To leave the bedroom was my most desperate mission, because behind me the chattering voices continued to holler and shriek and squeal and moan and because I knew that I could not bear to see who it was that made such noises, for so long, and in what dreadful company. They were coming behind me; they were coming for me. The first time, I screamed myself awake, waking K. in the bargain. He was understandably irritated with me. I named what had happened—"Bad dream"—but forsook any attempt at description. He drifted to sleep, while I lay in bed and mulled it over.

The dreams continued, as did the noises and the toothaches, and so I entered my doctoral program in a haze of unpleasantness and dread. I suppose that I began as I meant to go on. It was a weird place, the English department, just as weird and unwelcoming as anything in that town. The atmosphere of unpleasantness infected nearly everyone I encountered, which in this case had to do with an administration led by a very short and dimwitted man who seemed to have a special enmity for literature or, perhaps, for rigorous intellection of all kinds. There were few of us students, and resources were as threadbare as possible. The university had—as I learned on my first day—increased the teaching load required for graduate students to receive their stipends because it refused to hire additional faculty. I was fortunate in that I had received a first-year fellowship; my peers resented me for it, though the use I had found for my extra time took the form of unsavory punishment: an additional seminar, a course on the Middle English language that satisfied a breadth requirement. I learned swiftly how unhappy I would be. Meanwhile, K. had begun his own program in an even smaller and more beleaguered department (philosophy) but proved to be quite content there.

I visited a dentist in my third week there, who referred me to the Oral and Maxillofacial Surgery Center, which turned out to be about two blocks away from where we lived. All that time, the voices trailed me in the house, though they continued to be the loudest in the bedroom and basement. I began to sleep on the couch, which hurt K., who said he slept poorly on his own. I explained that my teeth hurt so badly I couldn't sleep. Anyway, it was true that I, the early riser, sometimes struggled to leave our bed where it lay shoved into the corner; all our furniture ended up in weird places because of the tiny rooms with their outsized vents.

Even in the living room, the voices shrieked at me, albeit more softly. The dreams of the house, its rooms extended so impossibly far, continued. Sometimes I thought I caught a glimpse of something behind me—a spiraling path in my peripheral vision—but the glimpses always faded upon waking up. Even so, in one of the dreams my oneiric eye caught the large vent in the bedroom. I understood that it led to the basement, that the voices trailed down and from there. It had a striking and utterly satisfying logic that did not abate when I awoke. And, when awake, I felt a low-level thrum of dread, and eventually K. did, too, which contributed to our frequent fighting. Even the dog seemed more excitable than she used to be. It was easy to reason that it was just our being in graduate school or living in a dump like this, and, yes, that was true, yet there remained something else that haunted us. K. also knew this, I think, even if the dreams and the noises seemed to latch onto me. He pointed out how frequently our neighbors moved and the generally ominous vibe of our street and the entire town. He began to mention the cellar door more frequently, and he focused his efforts on securing it from the inside. I knew this would do nothing besides providing a locus for his fears.

My surgery was scheduled for the beginning of October, when the leaves began to fall. My Middle English professor was deeply uninterested when I explained my looming absence. He peered at me through narrow glasses, rubbed his balding head, and said, "I see. Remember that I can't change the due date for anybody's weekly translations." Then he dismissed me. I remember the staff at the OMS Center as kind—they took note of my birthday, after all—and it surely helped that I went by myself. K. joined me only later, when he could; it was anyway ideal to present myself alone, lest the homophobia that most townies could not repress take over, compelling them to impertinence. They would have said, like our landlord: Is that your brother? They would have said: Your . . . *friend* . . . is waiting in the lobby. They would have acted like the woman at the BMV who seemed disgusted at the sight of two men who shared an address and sought, together, to obtain new driver's licenses—as we were in turn appalled by her behavior and her tacky, dated hair, which I barely restrained myself from pointing out. No, we did not wish for a repeat.

The four-day weekend felt like an inappropriate luxury, a foolish indulgence. Why did guilt overcome me, guilt for missing one day of the Middle English class I did not want to take—much of which was spent waiting for the professor to log into the computer? Nonetheless, it did, though, in the operating room, the drugs took over soon enough. Later, my limbs flopped as K. guided me from the office to the car and then up the treacherous stairs to our shitty house's backdoor. K. explained that I'd had a serious thought about the translation of a certain noun now lost to me, haphazardly explained through lingering nitrous oxide while doubled over on the stairs. I have an uncertain memory of glimpsing the family who lived across the alley, paused while loading their things in a van to gawk at us.

When we got home, I insisted on watching *Meet Me in Shaint Louish*, since I was then in the middle of a Judy Garland phase. I do remember lying in bed in a druggy, nostalgic haze watching Judy sing "The Trolley Song." I fell asleep while the dog wheedled her way into the bathroom and plucked blood-sodden cotton balls from the trashcan. The evening offered utter contentment while K. lingered in the kitchen and the dog sniffed out my blood's metallic tang. For a little while, the voices and the dreams left me alone.

I was back at it soon enough, diligently attempting my translations. I don't even remember what they were, but I do remember that, when I ultimately dumped my notes in the recycling bin in the alley outside, an old man rolled up and plucked the papers out, carefully inspecting each one. He didn't stop when he noticed me watching him. But he was a great inspector of trash. Even before my surgery, I had spied him digging through others' waste. Once, I watched through my window as a fight played out in the alley, where a woman had drug a whole heap of things and left them for the garbage truck to collect. A man burst outside of a back door, wielding a baseball bat and screaming at the old man who had begun to sift through it all. Neither the incident's cause nor its resolution ever became clear. But everybody on our street was constantly fighting or leaving. All of us must have clawed at ourselves and those closest to us in the same way, beset with the same dread and, perhaps, the same horrible noises. I imagined what it would be like for a man with a bat to bang at our cellar door and easily knock it down. What if he barreled into the basement? Just what might he find?

K. left the weekend after my surgery for a conference. Left alone to nurse my still softly aching jaw, I frittered my time away. I sat around and perused a message board whose members dissected the dumbest gossip I'd ever read in my life. The dog and I watched a TV show about straight people's problems and failed to relate. We walked outside and enjoyed—at least I did—the leaves and the way her little feet just barely made them crackle. On Saturday night, eating a bland pasta dish—the most I could bring myself to pull together—I dwelled on the voices. I could clear away my idiotic anxiety that my teeth somehow caused me to imagine the noises. And, without K., there was less to distract me. Perhaps his absence made me feel at ease, able to investigate—or to sit and stare at the wall and think about it—without raising his suspicions.

The voices howled all the time that I was in the house. The basement loomed in my mind, a palpable presence, but I did not consider going down there. I tried to distract myself by going back to the TV show I had been watching. Though it was unbearably dull, I allowed another twenty-two minutes to dwindle away. Then I rose and walked into the bedroom where, through the window, I had a direct view of the cellar door. In the encroaching twilight, nothing drew my attention. Tall, unmown grass and weeds spread across the backyard; the door was just barely visible in their midst. But then the door rose. It was barely perceptible, as though someone thudded it, weakly, from below. From the window, I watched as it happened again and again. The door moved in a syncopated rhythm.

I turned around and returned to the living room. I paced, observed with curiosity by the dog. The impulse to make a phone call—to K., or the landlord, or the police—overcame me. But I swiftly rejected it, as a result not of rational thought but of an unbiddable internal mechanism, some cog of the will I scarcely knew was there. I fetched the dog, picking her up and moving to the bedroom to place her in her crate, which I locked. Despite her indignant whine of protest, I left her there.

It must have been a desire, above all, not for confrontation or even resolution but witness. I realized that I did not feel as scared as I might have imagined. The dreams had misled me, plaguing me with a somnolent terror that, it turns out, I did not fully feel. Intuition, I suppose, confirmed that whatever resided in the basement was connected to the howling. Therefore, I was struck by a lucid realization: It fell to me to discern what resided below us. I wished to enter the basement and see what might be there.

A peculiar calm pervaded me, the calm of having made a sound decision. My feet moved with surety across the linoleum tile of the kitchen and the steps that led to the basement. From there, I watched as the cellar door continued its slight upward motion, apparently lifted by an unknown wind. Nothing tangible lurked in the dark, stumbling out to greet or to attack me. The sounds were louder than they had ever been and, in fact, crystal clear. I drew closer to the stairwell, where a succession of images made itself known. I put it that way because, just as the noises—the voices—roared like static in my ears, the images danced in my mind; they were thoughts I was not thinking. It was difficult then—and it's harder now—to confront them, to make sense of them. So consider the jumble, all of which poured into my mind at once: a spiral made of some dirty, moldering material, leading down and down; a vast and artificial canyon that, it was obvious to me, stretched beneath the entirety of the town but whose center lay right here, beneath our street; the many labyrinthine passages that honeycombed the canyon, every last one of which led ineluctably toward the spiral at the center; flesh slapping against flesh, bodies in motion, curled up, viciously torqued, and rolling down the spiral like marbles. The senseless voices were raised in agony and confusion and terror, clashing with the incandescent, hungry rage that pulsed from the depths like a hideous music. There was a thing I could not see, or if seen could not fathom, whose presence I could intuit all too keenly. It waited there, alone. All of this rushed into my head and then out, leaving me stunned. Whatever separated us from that region of cruelty grew thin in this little zone. Having registered this, I returned upstairs, where my dog was growing frantic.

Had the static then politely receded, it would have made for a tidy resolution. But it did not. Rather, I could begin to acknowledge it with a clear head, with the appropriate regard demanded by fearsome and uncontrollable things—floods and earthquakes, say, or a meteor aimed headlong at earth our home—but also with a certain humility. Whatever I glimpsed and however real it was, it could never be truly apprehended. There was no waiting for an imminent solution, for a better insurance plan or superior force of will that would permit me to confront the problem. Was it calming to recognize this? Not at all. But whatever knitted the house where we lived and the surrounding town to the images that invaded my mind had a peculiarly satisfying logic. The voices did not abate, and I did nothing to prevent them. Some things must be accommodated and borne, like varieties of pain or mortal limitations or this wretched town. It was enough, then, for me to serve as witness. But we did move across town as soon as we could afford it, joining the droves of others who had already fled our street.

We don't live there anymore, nor would we ever wish to go back, and even the few people we remember fondly have by now moved away. Come to think of it, we didn't make many friends there or put down any roots. When we got the chance to move to a city in a different state, very far from there, we felt thrilled. Even so, for over a decade now the Oral and Maxillofacial Surgery Center has dutifully sent me the same postcard on my birthday: that little cake never fails to find me, armed with its saccharine greeting. And while I have come to look forward, in a way, to the postcard's arrival, when I pull it out of the mailbox and inspect that rictus grin, that familiar sound seems to grow louder in my ears and I feel, too, a slight sense of loss.

⊠

Dearest Mother

~ Ellis Bray

Dearest mother,
I hope this letter finds you

wall, concrete

in your decision to
send
      me
            to
                  hell.

There is no safety here. No ambassadors. No H U M A N S.

It's the eyes.

THE EYES.

They glamper red and the

shadows.

There's too many shadows for how many venices there are.

Shadows
e   v
          e r y
                    w he r   e

reaching with arms like tines to consumpt me whole.

WHOLLY MOTHER.

If you must destroy me, at least feed JimJam.

Dearest Moth er

Tell me JimmyJames is all right.

You LEFT
me with monsters

  chattering and
               chantering
                    and cantering
                        and bantering
                           and calling upon satan and
satin and silk
  preying, mother

PRAYING
with their eyes
they follow me
with their eyes
up the staircases, down the hells, to the toilet

everywhere everywhere EVERYWHERE EVERYWHERE

A L W A Y S the eyes have it and so too the shadows
and I face it

                  alone
for my dearest fiend is a cat;
is immune.

Is away.

Dearest mother, I fear I am going mad. I dreamt of JamboJones last night and he walked me through hell and kept me safe and for the first time in weeks

WEEKS, MOTHER

I urinated in peace.

I am not mad
I am not mad
I A M NO   T M A   D
ANGRY, YES.
At

YOU

for your malfeasance, magnificent munificence, your malignancy, your malnutrition, your monstrosity, the monsters, mother, you are a monster, there are monsters here, but I am not mad, no, mother, I am not mad, for they are here, they are cantering and chantering and chattering and the halls are hallowed with their howling and I can hear them all through the night, their sibilant susurrus of sins praying to the Old One, the Great One, and his Might Throne descends upon us. Ia ia ia ia ia ia

I am angry but dare not show it for Jammy Dodger relies on your good heart for food and comfort.

Where do you hide

your   heart
mother?

Dearest mother, the blight of knowledge blinds upon me and the madness withdraws. Visit soon. Bring JimJam. Ever yours.

⊐

Armageddon, Now Available in Two Exciting New Colorways

~ Jessie Kwak

"I am perfect and whole," Barzabas murmured into the bathroom mirror. He straightened the knot on his tie, staring deeply—intently—into his reflection's eyes. Bright amber flecks danced in his irises, tiny pieces of eternal hellfire.

"I am enough," Barzabas said, voice stronger. "I have all the tools I need to achieve my goals. Every rejection brings me closer to my next sale. Every day, in every way, my revenues keep growing and growing."

Barzabas took a deep breath, feeling the warm glow of the affirmations deep in his bones. He smiled. He snuffed out the black candle with his fingertips—he'd read lighting a candle was a nice way to seal affirmations—then plucked the hot pink Post-it off the mirror and tucked it carefully into his toiletry bag among floss toothpicks and Trident gum.

This was the day. He could feel it. All his hard work was about to pay off.

The secret was in the morning routine. Whether he was staying in a zero-star motel or a four-star (he assumed; the Company had never put him up in a four-star, not like Damarius), Barzabas followed the same program.

He woke up early. Worked out. Meditated to a special playlist of tortured souls screaming in disharmony. Read for seven minutes exactly and journaled—all before he showered, shaved, and brushed his teeth.

The lit black candle and affirmations were the cherry on top of a guaranteed success sundae.

Barzabas lifted his chin to the mirror and buttoned his sport coat, rubbed at a spot on his shoes with a wad of toilet paper, swiped another finger full of product over his unruly cowlick, then grabbed his suitcase and his book of carpet samples and rolled on out into glory.

One of the wheels of his suitcase caught every third step, but Barzabas ignored it, because he was on the ladder to greatness. Today's sales call was going to be the one that made his career. For three months he'd been building a relationship with this local hotel chain, positioning the Company as the preferred carpet vendor for the upcoming remodel.

Today they were going to ink a deal.

The book of carpet samples under Barzabas's arm pulsed more than usual, a stringed instrument resonating in the presence of the perfect note. Barzabas had stayed at one of the Company's flagship hotel clients last night, and one of their most potent patterns blighted the hallways and lobby. The carpet swirled with chartreuse and gold and magenta, a design which might, from one angle, resemble birds of paradise. From another angle it might resemble the first and sixth letters of the Unholy Name of Our Lord and Destroyer.

Viewpoint was everything.

Evil was woven into every fiber of this carpet, charging with unholy energy at every step. This hotel was one of Damarius's big-time clients, which is why Barzabas picked it even though it was out of budget and he probably wouldn't get reimbursed. He wanted to feel the energy. Start the day on a high, because this was the first day of the rest of his life.

This was the day he finally contributed his share to the Unhallowed Name being woven across the surface of the Earth in carpet glyphs.

Barzabas wedged himself behind the wheel of his Prius, cursed the engine to life and eased into the traffic jam heading onto the highway. He fumbled for his headset when his phone rang, ulcer sizzling at the caller ID.

The Boss.

"You ready for your big meeting, Barzy?" Barzabas's boss sounded like he was chewing a breakfast burrito.

"I've got my pitch prepared, sir."

"Good, good. Anything you wanna run through?"

"I'm all right."

"You said that the last five times and look what happened." His boss belched. "But you know what, it's your own fucking funeral if you fuck this one up, too."

"I've got it." Barzabas was so distracted he almost waved a Subaru in front of him. He caught himself in time—an employee of the Company was never polite in traffic—and gunned his engine to cut the Subaru off, flipping off the drive and feeling the obscene glyph formed by the I-5 onramp charge just a little bit more at their rage.

"Budget's a little tight next quarter," the Boss was saying. "If you don't win today, I don't know if we're gonna be able to find room for you on the payroll."

"You can count on me," Barzabas said, and cut the call.

He glared into the standstill traffic, lips curling into a smile. "I have all the tools I need to achieve my goals. Every rejection brings me closer to my next sale. I am enough. I am perfect and whole."

Laura Keegan met him in the lobby of her family's flagship property, Juniper Springs. Impeccable ice blue suit, perfect manicure, no blond hair out of place. Barzabas surreptitiously smoothed a hand over his suit jacket, rumpled from the drive out, then flashed his most trustworthy grin.

"Ms. Keegan?" He held out a hand. "I'm Barzy."

"Call me Laura." Her teeth were brilliantly white. "Barzy, is that Eastern European, or . . . ?"

"It's unique, huh?" Barzabas grinned back—was he grinning too much? No such thing—and checked "A strong introduction" off his list. Moving on to "Build rapport with the buyer."

"This place is incredible! Wow, is this wood really all salvaged from the local railroad? Let me tell you, I see some amazing hotels in this line of work, but this one takes the cake. You have a real gem here."

Juniper Springs was indeed impressive, especially by Barzabas's standards. Most of his accounts were mom-and-pop drive-in motels. Saggy beds and leaky faucets and a steady trail of trucker grime ground into the carpet tread. On the one hand, there was an excellent chance of blood getting on the glyphs. On the other, those small-fry accounts couldn't invest in the truly powerful, violently stomach-churning designs a big hotel chain would.

The Keegans, though? They owned a few dozen funky, artistically reclaimed hotels and restaurants throughout the state. They were small enough that nobody like Damarius the Sales Champ wanted to waste their time, but interesting enough that Barzabas had a real chance selling a career-making colorway.

Yeah, yeah—and advancing the Unholy Name of Our Just Defiler and all that.

I have all the tools I need to achieve my goals.

"Why don't you give me the tour," Barzabas said, "and then we can take a look at the book."

"Absolutely." Laura led Barzabas to antique wooden stairs that curved over the front desk. "Like all of our properties, Juniper Springs is a historic site—it used to be a train depot." She paused on the mezzanine; the lobby below was bustling with the morning's check-outs. "The history of our properties has always been a big draw, but our demographic is changing."

"Millennials!" Barzabas grinned. It was always Millennials.

"They obviously love the historical kitsch, but they need hip, modern amenities."

"That's a tricky cookie," Barzabas agreed. "But a nice carpet really helps add a fresh modern feel."

"Exactly."

Maybe guys like Damarius were just looking for a sale, but Barzabas genuinely enjoyed his job because of conversations like this. Every day, he got to help small, family-owned businesses solve real problems—while also advancing Our Shadowy Savior's plan on Earth. A win-win.

"I have some ideas," Barzabas said. "We've got a few standout patterns that would make this lobby shine. Really elevate the experience."

Laura's smile was bright. "Excellent."

The rest of the tour went without a hitch while Barzabas made mental notes about which designs to show Laura for the common areas. Definitely SKU A717. It was a spin on the Company's classic bestseller, "The Serpent's Venom Consumes and Devours," but in a new colorway incorporating this year's Pantone Color of the Year. Acid orange and flame red shot through with cheerful periwinkles and lavender—A717 was going to be a hot seller.

"We won't need carpet up *here*," Laura was saying as they climbed a final set of stairs, "but no tour of Juniper Springs is complete without this view."

The stairs led to a charming rooftop terrace where the restaurant staff were currently resetting the breakfast buffet to lunch service. Barzabas followed Laura to the balcony, enjoying the warm spring sun.

"Wow!" He didn't need to act impressed, the view was amazing. Laura looked delighted. Building rapport? He was killing it.

"We have ninety-three acres of forest and working farmland," she said. "We grow our own hops! And from here you can see the mini golf course, our main concert venue, and the spa. But the unique thing about Juniper Springs is that it's actually our family home." Laura pointed to a small cottage at the center of the garden. "That's where my father lives. I was hoping we could look at a few designs to remodel the cottage, as well."

A bit of a weird request, but if Barzabas had learned anything in his centuries on the job, it was that hoteliers were a weird bunch. After all, they kept buying the objectively ludicrous carpeting the Company came up with—maybe they did like it enough to want it in their own homes.

"We don't normally do residential, but I can talk with my manager." Barzabas winked. "If you're buying for the entire Juniper Springs remodel, I don't see why we couldn't throw in some square footage for your dad's house."

"Great! I had a couple SKUs in mind. B445? We were thinking either the 'Rembrandt' or the 'Mardi Gras' colorway."

"Sure, we can definitely look at that." Barzabas started to turn away from the view, sensing that the time was ripe to start choosing patterns and inking deals. But something snagged a claw in his attention.

Wait. Laura shouldn't know about SKU B445.

B445 was a new SKU—so new he hadn't had a chance to send it over. Suzilith, the design team lead, had introduced it at the last product meeting along with a peculiar warning. Guys like Damarius tended to doze off in product meetings, but Barzabas had taken plenty of notes.

Suze had said that the new pattern, called—internally—"Our Lord's Wrath Shall Lay Waste Abundantly," should only ever be installed in a north-south orientation. Install it east-west, and it transformed from another glyph in the name of Our Sunless Mutilator Supreme to more of a . . . cage. A siphon. A trap.

"Install this east-west," Suze had warned the sales team, "and you could accidentally summon the Dark One into a human vessel. It would bring about an age of unspeakable horror."

Barzabas had raised his hand. "Isn't that what we're trying to do?"

"Not like this," Suze had said. "The Company's mission is to accelerate the just and judicious return of Our Twilight Overlord to bring balance on Earth. This would bend the wills of both dark and light to the command of a single, power-mad human. It would effectively destroy the universe."

Barzabas had raised his hand again. "Maybe we shouldn't be selling this SKU?"

The rest of the sales team, the design team, and the Boss had looked at him with scorn.

"It's got the Pantone color of the year in it," Damarius had said incredulously. "Kid, it's gonna sell like hotcakes."

Laura shouldn't know about B445, but that wasn't the only thing tugging at his attention. Barzabas frowned at the garden, at the cottage smack in the center. There was something about the way the garden paths intersected, and the way the colors of the tulips and daffodils and hyacinths were opening into the spring.

Oh, shit.

The layout of the gardens mimicked the new glyph perfectly. Installing carpet design B445 in the 'Rembrandt' or 'Mardi Gras' colorway would definitely complete that glyph. In an east-west orientation that would give a single mortal all-powerful control over the vast and terrible swells of darkness and light in the universe.

Oh, fuck.

Barzabas glanced at Laura, whose expression seemed perfectly, innocently excited about carpets. He could almost believe she didn't know what horror she was attempting to unleash on the human race, but he'd read all the books on negotiation tactics, and her tells said she thought she was getting the upper hand in this deal.

He took a snapshot of the garden and ginned up his best salesman grin. "I'm gonna need to loop my manager in on this one real quick," he said.

✱

"Hey, Boss." Barzabas was strolling the gardens now; Laura had politely pretended to have other business so he could take a private call. Barzabas's boss heaved a bellowing sigh on the other end of the line.

"Problems, Barzy?"

"Potentially." How to say this? "I just wanted to run something by you. You know that new SKU?"

"'We Unjoyfully Embrace the Hymn of Our Corruption?' Do they want it in 'Harvest' or the 'Tropical Sunset'? Because 'Bastille Day' is still on back order."

"No, no. SKU B445. 'Our Lord's Wrath Shall Lay Waste Abundantly?'"

"What about it?"

"I, uh." Barzabas cleared his throat. "You remember what Suzilith said about the east-west orientation, and how that would allow a human to summon Our Cimmerian CEO? I think this client is trying to do literally just that. Hold on, I'm sending you some photos."

The Boss snorted. "Barzy, you think some human hotel owner is going to capture the Dark Lord for their own nefarious purposes? We're talking—let me check my notes—a *midsized local chain. Family* owned."

"Yeah, but look at the photos! The garden looks like the glyph."

"If you're nearsighted, Barzy. Get back in there and sell them whatever the hell carpet they'll take. Don't make me do your fucking job for you." And he cut the line with a furious belch.

Barzabas stared at the phone, a trickle of sweat sliding down his spine, perspiration pricking his brow in the suddenly too-hot spring sunlight.

Or maybe it wasn't the spring sunlight that was too hot. From above, he'd been at ninety-nine percent that the unholy design was intentional; standing in the gardens, he was damn sure of it. The very pathways were charged with stickily pulsing energy.

He knew that sensation: that restless pawing, that stumpy, moldering grasping. He'd felt it in unfinished hotel remodels, when the pattern was half-laid and knew it was incomplete. The garden was *reaching.*

Beneath his arm, the book of carpet samples was pulsing sympathetically, responding to the polluted and foul glyphs half-formed in garish spring florals. The push-pull of energy—pure, wholesome evil versus this contaminated atrocity—churned his stomach.

Barzabas had to get out.

He had to get back to his Prius—forget this job, he'd take his concerns up the ladder to the VP even if it meant incurring the wrath of his boss.

"Hi Barzy!"

Barzabas's heart rabbited into his throat. He spun.

Laura Keegan stood directly behind him, a bright smile on her face and a coal shovel in her hand. She swung.

The world whirled drunkenly into darkness.

Barzabas opened his eyes to a splitting headache, the salted iron taste of blood, and what looked like the set of a low-budget horror movie. Unlike the exterior of the cottage, which had a charming-if-dated English countryside vibe, the inside was filled moodily with dripping candles and bones, the walls slathered in medievalish drawings of writhing human forms.

Laura Keegan stood beside an old man in an armchair. His ancient fingers clawed into the fabric, watery eyes swimming in the candlelight.

"What the hell?" asked Barzabas politely.

"We know you're a demon," said Laura. "There's no point in pretending."

Beside her, the presumed Keegan patriarch wheezed in his chair. "I'm here to strike a bargain with your master."

Barzabas cleared his throat. "Well, 'master' is pretty outdated language. But if you want to talk to the Boss, that's no problem. Didn't need to go through all this trouble, though. No ritual needed, we use cell phones these days."

"No," snarled the old man. "I don't want to speak to your *manager*. I wish for an audience with the Dark One."

Barzabas shook his head. "I don't think you do."

"Everything is prepared," the old man continued. "We're just missing the critical ingredient."

"Carpet can really tie a room together," Barzabas said brightly. "And my Company can help you take care of that. I obviously don't have enough to cover the whole floor on me—I drive a Prius! But let me hop on a call with our scheduling team and I bet we can get you sorted out as early as next week."

He didn't like the way Laura was smiling, and as his eyes began to adjust to the gloom, he realized why. The cottage's wooden floor was painted with a continuation of the glyphs the garden outside formed, save for a single empty spot at the foot of the old man's arm chair.

It was perfectly sized for one of Barzabas's samples.

"We were able to re-create the glyphs," Laura said. "But we need a true piece of carpet to charge it."

Barzabas relaxed slightly. Yes, that was *almost* all. He might still get out of this if they didn't know they also needed—

"As well as a drop of your accursed blood."

"We offer full-service installation," Barzabas said, desperation creeping into his voice. "And, let me tell you what, I can get you a great deal on the install. I'm not supposed to tell customers this, but I'm authorized to offer up to five percent off labor, especially if you're buying for multiple properties. But between you and me, I can definitely get you ten." He flashed his best smile at Laura and her necrotic father. "Let me talk to my manager. I think we could even go as low as fifteen."

"We have you," the mummified patriarch wheezed. "We have your sample book. We don't need your discount."

Beside him, Laura removed the unhallowed sample of SKU B445—'Mardi Gras' colorway—from Barzabas's sample kit. She began to chant, syllables twisting dark into the air. The room glitched around her, distorting in fractional ways Barzabas couldn't've put a finger on even if his hands weren't tied behind him. Hue by hue, color faded from the room as though leached out by the chanting; Barzabas's stomach churned as his life essence answered the tug and pull of the ritual, sloshing weakly around his gut like a greasy burger and fries.

The death of a salesman, Damarius had always said about fast food, because apparently Damarius had never been clubbed over the head and taken captive by an account who was hell-bent on siphoning the terrible, world-rending essence of Our Nightmarish Liege into his frail human body. This might bring about an Age of Unending Eclipse—and not in a good way.

The madness of true tainted evil chaotically contained in a human vessel would unpick the seams of the universe. It would transpose dark matter with light. The Earth would split at its very core. And that would be the best-case scenario.

Laura reverently set the sample of B445 into place, in the depraved east-west orientation, and lifted a ceremonial black dagger.

"Wait!" Barzabas yelled as Laura advanced on him. "Wait."

"No more sales pitches, demon."

"This isn't a sales pitch." He flinched back from the blade, grimacing. "You overheard my conversation in the garden, didn't you?"

Laura tilted her head, curious. "Yes."

"Then you know how much of an asshole my boss is. I've worked under him for centuries, and he still doesn't give me any respect. Believe you me, the tongue lashings this guy gives out are legendary."

"What's your point."

"Look. I've charged up our carpets a million times, and there's a trick to it. I'll tell you—but I want to make a deal. Once your dad ascends into Darkness, you'll need a minion who knows the ropes."

"You . . . want a job?"

"Best and worst part about being a salesman for the Company is there's literally no competition," Barzabas said. "I've wanted out for millennia, but where would I go? Believe me. I'm the guy you need at your side."

Laura glanced at her father, who nodded his skeletal head. "What's the secret?" she asked.

"It's the blood," Barzabas said, heart pounding against his ribcage. "First timers always underestimate the amount of blood they need. You really gotta soak the sigils to charge them."

Laura laughed. "You're serious?"

"Would I lie to you?"

"No, I mean, you seriously just told us that?" She shook her head. "You demons are such idiots. Thanks for the tip."

And she slashed the obsidian blade across his throat.

✷

The rest came in flashes:

The waterfall of blood pouring from his neck, drenching his best suit with gore, pooling at his feet, and soaking through the sample of B445.

The unholy neon blaze of grape purple and acid green and manic yellow as the carpet sample lapped blood to charge the glyph.

The first tentative gold sparks, crackling louder and brighter and finally brilliant enough to pierce even Barzabas's darkening vision as the carpet sample completely fucking overloaded in the flood of energy released by his blood.

The stupid looks on the Keegans's stupid human faces shifting from anticipation to confusion to terror as they realized shit had gone horribly wrong.

The agonizing rush of searing heat as the carpet burst into flames, engulfing Barzabas, the Keegans, and the entire accursed cottage in a ball of purifying hellfire.

Barzabas grinned as the world went black.

"Fuck me, Barzy."

Barzabas came to at his desk, migraine like a thousand dying suns crowded into his sinuses, whiplashed neck aching and stomach roiling. He vomited into his trashcan, then sat back up.

The Boss was at the corner of his desk, one hip hitched to half-sit-half-stand uncomfortably close to Barzabas's clunky office chair. Demarius stood at the Boss's side in a thousand-dollar suit, arms crossed and perfectly groomed eyebrow lifted.

"Did it work?" Barzabas asked.

"Did what work?" The Boss's tail twitched in irritation. "Did you blow a potential client to smithereens? Yeah, that worked. Do you know what a mess our PR team is going to have on their hands covering up that catastrophe?" The Boss scooted off Barzabas's desk with a disappointed glower. "I want a report by EOD, and it better be damned good or I'm busting you back down to the call center for the next century until I think you can handle being an account rep again."

The Boss slithered off, leaving a trail of sizzling acid behind him.

"You really outdid yourself, kid," Demarius said when the Boss was gone, and Barzabas straightened with pride. "I mean, there's losing a sale, and then there's actually destroying a client. What were you thinking?"

That stung, especially coming from Demarius the Sales Champ, but Barzabas kept his head high.

"The Keegans didn't trigger Armageddon, though? Did they?"

Demarius snorted out a laugh and sauntered away. "Seriously?" he called over his shoulder. "That's *our* fucking job, Barzy."

Barzabas sank into his desk chair, letting it slowly spin him in a circle as he prepared to compose the best damned report his Boss had ever read.

He couldn't stop grinning. Even Demarius's jabs and the Boss's threats couldn't pierce his mood, elated as it was with massive blood loss and the euphoria of success. Let the Boss bust him back to the call center, Barzabas had saved the world! And, more importantly, he believed in himself.

After all, Barzabas was perfect and (mostly still) whole. He was on the ladder to success. And each setback—so long as it didn't end in the wrong Armageddon—was just one step closer to his goals.

We Found Each Other on the Ocean Floor

~ *Tania Chen*

Perfect, like a photograph preserved through the decades plastic flimsy sheet protecting the mixed black and whites. Your grandmother's face a quiet echo reaching through time. This is your face now, the sum of all the trauma passed down generation to generation, until it rests firmly on your shoulders.

The wedding dress, silk and ivory: when you pull it out the closet the yellow stains betray its age; eighty or so years, seventy in storage. Stretched out on the California king-size bed it shivers under the weight of the ivory crucifix gaze above.

The lavender stalks protruding behind my head make an attempt at comfort, little appendages reaching out to brush salt water; the dried flower crown of your mother's First Communion in your hands. The cadence of her voice weathered by the years. You want to forget it.

Are you ready, your family asks, as if leaving the place of one's birth is an easy task.

Perfect, is what they say, ignoring the reluctance in the line of your stiff shoulders. Perfect, like how the past looks through the lens of nostalgia; a true liar if there ever was one. You wear your grandmother's face but you're nothing if not your own person. And me? I am the lover they denied you.

We walk into the bathroom. I feel your fingers reach to brush the thin filaments lining the stalk that stands as my body, the question asked by that simple touch. *Let's run away, elsewhere to be reborn.* Together our feet rest on the bathtub's wet porcelain and my smile is an open electric blue void as we make our escape.

We are perfect, like only frozen time can make everything.

*

Our steps on the bright green moss at the forest of the ocean's floor are loud. The moss scatters, swaying side to side and staring at you with disgruntled looks. We've woken them up, or rather you have, my own feet are used to this landscape: I float gently between, my webbed toes kicking.

The apple is sour, crunched between my teeth as we walk in the forest. Red with aquamarine tinge, not a poisoned apple like those from the fairy tales you grew up with: everything here is gentle. Quiet. Safe.

A couple of Amazon milk frogs fly past, taking residence on the nearest tree; the bark is all coral, porous and offering residence to tiny golden fish that peek through the crevices like spectators at a wedding.

Vestigial teeth wrapped around the skin of your arm cautioning before you step forward. The ocean's forest is deep, the canopy of anemone filtering out the sun; you walk further, past carved stones. The silence leaves, replaced by the choir of rainbow mantis shrimps: their thoracic appendages beating sand like a drum.

Your forehead against mine.

Unlike you, I am the sum of all my trauma, of each little love I brought here. And now what is yours is mine.

The wasabi green of my tongue and luminous pink of my skin, ribs pressed like trench lines, stretching the skin white stand out. Your trauma takes the shape of my spine, dorsal fin extending from shoulder to tail.

I say goodbye when it has finished growing, and your sorrow is part of me; for the silence between us is now its own song. You weep and so do I, our footsteps echoes beheld by silence.

I don't need to show you the way back; your feet find their footing among the open rocks; past the currents of salty waters, into lead pipes squeezed underground.

This time I will not follow you home—your new home—I am content to release you into a new life, away from the family that denied who you were, away from the trauma, away from me. Separation such a dull, familiar ache that it's become part of me, like a mango-coloured encasing around my heart.

Perfectly imperfect as love should be. It tastes just as sweet as the memory of your footsteps on the ocean forest.

The Fortunate Ones

~ Margo Pecha

When Simon and I finally married, it came as no surprise to anyone. His family was all too aware of the antiques dealer who lived and worked next door to his bakery and with whom he had been entirely besotted for the past ten years. The marriage made sense from both practical and business standpoints, and Simon had proved himself a steadfast companion in many of my misadventures in acquiring haunted or cursed objects; I couldn't deny his devotion any longer, and we were married in the spring.

And with the sealing of our nuptials came an endless stream of his relatives and their young children, the former poking about Esoteric Ephemera & Antiquities with ogling eyes and mouths agape, and the latter dashing and chasing each other around the displays of Dorflinger cut glass and hiding behind a cabinet of radium clocks.

I stood in the corner watching the chaos unfold, wide eyed and clenching my jaw, my whole body tense and primed for the impending tinkle of shattered glass. A permanent crick lodged itself in my neck from all the nervous energy coiled within my body.

So it was no great shock when Simon's mother decided she'd like to stay with us for a few weeks, and with her she toted a German porcelain bisque doll. I think I gasped when I saw it in her arms, which she mistook for excitement.

"For you," she beamed, presenting me with its stiff body. "I know you like these sorts of things."

I didn't, really, but I did like selling them.

"Thank you," I smiled, taking the doll. Her molded porcelain teeth grinned impishly at me through pink parted lips.

I knew there'd be an Armand Marseille stamp on the back of the head. My fingers twitched, itching to yank back the wig to validate my hunch. But I refrained and continued to smile politely instead.

"Is she a family heirloom?" I asked.

"Oh, no, of course not." Simon's mother waved her hand dismissively. "The women in our family have never been fond of dolls. I got it at an auction. Simon always mentioned how interested in antiques you are, and I thought this was just the thing for you."

"Thank you," I beamed.

The doll was dressed in a period ivory dress speckled with rosebuds and festooned with pink silk ribbons. The hems were trimmed with an abundance of delicate Chantilly lace, gathered and pleated, and accented with seed pearl beading. Her strawberry-blonde curls bounced with a life of their own. She'd been well taken care of, which was remarkable for a doll from the 1800s. She even had both her little shoes, which was no small miracle.

"You can't sell it," Simon hissed to me when his mother had turned her back to pet the cats, who were sleeping on an empty shelf of a bookcase. "It's a *wedding gift*. It's *sentimental*."

"I wasn't planning anything of the sort," I said, fingering the skirt of the doll's dress to inspect the condition of the cloth. "Besides, she got it at an auction. It's not like it's been passed down through the family or anything."

"You're appraising it right now!"

"I'm doing nothing of the sort," I responded, tilting the doll back to make sure the articulated eyes still worked, and they did, blinking once, twice, three times. Very good.

"I know that gleam in your eye," he whispered. "It's worth something, isn't it?"

"Perhaps. A couple thousand, maybe." I shrugged, feigning nonchalance. "It will look nice in our bedroom, don't you think? Sitting atop the vanity?"

Simon blanched. "Listen, I don't like it any more than you do, but you can't sell it."

"Fine," I said, smiling sweetly. I was already compiling a mental list of all the places around the house I could situate her to scare him.

And so we settled into married life, the doll providing months of entertainment—more so for me than for Simon, who I often heard yelp in surprise from another room upon discovering the doll in yet another compromising situation. One day he'd happen upon her nestled inside his biggest mixing bowl, clutching a paring knife, and the next he'd discover her in the basement leaning against a rusted two-man crosscut saw, grinning roguishly and gesturing an outstretched arm toward him. Tight lipped and with a flush spreading across his face, Simon would return her to the Chippendale wingback in the living room, shooting daggers in my direction.

We began to refer to her as Charlotte, and after a while our two cats, Karswell and Magnus, even grew fond of her, to the point where we'd often find their sleek feline bodies curled in her lap, sound asleep. A dusting of black fur now clung to her skirts, which I meticulously brushed off every morning in case Simon ever relented and let me sell her.

One afternoon I walked into our apartment and Karswell and Magnus were sitting in front of the chair, watching the doll. They were completely still aside from the occasional tip-of-the-tail twitch, seemingly entranced with Charlotte. A shiver worked its way up my spine, and I moved closer, cocking an ear toward the doll.

A hollow knocking seemed to come from her torso, like someone slowly tapping on a great metal door. But that couldn't be; the body was made of leather and stuffed solid with cork, there couldn't possibly be something *in* there. After a few moments of contemplation, I decided I was probably hearing the radiator clunking in the next room, or some liminal household noise I hadn't noticed before. I put it out of my mind and promptly forgot about it; a box of 19th century jewelry had just arrived at the shop containing a curious amulet, and I happily delved into inspecting and pricing each piece.

Spring conceded to summer, and summer gave way to fall. The antiques shop and the bakery kept us both busy, and Charlotte's novelty faded. Her station—now that Simon's discomfort had eased considerably—had somehow shifted from the wingback to our bed. I think Simon initially put her there in his own attempt to startle me, but it didn't, and I left her there. Eventually she just became another object to move before getting into bed at night, like a decorative pillow, and was then propped against them again in the morning after making the bed.

In October I began waking in the night to strange sounds. That metallic rapping again, tentative, halting, before becoming more persistent and percussive. I would lie in bed, Simon a slumbering boulder beside me, as the ringing pulled me from sleep to wakefulness. It was so reverberant that I couldn't determine where exactly it was coming from; it seemed to encompass the entire bedroom, and after a few nights when Simon hadn't woken from it, I tried, unsuccessfully, to convince myself it was nothing but an annoying and persistent bout of tinnitus.

Resonant, like a singing bowl, the sound haunted my dreams and occupied my waking thoughts. Most nights I would return to our apartment above the shop and have the uncanny feeling that I'd just missed something, a sound or a presence whose vibrations lingered in the air despite no audible proof. Simon would come up shortly after, and I'd search for signs, anything subtle in his facial features, that he'd felt or sensed something too, but I never noticed anything beyond the usual end-of-day weariness and a dusting of flour across his brow.

The cats became more agitated during this time. Restless and needy, their dark forms paced from room to room, pawed at my legs, endlessly yowled into the night. Not even a can of sardines could calm them. Simon speculated that it was reactionary—possibly the boys had seen a strange cat lurking about in the street—but I couldn't shake the suspicion that their sharp feline instincts were picking up a stronger frequency, something I wasn't privy to.

My customers began commenting on how tired I looked. Simon insisted I needed a vacation. I insisted I just needed more coffee and better sleep, perhaps a fresh doughnut from the bakery. But none of these things were true, of course, and no matter how many jelly-filled doughnuts Simon brought me, I remained just as tired and paranoid. I often crept up into the apartment during the lulls in my workday, hoping to catch . . . something. I didn't know what, only that I felt like the one friend who never understands the punchline to an obvious joke.

The end of the month marked another turn around the sun for Simon. We celebrated at a swanky new Italian restaurant on the other side of town, returning home around midnight after gorging ourselves on pasta and lingering at the bar for far too long. Leaving the house and shop had lifted my spirits, and I felt buoyant and giggly after a few too many glasses of wine. All thoughts of the mysterious nighttime sound, of being the butt of an unsaid joke, had left my mind.

But when we approached our apartment, entering through the back door in the storefront below, I was dismayed to once again hear the cyclical resonance bleeding through the walls.

Simon fumbled with his keys but suddenly stopped, cocking his head to the side.

"Do you hear that?" he asked.

"You hear it too?" I laughed, delighted, and sagged against the wall. "I thought I was losing my mind. I've been hearing it every night for weeks now."

"I've been sleeping through this?" he asked, incredulous. "Why didn't you say anything?"

I scratched my head, embarrassed. "I figured if it didn't wake you, I must be imagining it. Or only I could hear it."

"I'm a heavy sleeper, Tabitha. You know that."

He opened the door that led up to our apartment, and the boys were waiting on the other side at the bottom of the stairs. Karswell howled once at us, eyes wide in terror, then scrambled past us and into the darkness of the storefront to hide among the merchandise. Magnus clawed painfully up my leg and into my arms, tucking his wide head beneath my elbow. His tail curled around my wrist, and he trembled uncontrollably.

"Well, we'd better see if we can figure out what it is."

We ascended the stairs and moved cautiously through the apartment, Magus still tucked tightly into the crook of my arm. It became apparent almost immediately that the noise was loudest the closer we moved to our bedroom. Simon placed his hands over his ears and we entered, flipping on the light.

Charlotte sat on our bed where I'd placed her that morning, but her eyelids were flicking and her eyes rolling from the vibrational energy that seemed to be oscillating from within her. Her stiff body radiated noise energy, her body juddering. Then she flopped over, convulsing erratically facedown on the bed as if caught in an earthquake as the ringing escalated.

"It's possessed!" Simon cried, backing away. "I knew it!"

"Don't be silly, Simon. In all my years in the antiques business, I've never once come across a possessed or haunted doll. Frankly, I don't think they even exist."

I moved closer, curiously watching Charlotte as she continued to spasm. The commotion came from within—deafening and reverberant, filling the apartment with its haunting discord—and her arms flailed and bounced in tandem with the vibrational energy. And just as suddenly it was silent; all movement had ceased. The fine hairs on the back of my neck and arms lifted.

"What in the world?" I murmured.

And then the knocking began again, slow to start but sustained, building, and became so loud that Magnus bolted from the room, belly low to the ground.

"There must be something inside," I said, raising my voice above the noise. "Some sort of windup toy, maybe?"

"I have no idea," Simon said, hands clamped over his ears. "You're the expert. Just make it stop!"

And at his words, the noise did, indeed, stop.

We looked at each other, mystified. My ears were ringing, abuzz with the absence of noise. Magnus wailed from the other room, long and low and melancholic.

"Let's see what's inside Charlotte," I said, reaching for the doll.

We situated ourselves at the workbench in my office behind the storefront. I fiddled with the magnifying lamp on the countertop, adjusting it so its light shone brightly on the surface, and laid Charlotte beneath it. I lifted her skirt to expose the body, feeling rather obscene.

"Sorry," I muttered. "Now let's see what you're hiding."

The torso was fairly standard, soft kid leather worn shiny in areas from repeated handling. The leg joints were in good condition and moved freely when I bent them, the stitching tight and intact. No loose threads or ripped seams. I adjusted the lens of the lamp again, searching for any imperfections or the black bloom of mold across the body.

"Nothing unusual here," I said. "Probably worth more than I originally thought. The leather isn't even very dirty."

"You never appraised it?" he asked, incredulous.

I shrugged and reached up, tuning the radio on the shelf to the regional top-hits station. Cyndi Lauper's "Girls Just Want to Have Fun" flowed from the speakers, and I turned it up to drown out the slow knocking, which had picked up again. "You said I couldn't sell it, so I never finished looking it over."

I flipped Charlotte over so she was facedown. An incision ran along the length of her back, stitched closed with coarse black thread. The leather had puckered where the thread had been pulled too tight.

"Ah, here we go," I said, running a finger along the seam. "I suspected as much."

"What do you think's in there?" Simon hovered over my shoulder. "Gold coins?"

"Wouldn't we be fortunate?" I said drily, and I reached for my scissors. "I hope you weren't serious. How would coins make all this noise?" The knocking was building again, waves of vibrations cresting and echoing off the close walls of the workroom.

I felt his shoulder lift against mine as he shrugged.

I snipped the thread and tugged at it with my fingertips. Cold air puffed from the incision, fogging the magnifying glass. Something slender and black prodded between the loosened stitching. I paused, jerked my hand away, and it withdrew as well. The doll shivered.

"Woah," I said.

Simon placed a hand on my shoulder. "Maybe we shouldn't."

"Aren't you curious?" I asked. My pulse beat heavily, fear and excitement buzzing through my veins.

"Not anymore," he said.

Unbothered by his hesitation, I unlaced the stiff binding, pulling the thick cord with trembling hands beneath the bright illumination of the magnifying lamp. Then I swiveled the lamp out of the way and waited, holding my breath.

The doll quivered. A slender black appendage extended itself from Charlotte's cavity, impossibly long and lean. Bristly and sinewy, the leg heaved itself onto the workbench and braced itself against the surface as another leg wrested itself from the doll's back. Then another, and another, its feet skittering for purchase, knocking pens and pencils to the floor as the thing struggled and writhed before finally squeezing its bloated, hairy abdomen through the opening in Charlotte's back.

"Jesus Christ," I gasped, backing away.

"Tabitha," Simon moaned, "what have you done?"

Nearly as large as a basketball, it crawled across the tabletop in tentative, jerky movements. Its multitude of eyes glinted, as large as shooter marbles and just as slick. Its mandibles trembled and twitched, beaky and reminiscent of craggy crab claws.

It lurched toward the wall and began lumbering up. Its feet thudded against the brick, bits of mortar flaking off and crumbling to the ground as it progressed upward.

"Oh no," I said, and wrung my hands.

A movement on the desk pulled my attention away from its progression up the wall. Another leg was extracting itself from Charlotte, heaving itself up and out of an impossible confinement, testing and probing the surface of the desk. By the time its swollen abdomen was nearly out of the doll, another set of stubbled legs was waving in the air, scrambling, stretching and reaching for liberation. The noise was now deafening, hundreds of hands knocking on a door begging to be let through.

And then they poured forth, Cyndi Lauper's poppy proclamations about girls having fun bopping along beneath the shuddering rush of thousands of hairy legs scrambling and climbing, squeezing their impossibly large bodies from the back of the doll. They scaled the walls, knocking my tools and reference books asunder. Glass shattered. They clambered and scrambled over each other in a dizzying rush.

Simon and I backed away, until we were pressing into the wall behind the workbench. He clutched my shoulders painfully.

The arachnic wave swelled and surged, tumbling toward us. I lost my footing and fell to the ground, my shoulder connecting with Simon's nose, as I fought to breathe beneath the crushing weight of distended abdomens and prickly feet. Cyndi Lauper yipped and hollered. I blacked out.

We came to consciousness amid the wreckage of my devastated office. I don't know how long, precisely, that Simon and I had been out, but I was roused by his groaning and an intense throbbing building in my temples. My whole body ached.

A lump the size of an egg was swelling on Simon's forehead, and he probed at it gingerly with his fingertips, wincing, as he sat up and surveyed the room. His nose leaked a dribble of blood.

"Where . . . where did they go?" I asked.

Simon shook his head and wiped at his nose with the back of his sleeve. "Out," he said. "I saw them squeeze through the door, and that's all I know.

"The merchandise!" I cried, and I stumbled out into the storefront.

Almost everything was destroyed. Toppled cabinets slumped against bookshelves in domino rows, and books were strewn about, torn at their spines with pages cascading and crumpled. Shattered glass littered the floor like confetti after a party. The front door sagged on one hinge, ripped from the other in the spiders' clambering for freedom. Not a strand of webbing or speck of filament remained; the destruction was the only proof of their presence.

I picked my way through the wreckage to poke my head through the front door. The streetlights puddled pools of amber light on empty asphalt. Cold pinpricks of stars winked in the sky above. No cars crawled down the street; no shadows shifted along the sidewalk in midnight dog walk. If anyone had witnessed the stampede, no one remained to testify.

I returned to the office and shook my head at Simon. Tears blurred my vision, but my gaze snagged on Charlotte, still prone on the workbench with her skirt hiked up over her head. I stood trembling, clenching and unclenching my fists.

"How is everything smashed except that damn doll?" I sobbed.

Simon opened his arms to me, and I leaned into his chest, inhaling the near-permanent scent of vanilla and baked goods on his skin. I bawled at the thousands of dollars of damage, at the destruction of hundreds of unique and rare items I'd meticulously collected over the years. It was all gone with a single snip of the scissors. I wasn't sure I could financially recover from this.

"Do you think that was it?" Simon asked when my crying had calmed to intermittent hiccups.

"What?" I rubbed the tears from my eyes.

"Do you think there's anything else in her?"

I curled my lip in disgust. "Cobwebs, most likely. But by all means," I said ruefully, and gestured toward the doll, "see if there's any gold coins in there."

Simon carefully inserted his hand into the opening in the doll's back, sinking his wrist deep inside the cavity. His eyes grew wide, and his arm continued sliding down, deeper, past the workbench's surface and up to his elbow, then his shoulder, until his torso was pressed flat against the doll.

A shudder passed through him, and he straightened his body suddenly, yanking his arm out and shaking his hand as if he were trying to rid it of a clinging substance.

"Something touched me," he said gruffly.

Unable to help myself, I reached toward the doll, my fingers slipping inside before Simon put a hand on my wrist.

"Don't," he said. "I couldn't feel an end."

I withdrew my hand.

I stitched the doll up with shaking fingers. Though I pulled the binding as tight as I could, cold air still leaked from the seams.

We sat wearily at the workbench, observing the mess. My magnifying lamp had shattered, toppled to the floor under the scurrying feet of thousands. The radio was trashed, nothing more than a pile of broken Bakelite and smashed vacuum tubes. It was too quiet without Cyndi Lauper's bright vocals bopping off the walls.

"How much did you say you could sell the doll for?" Simon finally asked.

It took a long time to return the storefront to its former glory, but it didn't take long to find a buyer for the doll. Or, I should say, the buyer found me.

A man appeared in the shop a few weeks later as if drawn by some imperceptible trail. He said he thought I might be able to help him find something specific he'd been searching for. After enduring a handful of probing yet vague questions from him, I admitted to the existence of the doll and its strange properties and was persuaded to bring it forth for his scrutiny.

I retrieved Charlotte from the back room, where she'd sat on a high shelf since the incident. I could not determine whether she felt heavier or lighter than before, but something about her weight felt wrong in my arms as I carried her into the storefront and set her on the counter.

He regarded the doll before him for a moment before lifting her gently beneath her arms. He tilted her backward and then forward again so her sleepy eyes opened wide. He rapped his knuckles against her head, and that gonging sound filled the room once again with its haunting aura.

"Oh, aren't we fortunate?" he said, and his lips curled in a smile.

⊠

The Shivering Strings Shed Tears of Blood

~ Ngô Bình Anh Khoa

She walks toward the forest shrine
In streams of corpse-pale moonlight bathed,
A lonesome site few dare to tread,
Whose air makes lesser mortals flee.

In heavy layers of regal robes
With pure-white gleam unstained by dust,
She stands, a bright ethereal light
Against the mass of festered dark.

With blood divine in mortal flesh,
She greets the pit where she'd fulfill
Her clan's most secret, sacred task,
Decided by the lot she drew.

Amid the trees submerged in gloom,
Where tattered talismans are hung,
She places her blessed zither down
So that the ritual may commence.

The moon, a flawless mirror, shines
And casts its spectral web of light.
Her eyes are clear as she stands still,
Her mind a tranquil pool, unstirred.

She's now Salvation's instrument
Devoid of yearnings, wants, and thoughts
Of her twin toddlers left behind
(Whose future she's vowed to preserve).

The melody starts with one soft strum,
The sharp note piercing quietude's veil,
Whose lingering echo stirs the air,
And drooping leaves, arisen, hiss.

The following notes propel the song
Till every string, awakened, sings;
The breeze becomes a gust of chords
That sweeps across the quivering space.

The priestess's fluttering eyelids close,
But not once do her fingers slow,
Aglow with power as they dance
Across the pentatonic scale.

An alien presence starts to rouse
And rumble in the shrouded shrine,
Whose sealed door opens with a creak,
From which thick shadows, squirming, spill.

The gushing melody's now a gale
That fiercely rages on until
The shivering strings shed tears of blood;
They hum and shriek. They strain and cry

Beneath the heaven's silvery gaze
Till sunbeams grace the eastern sky;
The storming rush of music soars,
Unhindered by new grumbling growls.

Then, silence kills the final note,
And all the world begins to shake
As slithering shadows writhe and stretch,
Drawn to her light, which has grown dim.

Her final thought is of her twins
And how they'll get to grow up in

Her sisters' gentle, loving arms.
(May Fortune spare them from this fate.)

The shadowy tendrils claw at her
And drag her limp form toward the shrine–
Toward its abyssal, eager maw,
Where she joins those that came before.

The Ancient One receives his tribute–
The flesh and blood descended from
The priestess who first sealed him and
Who pledged to keep his hunger tamed.

The Ancient One accepts his tribute
And, for now sated, sleeps again,
Thus granting mankind three more decades
To thrive in peace—till next time comes.

◻

Hermit, Hound, Hand

~ Ben Curl

The first time the hand streaked past my picture window, I mistook it for a bat.

I felt no fright, no surprise.

Many large moths outside the cabin had performed the same basic feat—materializing out of the dark, swooping in spasmodic arcs, disturbing the silence with a faint flutter. I'd grown used to their erratic orbits. They no longer startled me. In fact, they brought comfort.

Deep as I was in my studies, I needed something or someone to claim as a symbol that my spiraling mind was not alone. These moths—this clumsy bat—would do.

I write in my journal most mornings. I write what my day will be.

Reflect on the night's visions. Gather firewood. Open the tome. Wait. Study. Write. Stoke the fire. Close the tome. Tea and prepare.

The day does not turn out this way. In my armchair, under the soft light filtered through the red feathered lampshade, while the nocturnal visitors flutter and grope about the single bulb on my porch, I revise the entry.

Reflect on the night's visions. Gather firewood. Take the long path through the dried-up creek, through the gauntlet of cracked boulders. Say a name. Open the tome. Wait. Study. Say another name. Write. Stoke the fire. Close the tome. Tea and prepare.

The second time it appeared, I saw it for what it was.

It floated by. The fingers pranced along a misty beam cast by the hanging bulb.

Steady, confident, perhaps material, the rising knuckles reminded me of the strutting of a show horse.

It floated by and did not return that night.

I wondered about it for some time, but because there was no mention of it in the tome, I forgot its existence over the following months.

The creek had run from a spring beside the barricaded mine entrance, until something shifted.

One morning, while I was wading through the tall grass and reflecting on a name which had been revealed to me by a footnote in the third subchapter of the third chapter of the third book of the tome, there was a loud crack from that direction. I froze.

A profound groaning of the earth. I stumbled. Something had slipped out of place, deep in the abandoned and flooded shafts. That much seemed obvious.

I didn't venture near the mine that day.

The next afternoon, I found only a trickle where the creek once had been its widest. Old coins gleamed in the dark loam.

I heard there had been many strange accidents in the mine.

Reflect on the growing absence of visions. Split the mushroom-ridged log. (How am I burning through so much firewood?) Take the long path through the dried-up creek, through the gauntlet of cracked boulders. Find a coin with the year of your birth. Say a name. Open the tome. Wait. Study. Say another name. Write. Stoke the fire. Close the tome. Tea and prepare.

I'd made a deal, you see, which had brought me to this cabin. Don't ask with whom. Part of the deal was that I must forget their name.

Time would be suspended for me. I would have as long as I needed, as long as I wanted, to read a book of indeterminate length. In its pages were written everything I was meant to know. Every novel, every treatise, every poem, every mystical aphorism, every letter, every theorem, every conjecture, every travelog, every proof and disproof of god—everything. But only what I was meant to know, nothing more.

I couldn't skip anything. As long as I read it all, I would know what to say.

I'd also know what to do and how to live.

In exchange, I must forget the deal maker's name.

Second condition: after reading everything I was meant to read, I must tell what it is I'm meant to tell.

There is, of course, a penalty if I do not fulfill my end of the bargain.

Out in the woods I found a small dog, or she found me—I can never say which is more true.

She was sniffing the path of coins. She urinated on the slab where I once had liked to sit and watch the creek flow. When she saw me, she twisted her ears, which ended in expressive wisps.

We walked toward each other, curious and cautious. When I crouched and reached out my hand, she leapt with her forepaws onto my thighs and licked my cheek.

I led her back to the cabin, neglecting the tome the rest of the day.

On her aged collar dangled an engraved tag: HARVEY.

Many years passed, but the seasons never changed. The trees remained perpetually half-leaved. The creek never returned.

Harvey kept me company in this land of changelessness.

Through tunnels of thorny branches we wandered, finding every once in a while another stray coin. Near the mine, she often found small hints of ancient human remains. At times, she dug up a deformed skeleton of a rodent I couldn't recognize. I'd let her chew it on the rug beside me in the evening, while I sipped my tea and stared at a blank page.

I didn't even try to write, to tell what I was supposed to tell. What was the point? No one would hear. There was no mailbox. As far as I could tell, there was no way out of the sea of thorns that surrounded the cabin.

The tome, which had seemed so promising at first (I had been ready to give up more than what the deal-maker had asked—far, far more—in order to spend an eternity among its pages), had now become an object of resentful obligation. It was an enemy to whom I was chained.

One day, sitting by the dried-up creek, with Harvey nestled in my lap, I realized my decision already had been made, pronounced by some unknown avatar secluded deep within the subterranean pyramid of my consciousness.

I would refuse my end of the bargain. I would not take in all the knowledge they had intended for me. I would make my own knowledge. I would defy the gods.

There was a penalty that had been described to me, though I couldn't recall what it was. Late in the evening, when the porch bulb sizzled out and the moths fluttered away, I sensed a chillness emanating from the far end of the woods.

"Harvey, if things get rough." I put her head between my hands and stared into her struggling-to-discern eyes. "You should leave."

Suppress the nightmares. Gather timber. Construct barricades. Inspect the dried-up creek, look for footprints. Set tripwire among the cracked boulders. Let the tome lie. Teach Harvey: 'stay' and 'fetch.' Tea and prepare. Wait for it.

Punishment still had not arrived, but the mists had grown thicker. Creakings arose from the bramble at all hours. As if they could foresee the approach of some terrible onslaught, the moths had stopped congregating on my porch.

In the meantime, Harvey had learned a reasonable number of commands, which she treated more like suggestions.

"Sit."

She sat.

"Stay."

(The cruelest command. She mustered the full force of her will. Her haunches looked like they would explode.)

"Fetch."

I threw a stick.

She bounded off the slab and down the dried-up creek (which had not fully dried out after all these years), then—with a flaring of her nostrils and the stiffening of her ear wisps—veered between two of the boulders, where she vanished into thin air.

Standing in the middle of the faded creek, tears welling in my eyes, I cursed the inevitable logic and perverse justice of the gods.

When I returned to the cabin, however, she was sitting on the porch, her wiry tail wagging. She dropped a hand at my feet.

Harvey watched with curiosity as I boiled a pot of water and made a hot compress.

The hand was injured but alive.

Enfeebled, bruised, swollen around the knuckles, it struggled to form signs that neither Harvey nor I could interpret.

Its gestures became more frantic. It trembled and pointed at nothing.

"Be calm." I rubbed the palm gently. "Rest. The mine was no place for you. You will live with us now." I looked at the mists coiling and unraveling outside the picture window. "For however long we have left."

What kind of mad torture is this?

Is this a torture?

We've waited for weeks, yet nothing has come.

The hand has made a full recovery. It helps with the tea and the dishes. It flips or bookmarks or rips out pages from the tome, depending on my inclinations. It sharpens my pencils. When my own hand grows tired, it writes for me, exactly the words I would have written. It throws bones to Harvey.

At times, when a loud snap arises from near the mine, it shivers and seeks refuge in the sleeve of my coat.

Nothing has come for us.

Nothing has come, but the mists have gathered tight around the cabin, pressing us in, squeezing us, suffocating us. We cannot see a thing outside the window. We never leave. If we crack the door for even a moment, the room fills with vapors. It takes an hour for us to be able to see across the living room again.

In these moments, lost in our own home in the inscrutable fog, I call her name, "Harvey, Harvey, Harvey," and she responds with a faint yapping from beneath the sofa: "YOU, YOU, YOU."

My heart relaxes.

And I find a warm hand in mine.

⛫

Tim and Tam Go to the Library

~ *Paul Jessup*

They weren't going to talk about mom's corpse anymore, they had bigger things to worry about. Like the constantly falling snow, their freezing feet wrapped in cheap shoes, their backpacks shoved tight with the last food they could make for themselves. Mostly sloppy peanut butter and jelly sandwiches, and some animal crackers, and the last of mom's cookies. The cookies were hard as rocks, but it didn't matter none to them. Food was food after all, and Tim found out if you put a cookie between the palms of your hands and counted to twenty, it would be warm and taste fresh baked.

Tam insisted they bring boxes of mac and cheese, but they didn't know if there would be a stove at the library. They only knew that there were books, and hopefully adults, and heat (HEAT!), and that they would be away from their mother's corpse. That last part was probably the most key out of all of them. The first day or so, they tried to call the cops and all the phones were silent. They tried to go online, but all the electricity was out, too. No one was coming, and their mom's corpse just laid there on the couch in the living room, waiting patiently. They tried to act like she was still alive, to wake her up, but there was no way that was going to happen.

She definitely did not look like she was asleep. Tim especially didn't like the way her eyes looked. They kept staring at them, even when they closed the lids, and her lips peeled back to reveal her teeth all long and ghoulish. Tam thought maybe mom would smell, but no. It was too cold for such things, their house freezing their bones even under three or four winter blankets. Tim thought that's how mom died. "They shut off the heat and she just froze up, her blood turned to ice in her body."

Tam wanted to ask if they were going to freeze up, too. But she decided against it. Some things are better left unsaid, and that was one of them. She was just glad she had her brother Tim here with her. She had no idea what she would do if she was all alone.

The snow outside was taller than their front door, and made it impossible for them to open. So they pushed open a window on the second floor, and flung their backpacks down. The snow was packed tight, hard, and the backpacks landed with a thump and didn't sink at all. It wasn't too far down, but far enough that it looked scary.

"We have to jump down and get to the library, remember? That's where we'll be safe."

"Are you sure? What if I break a leg or something…or what if I fall through the snow and keep on falling? We weigh more than backpacks, and you wouldn't be able to get me out if that happened."

Tim thought a moment, and looked across the street beyond in the evening air. It was January, and this snow came out of nowhere, and completely buried everything. They had never had snow in Madison before now, it was always a wet winter. Ever since Tam and Tim were really little. None of the lights were on in the houses, and the world was eerily silent. Not even the sound of wild animals, or people in the distance, talking. The streetlamps flickered here and there, still barely working, just enough light to guide their way into the dark beyond.

And there, about an hour walk away on the hill above the city, was the Madison Library. And it had lights. Golden, bright, spreading across the moonglow snow banks. Lights. And in those lights walked human shaped shadows.

"Okay, see? Look, there are people in the library, we need to go there and we'll be all right."

Tam grasped her shoulders and shivered briefly. Her lips felt numb. Could she even make it all the way there?

"What if those aren't people?"

"Wait, the shadows? What else would they be? Of course they're people, stop being stupid."

"But what if they're shaped like people, but they're not."

Tim sighed and grabbed his sister's hand. "We can't stay here, we'll die here, understand? Just like mom."

Tam nodded her head. She still didn't want to jump.

"Look, we'll jump at the same time, okay? Then if we fall through the snow we'll fall together, and we'll dig our way out."

Tam gulped. She didn't think it would be possible to dig her way out of something like that. It would only make things worse. She didn't say that, though. She looked at the trees lining the street and saw they were crystalized with ice. Beautiful, it caught her breath. And then she saw the corpses of crows frozen on the branches mid caw, unable to escape death, and knew that her brother was right. They had to go up and reach the hill. If they stayed here they would die like those birds, frozen and alone.

One, two, three . . .

They jumped, and landed, and didn't sink at all.

They've made this trek to the library billions of times in all their tiny little lives. It was close enough that they could go alone most days, once they were out of kindergarten and had library cards of their own. Though sometimes mom would come with, just to spend more time with them. They didn't mind either way, though it was very freeing when they would go by themselves, in a way that was almost terrifying. Barking dogs on tight leashes, strangers in their yards staring at those kids without a parent. She wanted to run past them and yell at the top of her lungs to *go away. This city was our city now.*

This time, it was very different. No dogs on leashes. No people staring at them as they walked by. This was terrifying in a completely different way, and was not freeing at all. Tam clung onto her brother's hand, tighter than she should have. She thought if it was too loose he would let go and she would fall away, into that darkness beyond the streetlamps. That terrified her almost more than anything else. Even the quiet emptiness of the street.

"I wish mom was here." She said as they began the steep climb up that hill. She wanted to apologize to her for always being late with her library books. She couldn't help it, she loved books too much to return them on time. Tim, on the other hand, only took out one book at a time exactly, and always returned it a day early.

"I don't, she's dead. What would that be like if she was here? A ghost? Or just her corpse following us, dragging itself behind? *Shhhk, shhhhk, shhhk.*"

"Tim, don't say that!"

"Okay, I'm sorry, I was trying to make you laugh, so you wouldn't feel so sad anymore."

It didn't make her laugh at all. She shivered, and wasn't sure if it was the cold, or something else. She kept looking behind, trying to see her mom's corpse crawling behind them. It was hard to see anything in the darkness down the hill. The streetlamps had already fizzled out in the city below, leaving only shadows behind.

The snow was deep on the library's stone steps, though not as deep as it was outside of their house when they left. The door was accessible, with lights coming in through the stained-glass windows. They only had to push away a few of the smaller drifts to clear their path in. On either side of the door waited two stone lions. This was an old library, Tam knew that. From before even when their grandparents were kids.

"Are you sure you want to go inside?"

The lights were still on, but all the people shaped shadows were gone now. Somehow, that made everything worse.

"Yes, can't you feel the heat? Even from out here, see? Touch the door. It's warm, like fresh bread from the oven."

Tam placed her hand against the door, and it was warm, but not like fresh bread. It was warm like a body is warm, and it seemed to move under her palm, like it was breathing. She closed her eyes and realized just how cold she was, and if she imagined hard enough, she could picture this door as something else. Something more comforting. Like her mom's back, the spine breathing against her palms. She knew she should turn around right now, but she was so cold.

"Come on, let's go inside, your lips are blue and you're shivering."

They unwrapped some of the sandwiches, but Tam didn't want to eat. She wasn't hungry. She just wanted to stay over here by the fireplace, surrounded by the warmth. It was odd, the fire was going when they came inside, but there was no one around. Not even a librarian or two. She knew that should freak her out, that maybe it should set off some alarms in her mind, but no. She was too cold to care at first, and now she was too warm to care. Though she hoped against hope that it was her favorite librarian, Miss Merryweather, and that she was just hiding somewhere else, maybe in the basement where they stored all the kid's books.

"You need to eat," Tim said. "It will help you keep warm."

And she sighed, and tried, but it was wet and mushy and tasteless, like eating newspaper in the rain. She retched for a bit, and he swore.

"We don't have that much food, you can't waste it like that."

"It tastes wrong, though."

"Your tastebuds might be frozen. You should eat it anyway, it will help, I promise."

He looked at her with such sad eyes. The same look he had on his face when they found mom's body on the couch.

"Okay, I'm sorry, I'll eat it. Please, just please, don't look at me like that anymore."

Tim went to sleep right after their makeshift dinner, curling up into a ball and just closing his eyes and snoring. She laid next to him, and tried to sleep as well, but could not. Every time she closed her eyes, she saw her mom's face. But not the beautiful face of her memories or photographs, no. The face that was now burned into her mind was the face of her corpse.

She tried reading. She walked amongst the shelves, taking out this book or that, but the words felt all squirmy, and she couldn't concentrate on them. She put them back exactly where she found them, in case she was right and Miss Merryweather was just hiding out in the basement, waiting for her to come downstairs and play. Maybe she should go down there after all?

She wandered around the first floor for a few moments more. There were only two floors in the Madison library, the first floor and the basement. The basement was where all the good books were stored, and where all the toys and masks and crafts were stored as well. Even if Miss Merryweather wasn't hiding down there, maybe she should go and look anyway? After all, she wasn't going to sleep just yet. She might as well go downstairs and explore.

Before she left, she wandered over tiptoe to the windows, and looked outside. The snow was still coming down. You couldn't even see the tree line outside of the window, where the pine forest sprawled across the top of the hill. It was all grey flurries, snow the color of damp mud. And already, the windows were half covered. She did not like this. They were going to be trapped in here until the blizzard stopped and all the snow melted. And mom's corpse would be there, waiting for them to return.

She heard footsteps behind her, and turned around. Nothing. No one was there. Just Tim asleep on the floor, curled up around a pile of loose books like a pillow.

Darkness greeted Tam at the bottom of the stairs. No lights were on in the basement floor. In a way, it wasn't really a basement. It was just the first floor, cut into the side of the hill. She always thought of it like a basement, since it was underground. She thought about all that packed earth overhead, all those books and stone blocks and wood planks right above, all that snow covering all the basement windows, and felt trapped under ground. Maybe she should go back up?

No. She'd come this far. She walked through the first floor, past the rows and rows of kid's books, and tried to flick the light on and off. No dice. She waited for a moment, her eyes adjusting little by little to the darkness. Shadows formed around her in the shape of shelves and chairs and racks of dvd rentals. In the corner was an old computer that was covered in crayon and stickers, with a sign posted on the front of the monitor. She couldn't read it from here, but remembered it from the last time she was here. It said Out of Order.

Everything was out of order now. She laughed, and then jumped back, surprised at the sound of her own laughter.

Something moved in the darkness. At first she wasn't so sure it was real or imaginary, so she stayed put, concentrating on the shadows. Another one moved, and another and another. They ran, these small shapes, and ducked behind bookshelves and under chairs.

"Hello?"

No answer. She walked forward some more, heard heavy breathing in the darkness, and the sound of footsteps down the stairs towards the first floor. Was that Tim, waking up again and looking for her? Oh. What if she'd worried him? She hoped not.

"Hello?"

Nothing. And then over in the corner, the House of Masks moved.

The House of Masks was the playplace built by a bunch of studious adults sometime in the nineteen sixties. They constructed it out of recycled wood, made to look like a perfect house in miniature. Like something out of a sitcom, or a Norman Rockwell painting. They'd slapped on bright colors, and covered the entire inside with a wall of brass hooks. And all along the hooks they hung masks for the kids to play with. Each mask was handmade, and every year more masks were created and added to the collection, with the librarians cycling them in and out when the kids got bored.

The ages were not kind to the masks, but the kids didn't care. The edges rubbed away, the paint dingy and filthy. Cobwebs from spiders lined some of the older, untouched ones, and a few that had been only paper mâché had rotted away to barely nothing.

Tam had never liked the House of Masks. Whenever she would go inside, it would feel colder than the rest of the library. As if the promise of the winter blizzard had nested in there, waiting to be born. The masks freaked her out, and the one time she put one on, she had nightmares for a week of strange lights, and dead children in the trees, their corpses smiling down at her, all teeth and eyes bulging.

And when she woke from these dreams she heard singing in the distance, and the bitter taste of snowflakes on her tongue.

"One two, one two, and true and true," the voices sang, "They run red, they said, and bleed blue."

The House of Masks should not move. It was too heavy. She knows it took at least four big burly men to move it from one side of the library to another, when they wanted to add the new desk for the librarians. Even if it was Miss Merryweather hiding there, she wouldn't be able to move it like that. This was wrong. This was so wrong.

The shadows around her stopped moving. She walked closer. She knew she should go upstairs now, go and see if Tim was okay, and if he was still sleeping. And maybe they could leave and go somewhere else? There had to be another house with heat, another place with electricity. It couldn't just be the library!

And then she remembered the snow outside of the window and felt sick to her stomach. Maybe it was too late.

"Hello? Who are you? Do you want to play pretend?"

Maybe it's a wild animal. Maybe one with rabies. A bear, yes, a bear would be big enough and strong enough to move the house like that. It might just be a rabid bear, come inside from the cold, seeking warm human bodies to devour. She shouldn't move forward. She should really stop and turn around.

The house moved again, side to side, side to side. A rattling on the walls, and then a pounding. She knew the door would open any second now, and a bear would come running out and devour her whole. A noise in the house, a chuckling sound, like a deep in the belly laugh.

"Miss Merryweather? If that's you, you should really stop. You're scaring me . . ."

And then a hand on her shoulder, like a whisper.

"Beware the Laughing Queen."

When she turned around the shadows scattered again.

She came upstairs and saw that the lights were off on the main floor now, and her brother was nowhere to be seen. Dead birds scattered across the floor and between the bookcases, and they looked unreal in the dim light from the windows. She touched one and it felt like a toy. So light, like it was made of sticks. And each of their eyes had been removed.

The blank, empty skulls stared at her. Emptiness from behind the sockets. Like the nightsky outside the library.

"Tim?" She called out. Worried now. Where did these birds come from? Where did he go?

She thought again of the House of Masks. Maybe that was him in there? No. That made no sense. And even if it was, she would not go back downstairs to check. It was not worth it.

And from the other end of the library, near the front door, she heard her brother singing a song. His voice so quiet and light, half a hoarse whisper of words.

"One two, one two, and true and true. They run red, they said, and bleed blue."

Tam wasn't sure about this. This all felt so wrong. But he was all she had left. That was it. He was the entire world to her now. She had to go over and find him. She had to see if he was okay.

The front doors were open, with a wall of snow avalanching out and into the library. It covered all of the door, and she could see that it went up over the windows, too. Tim was in the center of the avalanche, his arms wrapped around his legs, his cheek pressed up against his knees. His fingers were blue, and there were divots and grooves in the wall of snow where he tried to dig them out. And he was still singing that song, rocking back and forth now, not even seeing Tam as she walked up to him, curled up around him, and hugged his freezing body close.

She wanted to be a candle to warm him. To make him a puddle of human once again. He was too cold now, and shivering and she worried about him. Mom was the same way, right before she died, and Tam couldn't lose him, too. She couldn't. She wouldn't even know what to do with herself if she did.

He licked his lips and stopped singing. When he spoke, his voice felt older than his body and far away, like it came from somewhere else.

"I had a dream I was downstairs, and I heard someone singing this song in the House of Masks. I knew I was dreaming so I thought I was safe, and I went over to the house and opened the door and crawled inside. Mom was there, and she was alive, and she wore one of the bear masks on her face. It was the black bear mask, the one with really big eyes, remember? And a tiny gold crown that never stayed put and kept sliding off. Do you remember? It was that one."

He cleared his throat, and then pushed his head further against his knees, as if he was trying to crawl inside of himself and away from the world.

"She said Hi when I came inside and handed me a fox mask, but I refused to put it on. She laughed and laughed and laughed, but I knew it was a bad mask. There was a hole in the center like a keyhole, and there was dried blood all over it. She said okay, and then told me that she was still alive right now. She'd followed us to the library, but she was so cold it was hard for her to move, so it took a lot longer. She crawled all the way here, and she was waiting outside of the door. The snow was so big, she couldn't crawl through it, and so she needed our help. We had to open the door, and dig our way out to her."

She pulled him in closer, wrapping all her body around him. He was so cold and shivering. What had he done?

"I woke up and you were gone, where did you go? I was all alone, and there were all these dead birds around me, and the lights were off. I don't know what happened, and then I heard something moving outside the windows. I swear, I heard something scratching at them, like a wild animal. And if I listened closely, I think I heard singing. But I wasn't sure, you know? So, so, so. I opened the door. But mom wasn't there, there was nothing, just that wall of snow, and I tried, I really tried to dig my way into it, but it's so cold. It's so cold. Can you help me? Tam? Can you help me dig? Maybe there is a toy shovel downstairs in the basement we could use . . ."

She didn't say anything. She just listened to the silence beyond the snow. Waiting to hear what he heard. The sound of movement, the scratching noises, the singing. But, no. It was all just empty nothingness. She held him closer, and closer, and realized that she did not want to ever let him go. The minute she would, he would start digging again, and she didn't want to see what was beyond that wall of snow. She didn't want to go downstairs, she didn't want to go outside, she just wanted to stay here, with her brother. Hold him tight. Keep him safe and warm. As she listened to their hearts beating in sycophantic rhythm, the only sounds in the silence around them.

⋈

Palimpsests

~ *Simone Cooper*

Clean as a scalpel fresh from the autoclave. Clean as a laser. Clean as the whistle of a willow switch descending. That's how clean this patch of wallpaper must be before I can peel it back and get to work on the next layer, scrubbing away yet another attempt to summon an eldritch doorway. Given the age of this house, there's probably another layer beneath that.

I've been working this site, the topmost room of an abandoned Chicago rowhouse, for almost a week, the longest assignment I've been on in six years with the company. As of this morning, I'd cleaned and removed three layers of wallpaper, each fraught with desperate, scribbled drawings. It's tedious, detailed work involving math and fumes and a lot of elbow grease. Yet I must do it carefully, mindfully. Always attentive.

Never uncover all of any one drawing at once. If you do stumble on a complete one, such as upon first discovery, never look at the design in full. We wear special glasses with strategic squares blacked out across the lenses. The first time you wear the glasses in the field, the company warned us, you'll want to claw them off your face. You have to learn to focus past them. These are among the things the company teaches during orientation. We can clean away the angles scribed in ink, in chalk, in paint or blood. What we can't do is clean the sight of them from memory. Most of the afflicted try. Photographs of their eyeless faces accompany this lesson. They teach it well.

It takes a specific sort of person to do the work I do.

First, you have to have *seen* something. For me, it was one of those rare books so common to Lovecraftian tales. I used to study the history of theater design and its effect on public discourse. Burrowing down that rabbit hole, I'd found rumors of a "forbidden play" and a staging so connected to its text that its viewers were literally redefined by the experience. Once I learn about something like that, I have to know more.

Which brings me to the second requirement. You have to be boring. Focused. Obsessed. Also, educated or educable.

Third, you have to pass the company's equivalent of a security clearance. Being comfortable keeping secrets is a quality a lot of people think they have. They do not.

Finally, you need to have nothing else to live for.

My entire extant family died in a yachting accident when I was seventeen. Mother and father, brother, one aunt and two cousins. The only reason I hadn't been on that trip was I had dress rehearsals for the senior play, which I wouldn't give up for another of Mama's island-hopping summers. My chunky, overly square frame couldn't compete with her in the bikini department, and the fact that she'd shove me into one regardless, to reap the sympathetic noises of her "summer people" at the sight of my sad, pasty showings, had made the trips increasingly intolerable.

After the accident, performing lost its draw. Too much drama, honestly. Too many people you have to count on. But the language of the stage, the special relationship created between audience and text, shaped by curtain and proscenium and darkened theater, the transport of it! Those things still fascinated me. With the middling fortune I inherited, I plodded doggedly through university and beyond, following the tracks of this extremely unprofitable field. Unprofitable and lonely.

So many of the cultists, nihilists, and mad artists we oppose have a story just like mine. The difference between them and us cleaners is that the company finds us and intervenes. That, and, unlike them, I do not want this world to fall to the Elder Gods. Nothing I know of them from the company's teachings or my own research indicates they care for art, theater, poetry, or dance. Shakespeare to them is a frightened bark against uncaring chaos, the lowing of cattle comforting one another in the chute. Thank my mother, perhaps, but I've never been one to worship bullies. Fighting them, even just delaying them, is worth any risk.

The last question I remember from my company interview was, "Do you have any pets?"

"No." I'd replied. God no. What if something happened to me? What if I left one day and couldn't come back?

"Not even a cat?"

"No."

And so, I was in.

I'm lightheaded, I realize. My phone battery died, and the music in my earbuds cut out a while back. With the dormer window nailed shut, the room feels hot and cramped. Damn these Midwestern cultists anyway. Go back to New England where the summer is shorter and the humidity lifts once in a damn while. I throw the sponge at the wall. Inside their protective gloves, my hands are sticky and stinging in their own sweat.

Time for a break.

Before heading downstairs, I survey my progress. A two-foot width of the oldest wallpaper, yellow with tiny green flowers, blooms like a patch of sun from beneath the less flamboyant layers I've already cleared, brightening the odd-angled corner between the sloped ceiling and two walls. Before he'd disappeared, the most recent listed owner had painted the whole room builder's beige, wallpaper and drawings and all, in a doomed attempt to sell. This made my job much harder early on. The first and second days had been all about paint stripper, the discomfort of a respirator rated for chemicals, the maddening drone of the generator and the industrial exhaust fan it powered. That stage had been draining.

Plagued by tinnitus and cheekbones worn sore by the mask, my nightly check-ins with Stella in HR those two days had been more curt than necessary. I'll have to apologize to her when this is all over. She cares about us, and besides, it is her job to probe, however subtly, for signs of contamination.

I look down at my hands. The skin at my wrists is puffy and inflamed, making my always freckled arms seem mottled in the stark work lights. Ugh. I peel the gloves off, revealing fingers pale and wrinkled from hours trapped under latex. I foresee weeks of lotion therapy in my future. Maybe a manicure. One of those paraffin wraps would be soothing.

Then, hushed by distance, the doorbell rings. I'm surprised. In the guise of investors, the company had forewarned the neighbors they'd have people working here. And the neighbors had been so supportive! Someone just has to do something about this place! And, were we going to cut back the weeds? they'd asked. Because of the rats. You know.

I hadn't seen any rats.

I'm still holding the used gloves between the forefinger and thumb of my right hand. I shift side-to-side, stretching my hips. I'll head for the restroom as a matter of priority. Then food, then sleep. My bladder really aches, now I think about it.

The doorbell goes again.

I swipe sweat from my eyes with the sleeve of my t-shirt. On the damp floorboards next to the sponge I tossed are two flat, black, irregular shapes. I blink, squinting. Right! The broken halves of my glasses. Next to them, face up and spidered with cracks, is the cheery silver rectangle of my company phone.

Well. That's hard to explain.

"Hard to explain, yahp," someone agrees.

Yahp? I don't turn my head. Instead, I sigh. My thigh muscles twitch as if exhausted. "I, uh, can't move my feet."

"I can see that."

From the moist, gliding rustle across the floorboards, I can tell the speaker is moving around behind me. Closer. Closer. The smell is indescribable, but I'll try for the sake of completeness. There is ozone and rot, but also something my brain translates as banana esters and cinnamon. The smell is cold, if a smell can have a temperature, and it rides into my nostrils on air that seems very short on oxygen.

We cleaners have read all the stories, Lovecraft and Derleth and Smith and the rest. The company wants us to know that whatever we see, no matter how unbelievable, we should be ready to believe it. Whatever shapes. Whatever colors. Whatever geometries so distorted they must be inanimate yet are definitely, horribly alive.

The thin, pyramidal being sways into view a mere arms-length away. It is my height, void black, shot through with silver and a violet just at the edge of what I can perceive. The top of it, its head perhaps, swells like an orchid bud opening in slow motion. It seems to regard me, the spreading, oil-sheened lobes of its face glancing up and down. "Your friends aren't going to like this." *Ahn't gun ta lahk this.* The being has a Boston accent. "What will they do, do you think?"

Breathing is very, very hard. My throat makes a narrow, creaking sound, constricted to the size of a pennywhistle. The being is right. I know how the company usually responds to personnel contaminations. I even agree it would be right. Except. Except it's me, and I don't feel contaminated. I haven't suddenly decided the world needs to end. I don't feel any different at all. Except I see what I see. I haven't been careful enough, and the revealed edges of the designs have lined up, falling into some sort of completion. "Help. HELP!" I try with my scant air. It's like trying to shout in a dream. "HHHHelp!"

A bulging distortion rises near the thin top vertex of the pyramid, below the "face," and moves up and down. I think it's a shrug. "I would if I knew how," the pyramid says. "You're part in. Part across."

From the front door, two floors below, comes the clatter of locks turning. A much more solid voice shouts up, "Rose! What the hell?" It's William Ballard, bless him. "Rose, we're coming in!"

The relief is like an IV unfurling too cool through my veins. I do wonder why, though, why they're here. I mean, I'm grateful. Still, I wonder. I checked in every day. Six check-ins so far. They won't come until . . .

"Right. It's day ten," the being says.

I've lost time.

There is a dull boom and the sound of wood splintering once and again and a last time.

"And, you boarded up the door." The being nods with what feels like vaguely parental disappointment.

I don't remember doing that.

"Rose?!" echoes up the empty house, rattling. Ballard's voice again.

"I'm here!" I try. Nothing comes out but a whimper. Not being able to answer has become my topmost fear, which stops up my throat even more.

I feel my own rigidity, my elbows tight against my vibrating chest, my shoulders rising, neck tensing. My pulse pounds, whooshing past my inner ears. They won't shoot me, at least. I don't think. Too dangerous. Who knows what having a body stuck like this could do? Or if the blood would play a part, break the seals. More, I mean. More than I already have.

Many footsteps on the stairs and more voices. Quite a lot of them. I'm flattered. One shouts, "We're coming up!"

"They're coming up," the being says, sounding sad.

"I HEARD THEM!" I scream out, loud enough to surprise myself. Then my vision distorts, kaleidoscoping to a small window. Things go green around the edges, and I faint dead away.

"... Rose? Rose? You hanging in there?" Ballard is asking.

I'm on my back, maybe on a pad, with my knees up and my feet planted awkwardly on the floor. My left knee and ankle throb as if I've twisted my leg badly. I've wet myself. Light stabs my eyes when my eyelids flutter, and I put my hand up to block it.

"Hey. Hey, get those lights off her face." Ballard leans over me to block them. Haloed, he looks like a middle-aged angel with male pattern baldness. "Rose, are you okay?"

"Mm. Mmhmm." I test my voice. "I think so. Yeah."

He exhales, a relieved sigh. "Can you sit up?"

It's doable, though my feet are still maddeningly fixed on the floor. In the floor.

Ballard's hand hovers behind my back, ready to support me. The whole team is up here, seven people crowded into the room. A tarp hangs in front of my work area. Everyone has blocking glasses on. Someone had put a pair on me while I was out, a slightly crooked pressure on the bridge of my nose.

In the opposite corner, tucked hard against the wall, the being flickers through its alien spectrum. It appears to be wringing its hands. It does not have hands. I turn my head so I can't see it and instead look fixedly at Ballard and the others.

"What are we gonna do?" I try to sound positive. I try not to think about the company's decontamination rooms.

"First, we're gonna get you out of here. And before you ask, it wasn't your fault." I notice a few of the others seem skeptical, and I put my focus back on Ballard. He continues. "The design's baked into the architecture, not just in the artistic additions—"

"Like the witch house," Ellis speaks up. There's nodding all around, perhaps a touch more sympathetic. We'd lost three cleaners to the witch house.

Ballard nods. "Nobody expected this in Chicago. R&I went through the records before we sent you."

Research and Investigations. Pritchard is on that group, when she's between field assignments. She's here, too, arms crossed, trying not to scowl at this hint of blame.

Ballard continues. "Nothing suspicious in the era of the building or any renovations. We just have to keep you comfortable until we can get the demo specialists out. That should break whatever bridge you're on, let you go. Couple hours, is all. You'll be fine."

He doesn't say anything about my potential contamination, for which I am grateful. I can think about that later. "What about the neighbors?"

"We told them asbestos. The demo team will come in the environmental cleanup truck."

"Thanks, Ballard." I start to cry. "Seriously, thank you all."

Ballard squeezes my shoulders. "It's all good, Rose. All good."

I sneak a glance at the being, which is shaking its head. It's not all good, at all.

Hours later, I'm still here. They've brought me a thicker pad, a back support, some bolsters for under my knees, and more pain killers for my throbbing ankle. Also, some goggles and a mask and ear protectors for all the sawing. Everyone looks exhausted, hair stuck down with wood dust. Even the being seems slumped and smaller, crouched against the wall. I've gotten used to looking at it. As long as I'm on the threshold, I suppose, I will still see it.

At least I'm full and re-hydrated. Ellis and Pritchard and one of the men from the local demolitions team got in an argument about deep dish vs. cracker crust pizza being more Chicago-y, the result being us all taking a break for a pizza throw-down. I think I'm on team deep dish, but that might have been my hunger talking.

Ballard's on the phone with headquarters, trying to get an even more senior R&I person out here. There's been gesturing and swearing. People's expressions are getting kinder and more sympathetic, but they're also clustered on the other side of the room from me, like I have a terminal and contagious disease. Maybe I do.

Finally, Ballard pockets his phone and comes to crouch beside me. "So, look. It's gonna be maybe twelve hours before our man in Paris can get here. Levi's team is down the mines in Botswana dealing with an outbreak of children of Atlach-Nacha, so we can't—"

I squint at him.

"Spiders. The mindless joy of eternal service. You remember." He shudders.

I shudder. "Right. Right."

"So, yeah, we can't get a message to them any sooner." Ballard looks at his hands. "We'll . . . we'll get you a bed pan, okay? A doc on payroll is going to swing by in just a few minutes here, and make sure everything's all right with your feet. You can still feel them?"

I nod. We'd cut the tops of my shoes away. My feet look and feel fine, though that one ankle's pretty angry, but neither the shoe-soles nor my feet themselves will budge. "I understand. Nothing's getting worse, I don't think." I pointed up at the safety scaffold and the big hole in the roof, through which only I can see the dim outlines of the dormer's angles, layer upon layer of complex geometries glowing green like swampfire. "At least we've got some air."

After the doctor has been and gone, with everyone retired downstairs except Ballard sitting guard in a folding chair, I doze. I dream there is a weight pressing along my side. It shudders in little waves against me, like a dog recovering from a scare. I smell graham crackers and melted plastic. Of course, it is the being. Its orchid bud head is balled up tight, resting on my shoulder. It feels like oil or liquid silk or velvet. Above us, stars sweep across the sky, an alien Milky Way shaded green and violet that ripples like the northern lights.

When I twitch awake, the being phases away, leaving not-quite-invisible swirls in its wake.

On his flight over, Dr. Alpay, our man in Paris, had my notes and photos to study—piecemeal, of course—along with the few autobiographical details Pritchard had dug up about the owners and artists who'd contributed to this gateway. So, when Dr. Alpay gathers the others to my makeshift bedside, he's got good news and bad.

"Good news first, please," I say.

He smiles. It's a handsome smile. Dr. Alpay has dark, arching brows and a long nose and silver-shot hair, and looks far too much like someone's jovial uncle, if that uncle were a fashion model who wore a fistful of heavy, arcane-looking emerald rings. "Good news is, none of the people we think did this had the same vision. Better yet, none of them seem to have 'plugged in' to any of the greater Old Ones. No mention even of our local boy."

Local boy was our code name for Cthulhu, who waits dreaming near enough one should not speak his name.

"So where does the gate go?" Ellis asks.

"I don't know," Dr. Alpay says. He sounds a little delighted with the mystery, which makes me think he's a little less handsome.

I say, "That's the bad news."

Dr. Alpay laughs. "Not remotely. I said I don't know, because the original, architectural door could have been intended to go to several places. The builder himself had a friend who had reportedly read a near complete version of the play *The King in Yellow*—"

I perk up. That had been the focus of my own obsession, when the company recruited me.

"—but there's no indication he'd actually found the Yellow Sign. I think more likely he influenced the builder to construct this dormer, just so," Dr. Alpay gestures at the remaining roof corner, "and created a thin spot between our world and some nexus, a place of many possible paths. The others were drawn here by their own separate obsessions. Like at the observatory."

Ballard chimes in, "Which explains why the drawings differed from layer to layer."

I want to scream. Across the room, the being seems distressed, bending and waving. I swallow and say, "But it doesn't explain how I lined up any one of them well enough to fall through."

Alpay sighs. I wish he looked sadder. "That's the bad news. I think you lined up pieces of *different* drawings. We have no idea what percentage of which ones you activated. We'd have to guess at what construct might negate it."

"Which would mean, if you got it wrong, the door might open more." Would that be the worst thing? I wonder.

"More. Or *elsewhere.* Or partially. Your body . . ." Alpay sighs again, smiling like a reporter at a funeral.

See. That wouldn't be the worst thing.

They've started to test how far up my legs the effect goes. I've heard the word amputation several times. They're not even being coy about it. I squeeze the being against my chest like a stuffed toy. Nobody notices.

I'm getting lightheaded again. The ghost outlines above me pulse with weight the more I stare at them. I keep shifting my head to see past the glasses to different parts. I think I'm starting to catch the pattern, which lines belong to which space, where they interlink, where they displace.

The being says, "We can't go to where I'm from. You could hardly breathe there."

True.

Dread Carcosa where the King in Yellow rules also seems right out. I mean, the word "dread" is in the name. Though His Majesty is a drama fan, if the stories are to be believed.

Picking through the designs, I feel something happening in my mind, as if the lines of the drawings are a language I'm learning, their planes and angles a viewing window—a proscenium, if you will. I parse the drawings into smaller and smaller fragments. Angles and swoops align into reused symbols: worlds translated into stories, paragraphs, words. Phonemes.

The being vibrates against me, excited. "Oh! Yes! You could write a new story. Unlock it. Get out!"

My understanding unfolds, opening like a child's origami fortune teller.

Ballard is patting my shoulder. He has been for some time. "—Rose! Relax your arm. We're going to sedate you."

I shake my head. "I just need a little more time."

"Just relax your arm."

"Please. I can do it. Please." My face feels hot suddenly, stuffed with frustrated tears, and I can also feel the strange melancholy of the being, transmitted directly to my heart. "Ballard. William! Trust me. I can *see* the key. One more layer. Almost. I just need—"

Someone else has hold of my arm.

I just need another second.

The River Lethe washes me away, but behind me, there is a click, a change of pressure, a new world unlocking.

"Rose?" William calls from the kitchen. "You awake up there? Breakfast is ready."

"Mmm. Coming!" I call back.

Sunlight slips through the blinds and plays green and violet across the quilt. I yawn and stretch against the pillows, happy to be home with William, happy to awaken to the smells of bacon and pancakes and gingerbread. Somewhere, there must be a pot of coffee.

I set my feet on the floor, and the cat winds around my ankles, her black fur soft like oil or liquid silk or velvet. I bend to stroke her head.

"Good morning," she meows. She has a Boston accent.

"Good morning, Grimoire."

I get up and dress and head downstairs, already thinking of the work ahead.

So many doors left to open.

How the West Was Spun

~ *J. B. Kish*

Practical Knitting for Gunslingers is a trade booklet from 1865. It's twelve pages long with an introduction by the manufacturer in Dunwich, Texas. It contains 'seven necessary knitting patterns for the discerning cowboy,' multiple advertisements, and saddle stitching along the spine. The booklet offers one *BONUS* pattern—pattern number eight—meant only for the most serious of frontiersmen.

This is pattern one: *Bullets.*

Even a shadow knows better than to linger at high noon, when the sun is aloft, and our cowboy thumbs his knitting needles for a showdown. As he slowly lets out some yarn and ties one end into a slipknot, the townsfolk *yip* and slam their shutters tight. That's when the tumbleweed hitches a ride 'cross Main Street. Even critters—the untamed ones—get scarce; nothing is witless enough to mill about when two men such as this square off. So why does Knick feel like they're being watched? Everywhere he glances, some furtive shadow slips from view. Is his mind playing tricks?

"You ready, lil partner?" Cowboy speaks from the corner of his mouth. There's a frayed matchstick gripped between his molars; it rolls along each syllable like a wave.

Knick stares at the empty window of a nearby saloon. He's certain someone was there, watching them. Now, a single, white curtain waves back as if to say *too slow.* He hasn't been this jumpy since that run-in with a great horned owl.

"Still with me, Partner?" asks Cowboy.

Knick stares a moment longer, then scurries 'round the brim of Cowboy's hat. He jumps to the man's shoulder and unbuckles a tiny, braided lasso from his belt. Cowboy gives the pack rat a confident wink; he really is the best friend a rodent could ask for. The man is tall and muscular. Handsome. He wags a jawline as rugged as the West is wild. Whereas Knickknack is small, resourceful, smarter than most every critter. Together, they've claimed twelve bounties west of Texas. Even so, Knick has an unsettled and brittle feeling about this job. *Unlucky* number thirteen.

The other fellow—that *hangnail*-of-a-bounty down the road—is a man named Desmond Purl. He's wanted in Colorado for violent murders. And despite the unbelievable things Desmond's done with his bare hands, he's left speechless at the sight of a pack rat with a sidekick. Or perhaps it's that Cowboy's side iron lacks the traditional barrel, or sight, or hammer, or trigger. No matter. Desmond Purl is about to learn what a pair of knitting needles can really do.

It's not long before it's high time. The road dilates and the sky inhales. Purl is fast. Maybe the fastest Knick has ever seen. His pistol glints in the sunlight and fires two times: *bang, bang.* Cowboy is struck in the opposite shoulder and nearly tosses Knick to the ground. Bright red yarn bursts from the man's wound. Two long strands hiss through the air and coil into a perfect circle at his feet. Desmond Purl sees the yarn and stumbles backward in confusion.

"Took me by surprise," Cowboy says with a grunt. He sounds a bit embarrassed. "Still with me, little buddy?"

"I'm here, big buddy." Knick grips the man's collar with one paw. "Let's return the favor?"

"My pleasure," says cowboy. He draws his needles and begins casting on the stitches for a bullet, grunting the words from *Practical Knitting for Gunslingers.* They're unpolished and a bit rough, but they'll do. "I call upon the great plains," he says. "To the ancient one. *R'lyeh wgah'nagl fhtagn!*" He deftly finishes the bullet, and with an eldritch *BANG*, the adorable ammunition sails across the Sonoran Desert and inverts Desmond's right kneecap. The bounty wails, tossing his pistol aside.

"Vast skies—*S'uhn— S'uhn—S'uhn!*" There's another *bang*, and a second bullet flies off Cowboy's needles. It leaves an apple-sized bruise on Desmond's throat. The man gasps silently, unable to draw oxygen past a crushed trachea. Knick leaps to the ground and closes the distance between them. He races along Main Street, hops from a rock to the highest branch of a mesquite tree. With a soaring tumble, he lands on Desmond's chest, spins the braided lasso high above his head, and brings the loop down over the man's outstretched hands. With one swift jerk, the lasso tightens.

Applause erupts around them. Men, women, and children race outside to thank their liberators. Knick removes his tiny hat and dabs his brow with a kerchief. From behind, Cowboy's handsome shadow falls over the pack rat; his partner smiles down and extends an elbow of camaraderie. Knick scurries up the man's bicep and onto his shoulder. Together, they shake the hand of nearly everyone in town. They are triumphant. Purl makes lucky thirteen. And Knick's forgotten all about that brittle feeling in his stomach. Whatever he saw in the window, it was all in his head. The heat of the sun. Probably.

Practical Knitting for Gunslingers was published in Dunwich, Texas and is introduced by its Author, High Priestess Mama Lilith. In it, she talks about the origins of her church and her years spent studying the arcane. She hopes this booklet can help recruit like-minded individuals to her cause. While some of the patterns in this guide might seem daunting or immoral, Mama Lilith intentionally added a few that were just plain practical.

This is pattern Four: *Eye Masks*.

Few things are better than making camp beneath a Sonoran sunset, when everything below heaven is transfixed by miles of red and orange ribbon. As the sky gives way to freckled black, Cowboy knits an eye mask and serenades the coming stars. Knickknack jogs along the desert floor, collecting sticks and twigs for the fire. Before long, the watercolors above have dripped away, and the desert falls perfectly still. This is the hour of the nocturnal, though it's been a long time since Knick's had to worry about those kinds of predators. Now, he enjoys the safety of Cowboy's hat, which is placed on its side, opening toward the fire. Knick makes a nest of torn cloth and stretches all four paws in tired victory.

Cowboy knits a while before resting both needles on his lap. "Little-buddy-ol'-pal," he says, "I don't think there's anywhere else I'd rather be than holed up next to a fire with my best friend."

Knick yawns; his long, curved incisors open and close. "Me too, big buddy. Me too."

"Tell me something," says Cowboy. "What'll we do tomorrow?"

Knick considers the question. "I suppose we'll ride north and see if anyone's up to no good."

"Huh," says Cowboy.

"What's that?"

"Well," says Cowboy, "It's just that you never talk about heading home toward Texas. I wonder if we'll ever run out of desert and turn back?"

Returning home isn't an option, but Knick doesn't know how to explain that. After what he stole in Dunwich, he and Cowboy would be strung up if they ever showed their faces. "What do you remember of home?" he asks.

Cowboy makes a face like it hurts to think back that far. "Nothing. I've only ever known the trail. Chasing bounties with my number one pal."

"We've had fun, haven't we?"

"Most certainly," says Cowboy.

"Then maybe that's enough," says Knick, and he offers to take first watch. Cowboy nods, then finishes his eye mask and slips it over his face. Before long, both our heroes are snoring.

Are you tired of naysayers and backstabbers whispering behind your back? Wish you could know what they were saying without leaving the comfort of home? Then you need "Eldritch Transmutation," a vibrant incantation able to imbue small creatures with the gift of intelligence! Create an army of spies that can do your bidding! Recommended subjects include snakes, quail, lizards, cactus wrens, and pack rats. Send one dollar along with a self-addressed stamped envelope to the address below to receive your transmutation leaflet, brought to you by the maker of *Practical Knitting for Gunslingers*!

Knickknack has terrible nightmares; he's back in Dunwich, scurrying through walls, spying on the whole town. Turning people against one another. He collects secrets for his master: *searching, searching*, always *searching* for the key that unlocks the final pattern. The *BONUS*. Number eight in Mama Lilith's new book. Until that fateful day he accidentally stumbles upon it. Hidden in a pine wood box, stored somewhere by someone who hoped it would never be found. For days he keeps this secret from Mama Lilith, but there's suspicion growing in her eyes. She smiles too much. Gifts him scraps of cloth and extra food from her table. She means to kill him, he thinks, and he must escape before it's too—

—Knick awakens to a finger pressed to his lips. There's nothing left of the fire except a few winking coals. Their camp is eerie and dark, surrounded by the ominous silhouettes of saguaro cacti and flowering agave. Cowboy is kneeling above him. The whites of his eyes signals enough urgency for Knickknack to understand they're in trouble. The packrat nods and Cowboy removes his fingertip from Knick's mouth.

He motions with his hand. It's an ambush, three men. One north and two east of their position. Knick unbuckles his small, braided lasso and Cowboy draws his knitting needles. He lets out some yarn from the pouch on his hip and casts on the start of a bullet. He whispers a soft incantation but is interrupted by an unexpected *crack*: the sound of a twig breaking underfoot. Cowboy shouts the last of his incantation and the bullet takes off into the dark. There's a scream twenty yards away, and then everything happens very quickly.

Two figures appear in the dark and Cowboy's got just enough time to fire a second shot. It strikes one in the gut and they double over. But the third is too fast.

"Arid plateaus," they say. "*Y'hah—R'lyeh!*" Three shots ring out in the dark. Cowboy is struck. Two in the gut. One in the leg. He lets out a wail and Knick stumbles backward in shock. Those words. That voice. It can't be . . .

Cowboy falls to a knee. Red yarn spills out his stomach and splashes to the ground. "Little buddy," Cowboy grunts. "Run!"

Pattern Eight *of Practical Knitting for Gunslingers* is what they call an upsell: a sewing pattern so attractive that some would gun down their own family to have it. The catch was that it required a very specific kind of yarn—The Elder Yarn—in order to work. And the customer would have to travel all the way to Dunwich to obtain it. It was a clever mechanism for Mama Lilith to bolster the ranks of her church and was nothing more than a bait-and-switch. This 'Elder Yarn' had been lost decades ago. As far as Mama Lilith knew, it never existed in the first place.

This is pattern eight: Cth-*wool*-lu.

Knick runs. He doesn't know which way, but his rodent instincts guide him through the dark with precision. He makes it twenty yards before slamming into an unseen barrier. His small nose cracks like a twig and blood pours down his chest. For several moments, he's dazed, but eventually finds sure footing. That's when he spots the single strand of yarn encircling his camp, twisted and pretzeled in the shape of an eldritch glyph along the ground. He recognizes this trick. It's pattern number three: Snare Traps. That brittle feeling is back. After all this time, Dunwich finally caught up with him. *Why didn't he trust his instincts back in town?*

There's a loud scream from behind. Cowboy is shouting in pain. The campfire bursts to life and Knick spots someone standing above his friend. He scurries behind a prickly pear and takes cover, but the sound of Cowboy's pain is too much to bear. That's his best friend out there, and he's dying!

"You can't escape," says a familiar voice, and a chill runs all the way down Knick's spine to the tip of his tail. It's Mama Lilith. She's found him. "Why don't you come out, Knickknack. There's not much of your friend left."

Holding back tears, Knick walks into the fire light, his head hung low. Cowboy is a mess. Mama Lilith has used her magic and unspooled the man up to his chest. Everything below Cowboy's sternum is a rat's nest of brightly colored yarn all tangled in a heap. It will take weeks to put him back together, if Knick ever gets the chance.

"There's my pet," says Mama Lilith. She's a tall woman with pale skin and a thick drawl. But the thing Knick recognizes most are those horrible black eyes. The same black eyes that looked upon him the day she first plucked the pack rat from his nest.

"Don't give her nothing," Cowboy says. He's worse for the wear, propped up against a rock with all his threads spilled out.

"Is this a proper way to welcome your mama," says Lilith. "After I've come all this way to find you."

Cowboy spits. He reaches for his needles, but they rest firmly on the ground under Mama Lilith's foot.

"That was you I felt in town," says Knick. "I ought to have known."

"Don't beat yourself up about it," says Mama Lilith.

"Little buddy," says Cowboy. "Get out of here. I can take her."

Knickknack looks at the man with such deep appreciation. Cowboy truly is the best friend a pack rat could ask for; the two were made for each other. Literally. Cowboy may have been simple, but he was loyal, and Knick loved him to a fault.

"I don't think you'll be taking anyone, my unspooled friend."

Cowboy snorts. "I may just be a torso in the sand, but I know a thing or two about kicking ass. So let my little buddy go, or else." Cowboy produces two fists, raised high in the air like a boxer.

"Why did you come," Knick asks.

"You wound me," says Mama Lilith. "You act as if you're not happy to see me. Didn't I give you the gift of intelligence. A warm home. A place in my congregation—"

"You made me spy on our neighbors," says Knick. "And our friends. Some turned up dead; That's why I left."

"Really." Mama Lilith's black eyes narrow until they're practically slits. "I think you left because you found something."

Knick opens his mouth to argue, but nothing comes out.

"What's she on about?" asks Cowboy. "What did you find, little buddy?"

"I think he found The Elder Yarn," says Mama Lilith. "That which can unlock the final pattern. Awaken The Great Dreamer. The Old One. Cth-*wool*-lu!"

Knick's paw instinctively reaches for his lasso then freezes. It's too late though. Mama Lilith's eyes grow wide and land on the small braid. "It's true," she whispers. Her long, knobby finger points to the lasso. "The Elder Yarn. You truly found it."

Knick's small heart races. Mama Lilith takes a step toward him. He wants to escape, but to where? He's running out of options but knows one thing to be true: he can't let her have The Elder Yarn.

Everything he's read about pattern eight is horrifying. Without thinking, he hurls the lasso into the fire. His only hope is to destroy it, but Mama Lilith is one step ahead. She snaps her fingers, and the flames extinguish. *Damn her arcane knowledge!* Leaning down, she plucks the yarn from the coals and wipes it on her duster. Knick-knack curses himself; it was an obvious trick, and he should have seen it coming.

"Let my friend go," Knick says. "I'll go back to Dunwich. I'll spy on whoever you want."

"And rob him the opportunity to meet The Great Dreamer?" says Mama Lilith, her grin is so wide that Knick can see all her teeth by moonlight.

"Mama, please, don't do this!"

Mama Lilith removes her knitting needles; they're a pair of long, gnarled bones the color of shadow. She ties the Elder Yarn into a slipknot and pokes the tip of a needle through its opening. Knick runs to Cowboy's side and the man scoops the pack rat up into his arms. Suddenly, the glyphs around their camp glow brighter and a hot wind fills their ears.

"Caverns of old—" Mama knits furiously while chanting. "—Where the ancient one sleeps. *R'lyeh, Cth-wool-lu! Fhtagn, fhtagn.*"

The glyphs grow brighter still, and the desert is illuminated an eerie shade of green, as Mama Lilith knits even faster. "Cth-*wool*-lu," she chants. The Elder Yarn is glowing now. It vibrates between her fingers and begins taking shape. A small knobby creature is formed before them. Long tentacles shake loose from a quickly emerging head. A pair of knitted wings flap as they are freed from the needles, and before long, Knick and Cowboy are gazing upon true horror: pattern number eight. The Bonus. The Death Bringer. The tiniest, most adorable God. No bigger than a tomato. It floats up from Mama Lilith's needles, high above the campfire, and inhales deeply to scream. Knick and Cowboy hug each other tightly, ready for the end of all things—

—*Squeeeeeeeeeeeeak!*

What comes out the creature is an adorable sound no louder than a door hinge. Cowboy cocks and eyebrow, but Mama Lilith drops to her knees, bowing before the tiny Cth-*wool*-lu. She cries his name and begs his pardon. She offers herself in servitude. When he's had enough, Cth-*wool*-lu raises a small hand to silence her.

No one speaks. Cth-*wool*-lu points at Mama Lilith, then points to her knitting needles.

"What is it," she says. "I don't understand."

He points again, questioningly.

"I think he wants to know who woke him," says Knick.

"Right," says Mama Lilith, touching her breast. "I did." She climbs to her feet and brushes the dirt from her knees. "I have searched for the Elder Yarn my whole life, great Cth-*wool*-lu. I've built a church in your name. We've a congregation that would do whatever you ask for it—"

Cth-*wool*-lu motions to Knick and Cowboy.

Mama shakes her head, no. "They are nonbelievers. They have nothing to do with this. They are nothing!"

Cth-*wool*-lu hovers a moment. Then scratches his fuzzy butt. Finally, he flaps through the air, approaching Mama Lilith with arms stretched wide. A soft glow bathes the skin of her face. Like Jesus curing the blind, Cth-*wool*-lu places a gentle, wool hand on the very tip of her nose. Mama bursts into tears and lowers her head in sobbing thanks.

Knick sighs and rests his cheek on Cowboy's arm. He's spent so many months running from this very moment, hiding The Elder Yarn from mama Lilith. A small part of him is almost relieved it's over. He can stop hiding now. He tried. He failed. But at least he's with his best buddy in the end. That's more than any pack rat could ask for.

At some point Mama Lilith's sobs turned to groans, but Knick's only just realized. The sound turns to a wet gargle in her throat. When she looks up, the skin of her face is bubbling, as if her blood was run through a kettle . The small god turns to face Knickknack. He stares coldly as Mama's eyes and mouth disappear beneath swelling folds of skin. Knick is mortified. He thinks she is screaming but can't tell if it's her voice or the sound of her organs bursting. Sleepily, Cth-*wool*-lu rubs his eyes as the woman below approaches a breaking point. Mama Lilith attempts to stand, but her torso has grown three times in size. Her duster rips free, and because the weight is too much to handle, she topples over and bursts. Gallons of blood spray across camp! Knick and Cowboy are drenched, but they are too horrified to shield themselves. In an instant, the great and mighty High Priestess Mama Lilith is no more. She is an empty bag of blood on the ground, undone by her own ambition.

Turns out pattern eight is a *real* bitch.

With that, the wind dies down, and everything calms. Cth-*wool*-lu drops his arms and yawns. It's a cute sound, like saddle leather creaking. For long while, they all stare at one another, covered in blood and guts.

"What happened?" says Cowboy.

"I don't think . . . he likes being woken up," Knick says.

Cowboy wipes some blood from his jaw, then his eyes grow bright. "Hey, fetch my needles, little buddy."

"Why?"

Cowboy winks. "Pattern four."

Knick looks puzzled and then it dawns on him. For the next few minutes, Cth-*wool*-lu watches in fascination as Cowboy knits the most adorable, tiny eye mask you've ever seen. Practically giddy, the small god accepts the gift. He gingerly pulls it over his eyes, and then as if laying on some unseen bed, turns horizontal and begins snoring. After a moment, Cth-*wool*-lu unravels. The Elder Yarn falls from the air, and Knick jumps up to catch it.

Practical Knitting for Gunslingers is, above all, a friend for those brave enough to wander the untamed West. Mama Lilith knows all too well how welcomed a friend can be in challenging times. And so, this booklet contains a companion pattern for the wronged and weary. If you find yourself with no one to talk to, no one who understands just how hard this life can be, then look no further.

This is pattern seven: *Your New Best Pal.*

It'll take Knickknack weeks to knit Cowboy back together, and the desert is no place to be unspun. After a couple attempts, Cowboy is able to pull his torso onto their horse. Knick gathers the man's loose strings into a saddle bag so he doesn't drag behind, and as the early morning sun crests the horizon, our two heroes head into town for a well-earned bath. Knick's not sure what will become of Mama Lilith's congregation. There's more than a few men dumb enough to come looking for pattern number eight. But if anyone is clever enough to track The Elder Yarn all the way to Arizona, they'll have a surprise or two waiting for them. Not just a sleepy God or some well-knitted bullets, but the warm and immeasurable strength of true friendship.

⋈

Elder Bods

~ *Jonathan Wood*

Eric Bove had been a resident of the Sunny Hills Retirement Village for precisely twenty-seven hours when a member of the support staff popped her head into the recreation room and informed him that one of his new neighbors had passed away.

"Well," said the room's only other occupant, "that can't feel terribly auspicious."

Eric looked at the man. He looked a little like anthropomorphic oatmeal: gray and lumpy. "I'm Michael Murray," he said. "It's nice to meet you, but I don't matter very much."

Eric wasn't sure what to say to that. He'd spent most of his life preferring action over words. At this stage of life, though, that felt like poor planning.

"Normally," Michael Murray went on, "I'd say we lose someone about every six months."

"Is that . . . good?"

Michael Murray shrugged. "I've no idea, to be honest. But ignorance is bliss, etc. Well . . . actually, I can image a lot of situations where ignorance would be quite stressful. Crossing the road for example. But, well, that is to say . . ." He trailed off. "Do you like dominoes?"

Eric considered this in silence. He was here to make friends after all. To fit in.

"No," he said finally.

"No," Michael agreed. "Not many people do."

Eric's wife, Charlotte, had passed away shortly after Eric's eighty-third birthday. He would be the first to admit that he hadn't handled it well. But there had simply been no version of life in his head in which he outlived Charlotte. Charlotte lived and ate well. She made sensible decisions. Except the aneurysm hadn't cared about any of that. And all of a sudden, he'd been standing by a grave wearing a suit that didn't fit, living a life that didn't fit him either.

The drinking had gotten out of hand. He'd admit that too. And he understood why his children had been concerned. Hell, he was even reasonable enough to concede that asking them to deal with him twenty-four/seven was too much. And on a good day he would admit that the Sunny Hills Retirement Village was objectively beautiful, nestled as it was in the crook of two hills, overlooking wheat fields and a miniature lake.

But some days it still felt like he'd been shunted off into a corner while everyone else waited for him to die.

"Heart attack."

Eric had still not shaken Michael's presence. He wasn't sure if it was because he was unable or unwilling to do so. But now, as they sat together in the Village's dining hall, a woman joined them, speaking with relish. Eric thought people had probably once described her using the word "willowy." Over time she had hardened into . . . well, if not a battleaxe, then certainly a battleaxe handle.

"While I'm not a stickler for decorum," Michael said to her, "it seems early in the proceedings for so much glee."

The woman turned to Eric. "Ignore, Michael," she said. "He doesn't matter."

"That's fair," Michael conceded.

"Who are you?" Eric asked the woman.

"Julia," she said. "And while we are all insignificant specks in the grandiosity of the cosmos, I am far more significant than Michael." She ignored her plate of pork chops and mashed potato and opened up her chocolate pudding with zest.

"Julia was an astrophysicist," Michael said.

"And Michael," Julia said, "was a middle manager at the least important paper mill in the world."

"I was the associate floor manager at the fifth-most successful paper mill in the packing industry," Michael said.

"That's what I said," Julia said. "But I will admit you're very good at dominoes."

"Well . . ." Michael said.

"I'm trying to build you up, Michael."

"You just said I didn't matter."

"I don't want it to go to your head."

Was this, Eric wondered, his future? Was there anything else left other than letting friendly bickering wash over him?

"I was a gym teacher," he decided to add.

Julia regarded him. "What's your name?"

"Eric Bove."

"Did you shape the futures of any great athletes, Eric?"

"No."

Julia weighed this. "Would you call yourself a dominoes enthusiast?"

"No."

"Then you still rank above Michael."

"Seconded," Michael said.

"Did you know that this is the third death in a row at the Sunny Hills Retirement Village caused by a massive coronary?" Julia said, without any apparent concern for the prior direction of the conversation.

"I moved in yesterday," Eric said.

"You might have done some very specific research."

"Which," Michael added, "would have opened some interesting conversational avenues."

"I didn't."

"A telling fact in and of itself," Julia said, "but irrelevant to our curious clustering of cardiac calamities."

"I get the impression," Eric said, "that not much happens here."

"Well," Michael said, "there is quite a lot of dominoes."

"Eleanor in room 12C has some pertinent facts to the fate of our recently deceased neighbor."

Eric, who had given into the gravitational pull of dominoes, felt very glad for Julia's interruption. Michael, however, glanced up from his own collection of tiles with an air of aggrieved disappointment.

"Oh, don't give me that look," Julia said. "You're terrible at dominoes."

"You don't have to be good at it to enjoy it."

"I don't care. Now, the dead man's name was Joseph, and he was a charming widower with his own complete head of hair, which helps explain why Eleanor in 12C and Joseph were, in the common parlance, knocking boots."

Michael's brow furrowed.

"Coitus, Michael," Julia said. "It's like dominoes except a lot squishier."

"Sounds like I might like it," Michael said, and Eric had no idea if he was joking.

"While I am not one for idle gossip," Julia continued with no apparent regard for the truth, "this fact does add veracity to Eleanor's claim that Joseph had a robust heart, because he demonstrated it to her at least once a week after bingo."

Eric arched an eyebrow.

"There is more," Julia declared. "Eleanor, distressed by her lover's departure from the mortal coil, wanted to see the body. The staff tried to deny her, but they underestimated Eleanor's spryness, and she managed a single glimpse before she was dragged away. And do you know what she glimpsed?"

Eric did not. He waited to find out. He glanced at Michael. Michael looked at Julia. Julia stared significantly at Eric. To get around this impasse, Eric said, "No."

"Runes carved into flesh!" Julia said with significant delight.

"That doesn't sound likely," Michael said.

"It sounds suspicious," Julia declared.

"Has anyone screened Eleanor for dementia recently?" Michael asked.

"We must investigate!" Julia announced.

Michael gave his domino tiles a lingering glance. "Why?"

"Because," Eric cut in with significant feeling, "there's bugger all else to do around here."

Julia, it turned out, had acquired a spare key to Joseph's apartment from Eleanor. Inside, the room was strikingly similar to Eric's own. It had the same curtains, the same carpet, the same chair in the same corner. What had felt warm and hospitable upon his arrival, suddenly appeared institutional and impersonal. Only a few objects grafted any individuality to the place. And Eric hadn't hung half the photos Joesph had. He hadn't stacked half the silly little knick-knacks on shelves and dressers.

When he passed on, he wondered would there be anyone like Eleanor to mourn his absence? Would anyone bother sneaking into his apartment hopped up on boredom and gossip? Or would his belongings just be stripped away, and the world go on just as it had before?

"No pills whatsoever." Julia's voice emerged triumphantly from the bathroom. "A man in fighting form."

"Or, they already took them," Michael said, "so as not to leave medicine lying around."

"Runes carved into flesh, Michael!"

Michael shot a mutinous look in Eric's direction.

"Wouldn't there be blood somewhere," Eric asked, "if they carved runes into flesh?"

"Now there's someone who's thinking," Julia said, emerging from the bathroom. "However, we don't know that he was killed here, or that he was still alive when the runes were carved into him."

"Or if there were any runes at all," Michael said.

"Is this the sort of negativity you brought to the paper mill, Michael?" Julia asked. "Now, Eric, you used to be a gym teacher, help me move the bed."

"Why?"

"Clues!"

Eric regarded the bed dubiously. There was a time of course when moving it would have been a simple request, but now . . .

He was saved from embarrassment by the rattling of the apartment's front door.

"The bathroom!" Julia hissed.

There was a scramble then, the three of them bumping into each other, and Julia had only just eased the door entirely closed when the key clicked in the door outside and the sound of footsteps entered the other room.

"—think she really saw anything?" said a shrill cockney voice.

"I'll talk to her," replied a deeper voice, rich with Nordic vowels. "And if she did . . . It is a shame what happens to these old people.

Their hearts, you know, can give out like that." There was a snap of fingers and a low chuckle.

"She could be trouble though," said the cockney.

"She can only make trouble for herself." The Nord was very confident, and very cold. Eric shivered.

"What about these?" asked the cockney. Eric heard something rattle. "Shall I put them in the bathroom?"

The three of them froze. Eric found himself looking for a weapon and wasn't sure why. He felt very frail and very old.

"No," said the Nord. "Bedside table. Seems more urgent."

"And the family won't . . ." started the cockney.

"I backdated all the records. Everything proceeds as normal, and we move close to the day of awakening."

"Praise be."

A drawer rattled then, and the footsteps retreated. The door opened and closed, and Eric breathed for what felt like the first time in minutes.

"Did you hear that?" Julia flung open the bathroom door and marched to the bedside table. "A virtual confession."

"That was Adam Bennett and Anders Jensen," Michael said. "The physical therapists."

"Oh, Anders," Julia looked sad. "It will be so much harder to fantasize about sponge baths from now on."

"Come on, Julia," Michael said. "I think you're taking this a bit far."

Julia, rooted in the drawer and pulled out a pill bottle. She wielded it triumphantly. "Planted evidence, Michael. Now why would they do that?"

The next day, it was announced that Eleanor had died of a heart attack.

"Do you believe me now?" Julia asked.

Michael licked his lips.

"Yes," Eric said. "We do."

✳

Eric was assigned the duty of tailing Adam and Anders. He had been a gym teacher, Julia informed him, and was therefore athletic enough for the task. Eric, who had neither of his original knees, was less certain.

He was even less sure of himself halfway through his first senior Zumba class. There was, he thought, a savage glee in the instructor's eyes, and a zealot's fervor to her insistence that they thrust their hips first one way then another. Maybe, he thought, there was no plot. There was merely an over-enthusiastic instructor forcing the elderly into a death march of fitness.

He was so exhausted, he almost missed Adam and Anders walking past the open door of the workout room. Glimpsing them, he made vague gestures that could either be interpreted as the need for the bathroom or an incipient heart attack. The instructor merely flashed her canines at him more fiercely as he stumbled out after them.

Keeping up with their easy stride along the hallways and out across the sunny open spaces of the Retirement Village was almost more than Eric could manage. He huffed and stumbled along, stealth an afterthought at best. The only thing which prevented his discovery was Adams' and Anders' utter obliviousness to the elderly around them. Even when an octogenarian sent a friendly wave or "hello" in their direction, they moved on with barely a first glance, let alone a second one.

Maybe it wasn't just Eric who didn't matter. Maybe none of them did. Maybe they were all society's afterthoughts shunted out of the way, where they could do no harm except to themselves. Primarily through the medium of ill-advised Zumba classes.

The two physical therapists made a beeline for a small shed near the over-sized pond that was described as a scenic lake in all the brochures. Up close, though, Eric noticed there was a brackish smell to the water, and no wildlife dotted its surface. There weren't even birds overhead.

Adam and Anders disappeared inside the shed. Eric, grateful for the break, waited for them to emerge. It was, after all, a small shed. The wonders it could contain seemed limited.

After ten minutes, though, he approached cautiously. Which was how he noticed the keycard reader where the padlock should be, and how he saw that beneath the shed's aging wooden slats lay a steel door.

"The murder site," Julia breathed.

"They were in there for over three hours."

"Not to be indelicate," Michael said, steepling his fingers, "but have we considered that they might be lovers?"

"Not to be indelicate," Julia said, "but have you considered that you're an idiot."

"Just because I'm inconsequential," Michael said, "doesn't mean I'm impervious to hurt, Julia."

"There was a steel door, a keycard reader, and they are in a facility full of beds. What am I to do with your suggestion of a secret love shack, but to dismiss it as sub-par thinking?"

Michael contemplated this. "OK," he said finally. "I'll allow it."

Julia turned to Eric, who was grinning despite himself. "We need a keycard," she told him, "so we can enter the shed, gather evidence, and render these miscreants to justice."

"If we're making fun of things, "Michael said, "can I get a ruling on the word 'miscreants.'"

"No." Julia glared at Michael while Eric grinned. There was life in the old boy after all.

"I don't like this plan," Michael said.

"We are but cosmic dust in an infinite universe," Julia said. "Your concerns are of less than no significance."

"Well, that's disappointing."

Michael had relocated his standing Tuesday dominoes game with Jeffrey Johnson to the Fitness Center. He sat at a low table, shuffling his tiles. When they saw Jeffrey approaching, Eric and Julia left him there and went to stand in a corridor fifteen yards away, just outside Adam Bennett's office.

As the two men clicked and clattered with their tiles, Julia turned to Eric. "I know," she said, "that you think I'm cruel to Michael."

Eric, who didn't think this, said nothing.

"However, when he's like this," she went on, "in his own ridiculous world, I wonder if perhaps he's the only person who has it all figured out. Who has made his peace with all the chaos, and meaningless cruelty, and savage indifference. He's looked at it all, and found happiness in the clicking of little tiles with numbers on them. How am I supposed to live with that? How can I not try to bring him down to my level? I'm only human."

Eric had absolutely no idea was to do that information.

It was at this point that Michael stood up, tossed dominoes in every direction and screamed, "You conniving, yellow-bellied cheat!"

Shortly after this tirade began, Adam Bennett's office door banged open, and Adam Bennett himself emerged. He saw Michael seizing a bewildered Jeffrey Johnson by the scruff of the neck and cursed quietly to himself.

As the physical therapist stalked toward the two dominoes players, Eric slipped as nimbly as his incipient arthritis would allow him into the empty office. The place was a mess of old coffee cups and McDonald's containers and flyers for pieces of gym equipment. Rooting through them, Eric noticed a strange smell, and it took him a moment to realize it was the same faint brackish stink that the pond had held.

"What's taking so long?" Julia hissed.

Eric turned to explain this wasn't easy and found that it was. The keycard hung from a lanyard hooked to the back of the door.

"Nothing," he said, and slipped back out into the hall just as Michael started to pepper Adam Bennett with expletives and small plastic tiles.

The maintenance shed was not a secret love nest. Neither was it a shed. Rather, it was the entrance to a set of stairs leading down into the earth.

"This seems," Eric said, searching for the right word, "elaborate."

"And suspicious," Julia added.

They descended, albeit slowly and with care. At the bottom of the stairs was an earthen tunnel illuminated by the sort of lights used by construction workers, all strung together by a thick orange cable. The brackish smell had intensified, and Eric's mouth tasted sour.

"Do you have any hard candy?" he asked Julia.

"Am I just a walking stereotype to you, Eric?"

So they continued on in silence, and nausea built in Eric's stomach.

"Look," Julia said abruptly. "The walls."

Eric peered at one. It was rough, and earthen, and the brackish scent intensified, making his eyes water. But something had indeed been scratched or painted there.

"Runes," Julia said.

"Aren't runes angular?"

"What would you call them then?"

"Squiggles."

"We have a corpse with runes carved into its flesh, Eric. And now we have walls with esoteric markings. I think they can be called runes without an excess of quibbling."

Silently, Eric conceded the point. They went deeper. The stench was a physical presence, and Julia started to cough.

"Is your head . . . ?" Eric tried to ask, because buried memories were flickering through his mind: his wife in the hospital, looking inconsequential in the nest of equipment; old fights; old moments when he could have cared more, or been kinder, or made her life just a little easier. Missed moments. Forgotten opportunities to have been a better man. And all of it was drowning in putrid water. His head throbbed. His mouth tasted vile.

"There's something . . ." Julia started then coughed again.

"Yes," said a third voice. "There is."

Eric turned just in time to see Anders Jensen punch him in the face.

Eric had been punched before. There was a time when he was young, and rebellious, and out to make a mark. Nothing made the difference between then and now seem more stark to Eric than his return to consciousness in the tunnels below the Sunny Hills Retirement Village. He felt weak and weepy in a way he hadn't since he was child.

It didn't help that he was tied to a chair.

Julia was tied to another chair beside him. Michael was laid out on what Eric supposed was an altar of sorts—a great stone slab with more squiggles carved into its sides, raised on misshapen legs.

Michael was bound just as tightly as Eric and Julia and had an ugly bruise on his head.

Adam Bennet and Anders Jensen stood either side of Michael. They had stripped to the waist, and more runic scribbles adorned their chests.

Anders Jensen held a knife.

And yet, Eric could have borne all of this, if it hadn't been for the thing in the water behind the glass.

They were in a cavern. It had the same earthen walls as the corridors, except one was entirely made of glass, as if the space was some twisted aquarium exhibit. Except the animal on display, the thing suspended in that foul brackish water, the abhorrent knot of scale and skin and flesh and white, white bone . . . No. No-one should look at that. Eric tried to look away, but he couldn't.

"I'm sorry," Michael moaned from the altar. "Probably not my best turn as a distraction."

The thing behind the glass moved. A twitching of anatomy that made no sense. Plates of matter intersected with each other. And as the thing moved, more memories untethered themselves from the recesses of Eric's mind: not just the horror and regrets, but the good times too, the moments when his wife made him feel beautiful, the moments when the sun had kissed his face. And it was worse this time. Worse to have all that in his head, because under the unrelenting gaze of this eyeless monstrosity, it all felt meaningless. Every moment that had sparkled for him was revealed as an insignificant speck lost in the blaze of a million, million suns.

He was nothing. He was meaningless. This was the message of the creature in the water. This was the full scale, unfiltered truth that he had only scraped at in his lower moments. Humanity was nothing. And he was one of its least significant representatives.

"Well," Michael kept on talking despite it all, despite Anders advancing on him with the knife, "it's also my first turn as a distraction. So, I suppose it was my best. And my worst. Also an average performance for me. Not that any of this matters, of course, but-"

"Shut up!" Julia suddenly roared. Cords stood out on her neck. Spittle frothed from her lips. Even Anders hesitated. "Can't you see we're in the presence of a god?" she spat. "Your prattle sullies him."

Adam and Anders exchanged a look.

Julia shuffled her chair forward. "I felt it among the stars," she said. "For years. Something reaching out, yearning to be found. And you . . ." She stared at Adam and Anders. "Bring me closer to it," she said.

"No!" Eric yelled. Because he had to stop this madness. He had to give Julia a chance to repair her broken mind. But what could he do? Even in his youth he couldn't have torn free from these bonds.

"She believes," Adam Bennett said ignoring Eric's struggles

"Better to sacrifice her," Anders said, "and feed the Master her soul to hasten His awakening? Or better to have another ally?"

The thing in the water twitched again: a traumatizing shrug of cartilage and cilia. Eric's bile rose.

"He speaks to me," Julia breathed. "Bring me closer."

"An ally among the inmates could accelerate the recruitment of sacrifices," Adam Bennett said.

"Bring me closer," Julia said again, her voice full of yearning.

"I mean," Michael said, "I know I'm an insignificant man of insignificant opinions, but if I might register an objection to this whole . . ."

Adam and Anders paid him no heed. They lifted Julia and her chair, and she urged them on. "Closer! Closer!"

The thing in the tank—God, it must be the size of whale—spasmed again. Eric's vision blurred. When it cleared, Julia was thrashing against her bonds, shouting "Closer! Cut me free. Let me worship!"

Adam and Anders exchanged a look. Anders shrugged and slit Julia's bonds.

Immediately, Julia threw her bony elbow into Anders' face. He bellowed and grabbed his nose, dropping the knife. She kicked it straight toward Eric, who, still bound to his chair, stared at it, lying six feet away.

Adam Bennett shouted in surprise and anger and took Julia's knee to his groin.

"Come on, Eric!" she yelled at him. "You are meant to be a man of more significance than Michael."

Except of course he wasn't. He was a man shunted to the corner. A man without anything left to give.

"Come on!" urged Michael.

Anders was recovering. Anders was delivering a right hook to Julia that lifted her off that ground.

And what sort of man was Eric? He had certainly never been the sort to stomach a woman being punched in the face. Even here, at the end of things, even if nothing mattered, he didn't think he could stomach it. So, he rocked back and forth, then flung himself and his chair across the dirt. And somehow, something in that wooden chair cracked before his bones did. And screaming in pain, he scrambled free, diving for the knife, trailing rope and splinters.

He was moving slower than Anders, though, also going for the weapon. But Julia still had some fight left in her. She twisted her legs around Anders feet and sent him howling to floor.

Beyond this drama, the thing in the tank moved faster, excited. Eric wanted to throw up, but he seized the knife and stumbled toward the altar. As he crashed against it, one of the altar's legs collapsed, spilling both the plinth and Michael to the floor. Eric stooped and slashed, half-blinded at the other man's bindings.

Then Anders was up. Eric didn't know if Michael was free or not, but he had to bring the knife to bear on Anders. He had to hope that he could still have some impact on the world.

They both leapt at the same time, and for just a moment longer, Eric believed. Then the younger man twisted easily away from Eric's wild slash of the knife and cuffed him on the cheek, and Eric crashed sideways, tripping over the makeshift altar, and slammed to the ground. By the time his vision cleared, Anders had the knife again.

Adam Bennett had an arm around Julia's throat. He cursed, while she kicked ineffectually at his shins. Only Michael was free. He stood between the altar and the glass, and he held one of the rocks that had served as a leg for the altar. His arms shuddered under its weight.

Anders turned on him. "What are you going to do with that?" he said. "As if anything you could do would matter now. Get back on the altar if you want this to be quick."

But Michael just smiled and lifted his rock higher. "Perhaps I could counter that offer."

"I'm not scared of you," Anders sneered.

"No-one is," Michael said. "I don't really matter. But something here does." And then he turned, and he flung the rock with all the strength left to him at the glass.

Shock sublimated to terror on Ander's face. And then . . . laughter. The rock struck the glass and bounced harmlessly to the floor.

"Oh," Michael said. "Bugger."

"You're going to regret—" Adam Bennett started.

The crack ran along the glass like it was trying to flee the room. Like Eric realized they should all be doing.

The glass exploded.

Water gushed forth, a great tidal wash of filth. Eric was knocked off his feet. Air burst from him, and all that was left in its place was fear. Because that creature was in that water. There was no barrier left. There was nothing to prevent it from clutching and embracing and tearing and flaying and—

Screams echoed all around him. He saw Adam Bennett hoisted aloft on the end of spear of horn and bone, and ripped asunder into bloody rags. He thrashed through water up to his waist. He looked back despite himself. More dead-white tendrils of alien flesh flickered through the water, encircling Julia and Michael. Embracing his friends.

And there was nothing he could do. Because who was he? What did he matter?

But there had been so many times in the past few days when there was nothing he could do, and still he had done things. Still, he had come this far. Why not a little further?

Despite every impulse in his body, he waded back toward Julia and Michael. Above him, the ceiling shuddered. The walls rained dirt. Something snaked past his leg and he screamed unabashedly. He couldn't see Anders anywhere.

He seized Michael, who thrashed and spluttered. Julia clung to his arm. Eric's old muscles were tired and cold, but his will was gnarled and tenacious. He hauled them through the water after him, while the thing in the water smashed and thrashed at walls that confined it, while the ceiling started to crumble.

Somehow, he found a tunnel. Somehow, he was pulling them all toward higher ground. And perhaps he was still screaming, or maybe he was crying, or possibly it was both, but then it was all drowned out as the ceiling finally gave way.

When it was all over, he wasn't entirely sure how they'd made it out. But they had, and the thing hadn't, and the sun on his face felt like a childhood memory brought to life, and he sank down and just basked in it for a while.

"Well," Julia said, interrupting the moment. "I think we can all agree that if we're still alive at this point, we're unlikely to die of heart attacks anytime soon."

Eric wondered if he ignored the other two, they'd just be quiet.

"Well," Michael started, "there are still a lot of other potential causes of—"

"I meant, Michael, that we are unlikely to be murdered by two deranged cultists who worship a mutant cuttlefish."

"I know," said Michael. "What I think doesn't matter."

But that, Eric found, he could not bear in silence. That, he found, had to be put into words. "No," he said. "No, I think it does." He stopped, and then he found he still had more words to share. "I think it always has," he said. "And I think it's going to for a while to come."

"Well then," Julia said. But Eric was done, and lying back down with the sun on his face, he found he didn't care who saw him there, and who didn't.

◨

CONTRIBUTORS

Rachel Ashcraft

Rachel is a public librarian in the Midwest. She has stories published at Hungry Shadows Press, GrendelPress, Malarkey Books, and upcoming at Apex. The naval code book mentioned in the story is based on a real object found at the Lilly Library on Indiana University's campus. Find her on bluesky @rachiea. bsky.social.

Devan Barlow

Devan Barlow is the author of the *Curses & Curtains* series of fairy tales-meet-musicals fantasy novels. Her short fiction and poetry have appeared in several anthologies and magazines. She can be found at her website devan-barlow.com or on Bluesky @devanbarlow.bsky.social. She reads voraciously, and can often be found hanging out with her dog, drinking tea, and thinking about sea monsters.

Tyler Battaglia

Tyler Battaglia is a queer and disabled author of horror, dark fantasy, and other speculative fiction, who is especially interested in subjects that interrogate the connections between faith, monsters, love, queerness, and disability. You can find Tyler on social media at @whosthistyler and online at https://www.tyler-battaglia.com, where you can also find a full list of publications to date.

Megan Lee Beals

Megan Lee Beals writes cozy and fanciful horrors from her home in the perpetually soggy Pacific Northwest. She lives with her husband, her twin son and daughter, and the family's formally feral cat. When she isn't writing or chasing toddlers, Megan is drawing or sewing or building, and generally trying to accumulate hobbies at a truly unsustainable rate. She has been published in *Translunar Traveler's Lounge* and *The Iowa Review*. You can find more of her various things at www.meganleebeals.com.

Phoenix Bourgeois

Phoenix Bourgeois writes in Portland, Oregon where she co-hosts Northwest Speculative, a PNW Reading Series that connects readers, authors, and venues. She grew up bouncing from one library to the next. Now, Phoenix writes her very own fantastical stories—bouncing from one coffee shop to the next.

Ellis Bray

Ellis Bray is a science fiction author and artist who lives in the vaguely Seattle area, and he really hates the recent addition of a Fire Season to the regular Winter/Spring/Summer/Fall lineup. He is, however, a big believer in "pathological optimism" and strives to show that in his visual and verbal art.

He has a Master's degree in Medieval Scandinavian Studies and if you don't run away fast enough, he will download everything he knows about the Old Norse poem "Völuspá" at you. You can find his nonfiction in *NewMyths* (under SP Hofrichter); his poetry in *Eye To the Telescope* and *F&SF*; and his artwork on Instagram at @idreamofvikings.

Tania Chen

Tania Chen is a Chinese-Mexican writer and poet of living nightmares with a soft spot for pink stationary. Their work was selected for the *Brave New Weird* Anthology by Tenebrous Press, and has appeared in *Apparition Lit, Strange Horizons, Pleiades Magazine, Baffling Magazine, Longleaf Review, The Dread Machine,* among others.

They are a graduate of the Clarion West Novella Bootcamp Workshop of 2021, a recipient of the HWA's Dark Poetry Scholarship 2022, and a graduate of the Clarion West Writers Workshop 2023. Currently, they are assistant editor for *Uncanny Magazine.*

Simone Cooper

An avid reader and viewer of horror, science-fiction, and fantasy, Simone grew up on a diet of *Creature Features* and *Speed Racer* cartoons on Chicago's WGN-TV. She's played role-playing games since the late 1970's and was a major writer on the 2005 multiple ENnie Award winning *A Game of Thrones* RPG. She currently plays *Amber Diceless* RPG and other dice-light games and has organized more than 30 RPG conventions under the umbrella "AmberCon" in the U.K., Michigan, Portland, and on-line.

Ben Curl

Ben Curl is a storyteller and sigil-maker. His short stories have been printed and/or produced as podcast episodes by numerous indie publishers, including Underland Press, Tales from the Moonlit Path, Night Shift Radio, and Timberghost Press. He also teaches writing workshops and hosts the Capital Letters Eclectic Fiction Club in at A Novel Concept bookshop in Lansing, MI, where he resides.

Peter Damien

Peter Damien lives in the Seattle area with a million zillion books, a lot of tea, and a cat who probably won't do anything to save him if the books should ever avalanche. He's published short stories in an array of anthologies, magazines, and web-sites over the years, from *Fear and Fables*, to *Literary Hatchet* to *Something Wicked* to *European Monsters*, and lots of other places. His non-fiction has appeared on *BookRiot*, *QuirkBooks*, *SFSignal*, and *The Future Fire*. He plays more *Minecraft* than he cares to admit.

Lauren Elise Daniels

A 2023 Bram Stoker Award® nominee, L. E. Daniels is an American author, poet, and editor. Lauren's novel, *Serpent's Wake: A Tale for the Bitten* (Interactive Publications) is a Notable Work with the Horror Writers Association's Mental Health Initiative. Recent publications include historical fiction/horror, "Silk" in *Hush, Don't Wake the Monster* (Twisted Wing Productions), "Darkness Repeats" in *Monsters in the Mills* (Interactive Publications), and "Hangman's Coming" in *Where the Silent Ones Watch* (Hippocampus Press). Her poem, "Night Terrors" (HWA, *Of Horror and Hope*) was a 2022 finalist for the Australasian Shadows Award. She lives in Australia.

Luke Elliott

Luke Elliott is a writer and podcaster living in Portland, Oregon, where he participates in a thriving speculative fiction writing community. His shorter fiction has appeared in *Reckoning*, *Metaphorosis*, and the *Buckman Journal*, among other magazines and podcasts. He has also been the co-host of the *Ink to Film* podcast and YouTube channel since 2017, where he and a filmmaker co-host discuss books and their film adaptations from a craft perspective.

He has an MFA in Writing Popular Fiction from Seton Hill University and is a graduate of the Viable Paradise writer's workshop. He'd love to chat at the next big genre convention, where he often appears as a panelist who's always excited to talk about books, movies, or podcasting.

Daniel David Froid

Daniel David Froid is a writer who lives in Arizona and has published fiction in *The Masters Review, Lightspeed, Black Warrior Review, Post Road*, and elsewhere.

Andrew S. Fuller

Andrew S. Fuller writes and edits horror, fantasy, and science fiction. His work appears in several magazines, anthologies, short films, and the collection *Constellations of Ruin* (2023, Trepidatio). Since 1999, he's edited the fiction magazine *Three-Lobed Burning Eye*. He lives in Portland, OR between two rivers and near several extinct(?) volcanoes. Visit him online at andrewsfuller.com.

Brian U. Garrison

Brian U. Garrison (he/him) writes poetry for children, adults, and grand adults. His chapbook *Micropoetry for Microplanets* (Space Cowboy Books) celebrates the smallish to medium rocks that circle our sun. The book also provides a fun excuse to talk to students about space (and what a lovely, inhabitable planet we have here on Earth).

He serves as Managing Editor for *Eye to the Telescope* (eyetothetelescope.com). Find him online at bugthewriter.com or enjoying the vegan biscuits and gravy at Shoofly Cafe in Portland, Oregon.

Maxwell Gold

Maxwell I. Gold is a Jewish American multiple award nominated author who writes prose poetry and short stories in cosmic horror and weird fiction with half a decade of writing experience. He is a five-time Rhysling Award nominee, and two-time Pushcart Award nominee. Find him at www.thewellsoftheweird.com.

Erik Grove

Erik Grove is a writer, writing teacher, long distance runner, and little dog wrangler living and doing things in Portland, OR. You can find his work in places like *Nightmare, Escape Pod*, and the *Space Cocaine* anthology series. He teaches writing and mentors writers with Working Title (www.workingtitle.us).

Check out his webpage www.erikgrove.com for links to his published work, dog glamour shots, marathon training nonsense, and sundry writerly shenanigans.

Elad Haber

Elad Haber is a husband, father to an adorable little girl, and IT guy by day, fiction writer by night. He has recent publications from *Lightspeed Magazine, Underland Arcana,* and the *Simultaneous Times* Podcast. His debut short fiction collection, *The World Outside* was published by Underland Press. Visit eladhaber.com for links and news.

Paul Jessup

Paul Jessup is a best-selling video game designer and award-winning short fiction writer. He's also an active Pro Member of HWA. He has three books coming out within a year from Underland Press: *Glass House, Skinless Man Counts to Five and Other Tales of the Macabre,* and *Daughter of the Wormwood Star.* Another is forthcoming.

Chris J. Karr

Chris J. Karr is a software creator in Chicago, where he builds new systems to push the borders of scientific knowledge for research clients. A decade ago, he created *The Pnakotic Atlas,* an illustrated map to the Lovecraft Mythos for mobile devices. Most recently, he is one of the co-founders of "Weird Fiction Quarterly" where he publishes anthologies of weird flash fiction four times a year.

His (chronically outdated) website is online at aetherial.net and he periodically posts at notesfromthevoid.cc. You can find him on the Fediverse at @chris@omgwars.com.

Ngô Bình Anh Khoa

Ngô Bình Anh Khoa is a teacher of English in Ho Chi Minh City, Vietnam. In his free time, he enjoys reading fiction and writing speculative poetry. His poems have appeared in *Weirdbook, Star*Line, Spectral Realms,* and other venues. He also writes haiku on occasions, many of which have received honorable mentions and awards in various contests in the US, the UK, Japan, Canada, and elsewhere.

J. B. Kish

J.B. Kish is a horror and weird fiction author living in Portland, Oregon. His work has appeared in *Cosmic Horror Monthly, Metaphorosis Magazine,* and Unsettling Reads' *Still of Winter* anthology. When he's not writing, Kish teaches workshops that help emerging authors design strategies to reach their goals. He has one wife, one cat, and one dog.

John Klima

Over the course of his career as editor of *Electric Velocipede,* John Klima received the Hugo Award as well as multiple nominations for the World Fantasy Award. He lives in Wisconsin with his family, where he does secret work for a large public library. Occasionally, he writes fiction.

Jessie Kwak

Jessie Kwak is an author and business book ghostwriter living in Portland, Oregon. When she's not writing, she can be found sewing, mountain biking, or organizing the Author Alchemy Summit.

She is the author of a supernatural thriller, two series of space scoundrel sci-fi crime novels, and a handful of productivity books including *From Chaos to Creativity* and *From Big Idea to Book.* You can find her at jessiekwak.com.

Jon Lasser

Jon Lasser lives in Seattle, WA with his wife and two children. His stories have appeared in *Lightspeed, Interzone, Galaxy's Edge,* and elsewhere. He's a graduate of the Clarion West writers workshop. Find him online at twoideas.org.

Basile Lebret

Basile Lebret is French and lives south of Paris where the cities meet the trees. His work has been published in SlicedUp Press' *Monstroddities,* Atonic Vision Press' *Strange Weeds,* Bag of Bones' *Step Into the Light,* Off Topic Publishing's *Home, Carnage House* and in France in Lufthunger Club's *Les Feux de la Révolte.* Find him on Twitter: @evoripclaw or Medium: https://basile-lebret. medium.com/.

Buffy Mitchell

You can call her Elizabeth, Buffy, or Elle Mitchell, just don't call her after 10 P.M. She's a disabled alchemist who turns pain into art, a dark fiction and crip fic author, an essayist, and a co-chair of the HWA's Oregon chapter.

Whether gaming, going for short walks, or creating new recipes, she needs more downtime than most. Being a woman with several invisible illnesses, she enjoys living a semi-horizontal life with her husband and spoiled furbutts in the PNW.

Margo Pecha

Margo Pecha lives in southwest Washington state and writes about the things that fuel her anxieties. She studied creative writing at Eastern Washington University and completed graduate work in writing and publishing at Portland State University. When she's not reading and writing, she's wrangling chickens and working in her extensive gardens.

Kate Ristau

Kate Ristau is the author of two trilogies for tweens and teens: *Clockbreakers* and *Shadow Girl*. She also wrote *Wylde Wings* and *Mythwakers*. This is her first cosmic poem, and she's worried that the words will keep eating themselves until the only thing that's left is cotton candy. Make sure she's okay at kateristau.com.

Matthew Ross

Matthew Ross (he/him) is a writer, editor, and English professor living in Los Angeles, CA. He is an associate member of the SFWA and an affiliate member of the HWA. His fiction has appeared in *Andromeda Spaceways Magazine*, *Etherea Magazine*, and *Sci Phi Journal*, amongst other places. Find him online @matthewrossphd.

Kevin Wetmore

Kevin Wetmore is a five-time Bram Stoker Award nominee, the author or editor of almost three dozen non-fiction books and many, many short stories, including his other Lovecraft mashups, "Tales of a Fourth Grade Shoggoth," "Are You There, Azathoth? It's Me, Margaret," and "The Statement of Eeyore Carter," as well as other Lovecraftian stories in such anthologies as *Fall of Cthulhu II*, *Whispers from the Abyss 2*, *Urban Temples of Cthulhu*, and *A Lonely and Curious Country*. Learn more at www.SomethingWetmoreThisWayComes.com.

Jonathan Wood

Jonathan Wood is the author of 8 novels (The Hero series, The Dragon Lords series writing as Jon Hollins, and *City of Iron and Dust* as J.P. Oakes). When not writing he spends far too much time playing videogames and sharing memes on facebook while society collapses around him. He can be found online at jpoakeswrites.wordpress.com.

EDITORS

Frances Lu-Pai Ippolito

Frances Lu-Pai Ippolito (she/her) is a Chinese American judge, mom, and writer in Portland, Oregon. Her writing has appeared in *Nightmare Magazine*, Flame Tree's *Asian Ghost Stories, Chromophobia, Mother: Tales of Terror and Love, Death's Garden Revisited*, and *Unquiet Spirits*. She is the founder of game and book publisher Demagogue Press and the nonprofit, Qilin Press, which focuses on diverse, marginalized voices. Frances also co-chairs the Young Willamette Writers program that provides free writing classes for high school and middle school students.

You can find her on IG @francespaippolito, FB Frances Pai, and at www.demagoguepress.com/.

Mark Teppo

Mark Teppo is the publisher of Underland Press. He has written more than two dozen novels across a wide variety of genres, including historical fiction, eco-thriller, horror, western, mystery, science fiction, and dark fantasy. He lives in the Pacific Northwest, where he is busy making things.

His favorite Tarot card is the Moon.

You can find him online at https://www.markteppo.com/.

For more information about Underland Press, please visit the website:

underlandpress.com